FEROCIOUS

THOMAS LAIRD

Black Rose Writing | Texas

ISBN: 978-1-68433-992-1
PUBLISHED BY BLACK ROSE WRITING
www.blackrosewriting.com

Printed in the United States of America
Suggested Retail Price (SRP) $21.95

Ferocious is printed in Calluna

*As a planet-friendly publisher, Black Rose Writing does its best to eliminate unnecessary waste to reduce paper usage and energy costs, while never compromising the reading experience. As a result, the final word count vs. page count may not meet common expectations.

FEROCIOUS

CHAPTER ONE

"All human beings, as we meet them, are commingled out of good and evil: and Edward Hyde, alone, in the ranks of mankind, was pure evil."
— Robert Louis Stevenson, *The Strange Case of Dr. Jekyll and Mr. Hyde*

When Karras arrived on scene, he came alone. He had no partner since Ed Bailey retired, and Nick rather enjoyed working on his own. He'd been assigned to Homicide since 1967—five years now—and Ed was his first and only partner. Karras was a creature of habit and breaking in a new guy wasn't something he looked forward to.

The ME was still present on the scene, but he was finishing his preliminary examination of the deceased, a twenty-something female who lay on her back in the middle of the living room floor inside the apartment near Lake Michigan on the near north side. It was walking distance to the beach, but it was mid-December, and no one hit the sand, pretty much, until Memorial Day.

Then he looked down on her more carefully and saw what had been done to her. There were ligature marks on her throat, but what grabbed Karras' attention was the damage below. She was a pale strawberry blonde, thin, maybe even gaunt, and her nipples had been severed from her small breasts. Blood ran onto either side of her chest from the wounds.

Last, he noticed that her toenails had been torn from all ten digits. He thought the perp might have used pliers.

He didn't gasp. He couldn't. But he'd seen these markers before.

•   •   •   •   •

Nick looked out his office window onto Michigan Avenue, here in headquarters. The men on the other side of the building had a primo view of the Lake, and he sometimes felt jealous of them. His colleague, Jimmy Parisi, had the best view of the water. It was a stark blue on some days in the summer, but in the winter the Lake appeared a cobalt-gray, and it was chilling to observe in December.

He didn't mention the similarity to anyone else in Homicide. The first one had happened back during his first year in this position, and the person it had happened to was his daughter, Penelope. Penelope, who now resided in the Elgin State Mental Facility. But his girl had survived the rape and the mutilation—if you wanted to call it surviving. She was catatonic and unresponsive and had been in that vegetative condition since 1967, when it took place.

Penelope was what they called a 'problem' child. The problems began when Carole, his ex-wife, had taken off on them both when the girl was only six. Carole had a diagnosis, as well. Manic-depressive. She had extreme highs and lows, and the final result was that she bolted without notice just after Penelope's sixth birthday. To say it was traumatic to his daughter was a prejudicial understatement. Carole started 'presenting' her issues a few years after they were married, in 1953 when Karras got out of Korea and the United States Army.

His wife became pregnant almost immediately after Nick returned from the service, and Carole had been obvious about the fact she never wanted a child. She used birth control, but the girl arrived, nevertheless, ten months after they'd been wed.

Penelope started running away as soon as she hit her teen years. Nick was able to retrieve her each time she rabbited, but when she hit fifteen, she hit the bricks and didn't return and Karras was unable to locate her, and neither did Missing Persons.

Only when she was found in a Clark Street alley did he reunite with her. And shortly thereafter, she was committed to Elgin.

Her case was hopeless, the doctors told him. They didn't want him to think she'd miraculously come out of it, he was warned. They'd tried electro-shock therapy and the results were negative. She was non-communicative, and the shrinks didn't hold out a chance for her to return to the world. She was lost, forever lost.

Nick looked into the matter personally, although his job was homicide. Penelope was alive, after all, but he searched anyway on his free time. All he had was the job. There was no wife, and then he lost his kid, too. She was disappeared, but her body still sat at Elgin.

The mutilation was exactly the same. The problem was that there had been no cases like it—until now. Karras started to think, as time passed, that the rapist had ceased to operate or that he ceased to exist. It didn't seem likely that this was a copy-cat thing. They had kept Penelope's case out of the papers because she was a minor. Papers didn't print the names of victims like his daughter.

This time it was Karen Manski, a college student at Loyola, downtown. Twenty years old, she lived alone in an apartment her father provided for her in order that she live closer to campus.

Nick interviewed everyone who lived in the three-flat. Karen occupied the bottom floor apartment, but no one in the building heard anything on the night of December 12th. The girl never talked to the other residents, and she was only seen going out to school in the mornings and coming home sometime after 7:00 PM, usually, when she returned from Loyola.

He interviewed some of the other students from Karen's classes. They didn't seem to know much about her, either, other than the fact that she was an English Literature major and a junior at the university. Karen didn't have any close friends at the school. She appeared to be a loner, several of her classmates told Nick. She never hung around after class, never drank coffee at the Union with the other class members. She went to class, she studied in the library, and then she disappeared until the next class

3

meeting. Karen Manski was a name on the roster in each of her class sections. Her instructors noted that she infrequently participated in discussions.

She occupied a seat, and she was an A-B student. Very bright, as far as the exams went.

It wasn't much to go on, so Karras scheduled a meet with the parents.

•   •   •   •   •

They lived in Northbrook. Carl Manski was a lawyer, a criminal attorney, and he was well-known among his peers. Nick checked him out. You had to look at the family, but it didn't seem likely that her father would fall under the microscope. His demeanor displayed genuine grief, Nick thought. The mother, Nicole, was a fashion designer who worked downtown. Both parents seemed successful. The house was more like an estate that rested on a half-dozen acres on the periphery of Northbrook, a fairly affluent suburb that lay north and west of Chicago.

They talked to Karras in a spacious living room with a wide bay window that looked out onto their impressive property. Carl Manski was approaching fifty, but he was tanned and fit and had silver streaked hair on either side of his handsome, masculine face. He was dressed in a polo shirt and some expensive trousers that never came off a rack. Nicole was thin and tall and could have moonlighted as a model for the clothes she designed.

Nicole displayed a long stare, something like the thousand- yard variation that Nick had seen often in Korea from fellow combatants who'd experienced and observed too much carnage in battle. She appeared vacant, it seemed to the detective.

The father was more alert, and he answered all Nick's queries without hesitation. But the mother was dazed and far away, so Nick let it be, with her.

The interview took twenty-five minutes, and Karras left them to attend to their loss.

·　　·　　·　　·　　·

He knew Captain Magrette for a long time, longer than he'd been in Homicide. Nick worked Robbery/Auto Theft before he arrived in the most elite division in the CPD. Magrette had worked Robbery, as well, so they had some history.

The Captain was tall, maybe six-five, and he carried his bulk well. Nick was a good six inches shorter and he weighed in about seventy-five pounds less than his boss. Magrette had some French blood in his veins, and he actually spoke the old country's language. Nick knew a few words in the Aegean tongue, but his parents had been born in the States and had lost hold of their ancestors' tongue. The Captain and the Homicide detective were a study in contrast. Magrette was tall and fair, and Karras was shorter, lighter, and swarthier.

Nick sat opposite his commander. It was a straight-backed wooden chair, as opposed to the plush leather seat that Magrette perched atop.

"I read the report," the Captain said.

Nick squirmed a little on his rock-hard seat.

"Why didn't you come to me earlier, Nick?"

Karras had no reply.

"Then I'll say it. It's the same MO from your kid's perp. Isn't it."

"It is. Yes."

"Maybe you ought to pass it on, then."

"No. I'd prefer not to."

Magrette swiveled his chair toward his office window that overlooked State Street.

"Have you seen Penelope lately, Nick?"

"Two weeks ago."

"And?"

"No change, Captain. The way it always is. She's in an invisible cocoon, and no one can touch her."

"I'm very sorry...But it might be the right move to give this one to someone else."

"I'm asking you...I'm pleading with you not to take it away from me, Captain."

Magrette swiveled back toward him.

He lay his folded hands atop his large, mahogany-surfaced desk.

"You want to kill this guy, if it's him. Right?"

"I don't operate like that, Captain Magrette."

"Everyone operates like that if it's his kid. If I left you on this one, there'd be a shadow cast over the investigation."

"I'll do it by the numbers. You have my word...And like you said, it might not be the same guy."

"The modus operandi troubles me. It's identical, no?"

Karras didn't respond.

"We're a little light on manpower at the moment. Don't make me sorry, Nick."

Karras looked up.

"By the numbers. You cannot get personal with this one, Nick. It might not be the same guy. But those details never made it to the media, in either case, so what are the odds it's a new guy on the block?"

Magrette separated his hands and rested them on his arm rests.

"Don't make me sorry, Nick."

•   •   •   •   •

No fingerprints, no fibers. Karen Manski's apartment was clean. There was no body fluid, either. She'd been raped. The vaginal tears were evident with the Medical Examiner's investigation. But no sperm, no remnants of the rapist other than the savagery that he'd left behind himself.

"Ferocious."

That was the word the ME had used. One word.

•   •   •   •   •

There had been problems ever since grade school with Penelope. She didn't play well with others. She was moody, rebellious. She had to spend time in the principal's office, and Nick had to take time away from work to collect her and take her home.

Karras never manhandled her. Never slapped or spanked her. He figured being deserted by her mother was punishment enough. But he couldn't talk to Penelope, couldn't get through to her about her self-destructive behavior.

There were counselors and child psychologists. He even popped some big money for a shrink. Nothing seemed to help. It would've been easy to become enraged with Penelope, but Christ, she was only six when it began.

Then she seemed to concede that her bad behavior wasn't getting her anywhere. Maybe she tired of the principal's office and the defeated look on her father's face when Nick was called to the school to take his daughter home. So, she seemed to calm herself to the point that she wasn't a sore spot, a distraction in her father's life.

She kept a low profile and got through the next few years. The girl still seemed distant, isolated, but she didn't require disciplinary action any longer.

In retrospect, Nick thought she was simply preparing to take off when she felt old enough and strong enough to run away. She waited until she was fifteen, and she remained lost until they picked her up naked and torn apart in an alley on Clark Street.

Nick remembered the patrolman at his door, remembered the sad look on the guy's face when he told Karras that he needed to go for a ride with him in the squad down to St. Marion's Hospital on the north shore.

When he walked into the ER room, the doctor had the same look on his face as the patrolman had. He IDed his daughter. The shock didn't hit him until they transferred her to Elgin. When they dropped her off from the ambulance to the mental facility, the doctor wouldn't allow him to stay with Penelope. He had to drive back to his north side apartment, and as he drove it finally hit him.

It wasn't sorrow. There were no tears. There was only an animal rage. He almost rammed into the car in front of him on the Stevenson Expressway, but he managed to get home. Nick didn't tear up the apartment. He didn't break anything. He couldn't sit down or lie down. There was no sleep for him that night or during the next. He walked back and forth in his studio for hours. He didn't eat. He stayed away from work for four days.

And then he returned to the job. His lieutenant tried to convince him to take more time off, but Nick refused. After a day back at work, he came home and collapsed on his bed and slept for twelve straight hours without twitching a muscle.

He did not dream in those twelve hours. If he hadn't been breathing, someone might have thought Nick Karras was dead.

•   •   •   •   •

After Penelope was committed, Nick began to attend night school at Northwestern University in Evanston. He was able to use the GI Bill to take a few courses. Otherwise the tuition might have been a bit too pricey. But he couldn't sit in his flat by himself any longer. He visited Penelope on his days off, but the visits were becoming too depressing, too difficult, and he went to Elgin maybe once a month, after a while.

He took American Literature classes on Tuesday and Thursday night because he was working days. The classes were an opportunity to get away from his isolation for a little while, at least. The courses were about 19th and 20th Century American writing, and he found them interesting. He'd only gone to a junior college for a year before he left for Korea, and he figured he might pursue a bachelor's degree. It didn't matter how long it took. The classes took him out of his box of an apartment for a little while, at least.

He met Nora in the 20th Century American Novelists section on Tuesday nights. He noticed her because she seemed to be older than the other students—he and she were the 'senior citizens' of the group, although she looked approximately Karras' age, just shy of forty.

There was no ring on her finger. She didn't dress in blue jeans like the kids around them. It was 1972, and everyone seemed to be swathed in denim. The new war in Asia was souring in everyone's minds, and the age of revolt had returned. There were demonstrations on campus and in the city. The hawks had turned into doves, and the peace emblem seemed to be everywhere.

He asked her out for coffee at the Student Union after he gathered the courage. Nick hadn't been with a woman in the biblical sense since Carole boogied, all those years prior.

Nora worked in an art studio in the city. She'd never been married, she told him as they sat in a booth in a mostly deserted Student Union. She was as dark-skinned as he, and she was a kindred spirit, a Greek. Her name was Papanickolas, and her parents, both deceased, had migrated from Athens to Chicago.

She reminded Nick of the Greek actress Irene Pappas. She wasn't the movie star's double, but there were similarities.

"I read palms," she told him.

Nick began to wonder about connecting with her, but he reached out his hand.

She took it and clasped her fingers around it.

Her face became somber, distressed.

"You have suffered a terrible tragedy," she told him.

Her brown eyes pierced his gaze.

"I am so sorry, Nick," she said.

CHAPTER TWO

He loves watching the countryside pass by him on the driver's side window. It's one of the perks with driving transcontinental. He's seen the entire fifty states and some of Canada and Mexico, as well. As a hauler, there have been countless diners where he's eaten, some better than others.

He lives in the city, but he knows you never shit where you eat—except for two occasions. But the incidents were separated by years, so he thinks he's got all his bases covered. Whenever someone shows up on his radar, there are hundreds of miles of separation. So, the police don't connect the dots. Not unless the FBI catches wind that he's crossing state lines.

There have been twenty, so far. Some he lets live and others...The compulsion to hurt them becomes carried away, now and then. It depends on how much they struggle, how hard they fight back.

With the most recent one, it wasn't a matter of her fighting back. He'd simply been swept up by things. She was too innocent looking. He knew the type. College girl. All wrapped up in herself. Rich parents who bought her an apartment.

He always talked them up before he got around to the main event. The talking put them at ease.

He found her walking back to her building. He approached her and asked her why she was walking alone in this neighborhood. Her breath puffed out in a small gray cloud because he'd apparently startled her. Her mother must have taught her to avoid strange men because she didn't respond to him at first, but then he offered to walk her to her door, and she loosened up. Well-bred suburban girls didn't have the common sense inner city kids did. A city kid would've told him to go fuck himself and then dragged out an aerosol can with bear spray or some shit and have threatened to douse him.

But as he walked with her, she opened up. She sounded lonely. She was only a kid, maybe twenty, and she probably didn't get a lot of friendly vibes from people in this town. Chicago could be hard and brutal and cold. So, it might have been that she was relieved to find someone to talk to. After the few blocks walk, she warmed to him.

He was good-looking and not much older than she. When she got a good look at him in the glow of a street light, she saw that he was tall and well-formed. In fact, he had a kind of baby face, a look of innocence that seemed to work on women.

By the time they reached the building, he stopped at the entrance.

"It was nice meeting you," he told her.

It was cold out, in the lower twenties. She looked at him carefully.

"Would you like to come in for some coffee?" she asked.

She was thin and fair-skinned. He was attracted to the type, but he'd done things to various types and shapes before. Colors, races, didn't matter, either. He'd done brown and black and Asians. He had no bones to pick with one category. They were all equally targets to him.

"I shouldn't," he told her. "We've only just met. I'm sure you've been warned about strange men."

"You must be cold...How far away do you live?"

"A few blocks. Not far, down there."

He pointed to the west. The Lake was behind them.

"It's awfully cold. And I never talk to many people, and you were so nice about walking me here."

"Okay. But only for a little while. I've got to get up early tomorrow."

She unlocked the entry, and he followed her inside.

•   •   •   •   •

They were always taken by surprise. He really was a charmer, after all. It was the way he worked his way inside. With some of them, he drove them in his truck to their places. Some lived in apartments, and some lived in trailer parks. It didn't matter. He found his way in no matter where they lived. Once he was inside, it didn't matter where they were located. He found them on foot. He found them at diners. He found them coming out of stores and libraries and gyms. But he found them.

This one he discovered just by walking the blocks just west of the Lake. He enjoyed taking the air even when it was as frigid as it was that evening. He found them by chance. Stragglers from the herd, usually. Walking alone to wherever they were headed. Easy pickings. It was truly amazing that women ventured out alone after all the publicity about what happened to solo females traveling about.

They were more difficult to locate in small towns, but they were available nonetheless. He figured it was their false sense of security. But then he came across to them as a nice guy, gentlemanly, offering to take them home so that the boogie man wouldn't swoop down on them.

It was, of course, too late when they found out he *was* that infamous creature of the night. And they always invited him in. He never had to force his way into their lodgings. And his good looks helped things along. And his age didn't work against him; he had just turned twenty-five.

When he got inside her apartment, he didn't waste time. Before she could turn to him, he was behind her and he wrapped his arm around her throat. She slumped to the floor directly, but she wasn't dead yet. He tore off her clothes as she lay on her plush carpet, and she moaned as he stripped her.

He dropped his pants, and then he found the condom and put it on his semi-erect member. When he looked at her child-like body, he became fully taut and aroused. She groaned again when he thrust himself into her, and he finished rapidly. Her eyes were only half opened.

He rolled her onto her stomach, and then he pulled out the cord and yanked her head off the floor by her hair and wrapped the thin rope around her neck. He throttled her until he felt her go limp. But he didn't want her dead yet. So, he turned her over again. The girl looked up at him with glazed eyes, barely alive.

He choked her until she was fully unconscious, and then he did the cutting. The pieces of her were his trophies. Finally, he tore off the toenails with a pliers he had in his jacket, along with the scissors that procured his two other trophies.

When she opened her mouth to scream as he tore off two of the nails, he applied the cord once again, and this time she stopped breathing. Her eyes were fully opened and her mouth formed an imperfect circle.

He finished his work with the pliers. When he was done, he put her fragments in a plastic bag.

He went into her kitchen and found a dish rag, and then he wiped her body down to remove any fibers or prints. He wiped anything he might have touched, but she had opened the door. He'd use the rag to wipe the nob on the way out. He flushed the used condom in her toilet and made certain it didn't come floating back up again.

When he was satisfied that everything was as it should be, he left her lying on that plush, red carpeting, and he walked out her door using the rag to cover his hand.

It was colder outside, now, and he turned up his collar on the peacoat. It was six blocks to the building where his apartment was. He always parked the truck a few blocks from where he lived and then he would walk home. It didn't seem like a good idea to leave his livelihood too close to his residence. A rig like his was sure to draw attention to itself.

• • • • • •

Nora was unusual. He didn't want to classify her as some kind of psychic spook, because she wasn't some kind of loopy woman who read tea leaves and had a crystal ball to tell the future with. She explained it as some kind of heightened sensitivity, not as something paranormal or unworldly.

But it had caused her some pain, back in the day, she told Nick.

"I didn't have many friends, back in high school. They thought I was strange. Boys were attracted to me, so there was that. But I kept them at arm's length, mostly, because they looked at me oddly, like the girls.

"I made the mistake of telling someone that they needed to be careful driving home, and then they got into a wreck a few blocks from their house. So, they naturally thought I was some kind of gypsy or witch, and they kept their distance.

"I didn't mind all that much because I've never been much of a social animal."

They were under the sheets at Nick's studio apartment. They were heated up after a long and fairly intense encounter. Her body was as slick as his was, and she ran her fingers down his side.

Nick shuddered with pleasure.

"You're ticklish?" she grinned.

"You've found me out."

She looked about the small flat.

"I like this place of yours. Cozy, not cramped."

He traced his right forefinger between her breasts down to her navel. She didn't shudder, but she smiled lazily.

"I'm not ticklish, however."

He rested his palm flatly on her belly. She was lush, but not overly so.

"Why have you been single all this time?"

"Convenience, I guess. Couldn't picture cohabitation with anyone. I like my space and my privacy, too."

"So why am I so lucky, then?" Nick grinned.

"First of all, you're Greek. And I'm not fond of most Greek guys, but then you seem different."

"You don't like lily-white Anglo types?"

She laughed. He liked her laugh; it seemed authentic.

"It's just genetics. We lean toward our own species."

The smile betrayed her sarcasm.

"You are very unique," he told her, straight-faced.

"Isn't that why we're together? We've both suffered, for our own reasons. We're kindred spirits in a very hostile environment. This planet, I mean."

He watched her brown eyes.

"How'd you know about her?"

He'd told her the story about Penelope before they wound up in bed.

"It's like an aura. Maybe it's just some kind of sharpened instinct."

"I read about the studies at Duke University. Apparently not all of it is parlor tricks by illusionists."

"My parents took me to the University of Chicago. They had me do the card tricks."

He studied her more intently, and then he traced the same digit down her torso. She replied by taking hold of him.

"I really like your resilience," she beamed.

"I haven't been with anyone since my wife...took off."

She didn't let go. He rolled onto her and held her hands up against his headboard and then they were joined and moving against each other.

When it was over, he rolled off.

"It's December and I'm sweating like it's July," he told her.

"We're both liquid animals. I don't find it offensive. Do you?"

He shook his head.

"Did you love your wife?" she asked.

"I thought I did. We were young. I just got back from the war. You never know anybody until you're under the roof together."

"So I've been told."

"By who?"

"You. Just now," Nora laughed.

He had to let loose with a snort.

"So, what happened?"

"She had problems. Mental, it turned out. They said she was manic-depressive. Big, bad mood swings. And then when Penelope turned six, she hit the road on us."

"That must've been hard on both of you."

"Mostly with my daughter. I was relieved she left, to be honest. Every night I came home, I never knew what mood she'd be in, and mostly it wasn't pleasant.

"But Penelope took the bigger hit. She wound up with the same diagnosis as Carole—manic-depressive. She was troubled. Then she started taking off on me. When she hit fifteen, she was gone. And then..."

"She wound up in an alley, like you said. And then Elgin. It's a lot to take."

She put her hand on Nick's cheek and stroked the flesh gently.

She bent over and kissed him. It started them up again, and they continued through the night.

•   •   •   •   •

When it was light, about 7:00, he looked over at her and found that Nora was awake, too.

"I don't want to scare the hell out of you, but..."

"If you want me here, I'm here."

•　　　•　　　•　　　•　　　•

She moved in the next night. He rented a U-Haul and carried her sparse belongings to his apartment. There were clothes, a few personal items, and no furniture. Her flat had been furnished. Nora traveled light.

He took her out to Diana's on Halsted Street to celebrate their cohabitation.

"People will think we're nuts," she smiled over a glass of red wine.

"What makes me think neither of us cares?" he toasted back.

"It's too soon for the L word, isn't it?" Nora asked.

"Probably. As I said, I don't want to frighten you off. If you feel the need, you can let me have it. The only issue is who says it first, I guess."

"We won't play board games, Nick. I hate games. I despise one-upsmanship."

"It's agreed, then. No maneuvering. No ties, either. You stay because you want to. If you don't, no scenes. Not from me."

"What could possibly go wrong with a plan like ours?"

"It feels right, though, God help us. We've only known each other a week and...God help us, Nora."

"Don't look for help from Him," she replied.

Diana's was famous throughout the city for its Greek cuisine, and they had the strolling musicians who passed your table. All very authentic, Nick had read in the reviews. He'd never been to Greece and neither had his new roommate.

Maybe roommate wasn't the right word. She seemed more than a cohabitant.

And it was too soon for the L word. Nick didn't think it was impossible that he might gush forth with it. But he was determined not to get ahead of himself in this relationship because it was at least a *relationship*.

It felt like something more, but he was hesitant to utter his feelings aloud. He didn't want to rush things the way he had with Carole. He was quite aware how all that had turned out, and he wasn't looking for a sequel to the first disaster.

Nora had remained unattached for all these years. She'd sprung forth with her age—38. He was two years her senior, so they were at least age-appropriate.

It wouldn't have mattered how old she was or if she'd had baggage from a first marriage or relationship. He had truly never known anyone like Nora Papanickolas. Her being Greek didn't seem to count, either. He thought he'd loved Carole, and she was of Lithuanian descent.

One week in and he felt happiness as he'd never experienced happiness before. There was all that anger and anxiety and sadness with his first wife and with his daughter.

The mortality rate of cops' marriages was a concern, too, but marriage wasn't on the horizon after a mere week together. Nick tried to tell himself all the downsides to a hasty joining with Nora, but his doubts rolled off him like water slides down a duck's backside.

He reached out for her hand and he found it waiting for him across the table.

CHAPTER THREE

He went alone to Karen Manski's flat on Lafayette Street. Even in the chill he could smell the lake water. The wind came in out of the northeast, The Hawk, city dwellers called it. It crept up your spine and nothing could seem to relieve the clamminess. It was one of those things peculiar to Chicago, and people in this town learned to adapt to it. There was no escaping it after the fall moved into the ice house of winter.

There were no signs of forced entry. He checked the doorway near the lock. She had a deadbolt and a chain, and there were no signs that anyone had bulled their way inside.

So, she knew whoever it was that had killed her, or at least she had consented to let him inside. Unless he threatened her at gunpoint or unless he held a blade to her throat. In either case, he'd be taking a chance that someone outside might have noticed and that someone might have called the police. Nick had the feeling that she simply allowed him inside her flat. It was a gut call, but instinct was all he had to work with.

Instinct was an underrated tool in his business. Facts were necessary, even crucial to bringing it to the prosecutor, but you had to find your way to the evidence before it lay before you. No prints, no fibers. Jack shit, that's what he was left with.

There were only traces of some kind of kitchen soap that he'd used to wash her off. It was a slight residue, but it had remained on her flesh.

He couldn't shut out his memory when it came to his kid. She'd been mutilated in the same fashion, but the big difference was that he'd left her alive—if you could call Penelope's existence 'living'.

Nick looked through old files back at headquarters for similar kinds of slashing and tearing, but he couldn't come up with a match. There were instances of cutting, with breasts, but that form of savagery was somewhat common with these kinds of murders. The thing with the toenails showed up on a few solved cases where the perp was rotting somewhere in a cell or where the guy had died. There were no identical kinds of method that he could find, so far. Checking files took hours. It took the bulk of his time as an investigator, and everyone knew the old truism about how the longer the killer was out there, the less chance you had to pinch him.

So, who was it that she knew well enough to open the door for him? Nick already interviewed her parents and her instructors at Loyola and some of the students she shared a class with, and it was all pretty much the same story. Karen Manski had gone through three years of college and had made no tight connections with anyone. No boyfriends or female bonds. She remained aloof.

But her father told Nick that it was the same throughout most of her brief life. She got close to no one. Not even her parents, Carl Manski told Karras. She kept herself apart. Karen wasn't a joiner or a herd creature. She stood alone in life and in her terrible death.

Penelope was like this young woman, that way. Of course, her lot in life was perhaps more terrible than Karen's. At least this murdered girl's suffering was finished. There was no telling how long Penelope was to remain in her horrible captivity. With the vic, it only took minutes to suffer her agony. Nick's daughter might have a lifetime yet to endure.

Karras couldn't go there anymore. He had learned to file his daughter in some distant compartment, only to be visited when he went out to Elgin to visit her. It was a struggle to go there on his monthly duty.

Who did you let through that door, Karen? What prompted you to take a chance on someone you likely only just met? He thought she might have run into him accidentally, but if it were chance, why would this guy be out for a walk on a night that would prohibit most people from venturing outdoors?

He didn't just land at her door out from left field. The guy had to be local. He had to live somewhere close to head out into The Hawk.

But there were hundreds, thousands, of males in this vicinity, so where the hell would he begin to look?

This creature was a predator, of course. A hunter. If he went out looking for quarry, maybe he'd try it again. Maybe it was his first time out.

Nick didn't think it was his premiere sally. He'd been too careful; he made no mistakes. Karras had taken the course at Quantico the summer before last. He was in Virginia at the FBI campus for six weeks, courtesy of the CPD. They wanted all the Homicides to take the course. They called them serial or series killers.

The problem here was there was no series. There was just Karen Manski.

It was back to his intestinal insight, his gut. This guy hadn't done just the one. That's what his instinct was telling Nick. There were others. He simply hadn't located them yet.

If there were other slayings, perhaps the reason he couldn't find similar cases might be that this particular murderer-rapist had pulled his numbers elsewhere. If that was so, his theory about the guy being a local was doomed. You couldn't have it both ways.

Unless he was a traveling killer. Maybe he lived here, and perhaps he did his thing interstate. Nick was going to have to consult the federals and find out what they had in their vast bank of homicidal horrors.

The apartment had been cleaned by now. The evidence crew had finished their examination a week ago. It was mid-January, already, and the surprisingly small amount of blood had been steam cleaned from the carpet. There was a sign for a vacancy on the entry door of the building.

Nick wondered who would want to live in a flat where a murder had happened. He didn't know if apartment managers were compelled to hand out 'full disclosure'.

Nick remembered how Nora had blurted out her sense that he was suffering loss. The story about her being 'tested' at the University of Chicago suddenly came alive in his memory.

There was a phone on the kitchenette counter, and surprisingly it hadn't been disconnected yet.

He called their apartment. Strange. It was 'their' apartment now after only being together a few weeks.

Nora answered on the third ring.

"I thought you were working the late shift," she said.

It was four to twelve, in fact. Midnights was the least likeable tour of the three. You never knew what time it was.

"I'm going to ask you something that might sound a little weird," he told her.

●   ●   ●   ●   ●

"I thought you weren't allowed to bring civilians into places like...this."

"I'm not. Don't tell anyone," Nick smiled wanly. "If this is too odd for you, we can leave."

Nora looked around the small apartment.

"It looks pretty standard for a studio type thing. I don't like the red carpet, not even a little."

But she wasn't making light of the flooring.

"Why am I here, Nick? Couldn't bear to be without me?"

Now there was a slight smile on her full lips.

"You didn't bring me here to seduce me in a new spot, I take it."

"I like it at our place, thank you. I just wanted to see if..."

"I'm not all that comfortable, if that's what you mean. This is where something very bad happened, isn't it."

"Yes. A young woman—"

"Was murdered here. Yes. If it were a smell, it would be death."

"I'll take you home. Maybe this was a very bad idea."

"You wanted my impression," Nora told him.

"Yes. There's nothing else I can figure to do, here. There was no forcible entry. I'm pretty certain she let him in."

Nora walked into the kitchenette. Then she walked out into the tiny living room, and then into the single bedroom.

"She was lonely, alone. She was someone who kept people away from her. I can't see the other. I don't think she knew him very well. But she didn't want to be alone. She wasn't afraid of him, I don't think. It might have been the first time, maybe the only time that she'd ever seen him. I think she might have been attracted to him, and she'd been by herself for a very long time.

"She was alone constantly. I can see her, but I can't see him.

"It turned ugly right away."

Nora stopped. She put her right hand to her mouth, and then she hurried into the bathroom.

Nick heard her being sick, and then he heard the flush of the toilet.

When the door opened, he grabbed hold of her.

"This was a very bad idea. Forgive me. Let's get the hell out of here."

•   •   •   •   •

He drove her back to the apartment just as his shift ended, midnight. He held her all the way inside to their door.

She seemed better once they got into the flat.

"I'm sorry, Nora. It'll never happen again. I don't know what I was thinking."

"The things he did to her."

"Forgive me."

"It's all right. I'm all right now."

"I thought you might…"

"I know," she said, "and it's all right, now."

He held her tight as they sat on the couch. It was late, and she had to be at work in the art studio at nine.

"How do you do what you do, Nick?"

"I can't think of an alternative. Somebody has to stop them. I don't know what else I'm any good at."

"Do you catch many of them?"

"Most of them aren't like this. Just stupid brutality. Domestic fights that get out of control. No-brainers. It doesn't take a super-sleuth to locate them. They're pretty stupid, mostly."

"But not all of them."

He looked at her, and then he held her face in his hands.

"I'll never do that to you again, I swear."

"Other than losing my three meals of the day, it was a little exciting. I've never been on a murder scene before. Only in the movies."

"It's not like the movies or the TV."

"No, it isn't. She was alive, and then she wasn't. She was always at odds with herself, Nick. She wanted to connect, but she never knew how. She never got the chance."

"You better get to bed. You can't sleep late. I have to go in early to make a few phone calls before my shift begins."

She looked at him, and then she kissed him.

"Excuse the odor. I've got to brush my teeth. Sorry for the weak stomach."

"There's plenty of that from professionals. You'd be surprised. But then you get numb to it."

"You're not numb, Nick. You never will be…Come on, let's go to bed. First, I have to de-stinkify myself."

She rose from the couch.

"I love you, Nora."

"You sure pick your spots. But I love you, too."

Nora went to the head, and then Nick walked into the bedroom.

• • • • •

There were hits from sixteen different states, and all of the cases had occurred within the last twenty-eight months.

The FBI agent's name was McNally—Harold "Harry" McNally. He was one of the top profilers at Quantico.

"The breast mutilation and the toenails thing don't match exactly in all sixteen cases. There's some slight variation, but it's very similar. Occasionally he helps himself to the pinky toes. But I'd say it's quite possible the profile fits your man."

Nick explained the similarity between Penelope's assault and the Karen Manski murder.

"Sometimes they let them live. Only four of the sixteen we talked about were still breathing when they were found. I can't say that those four went back to life as usual, unfortunately. Like your daughter, three of them were institutionalized, and the other had to go into rehab with a morphine addiction.

"I'm sorry about your kid, Nick. I'll get back to you with anything new we hear about.

"I think we have a traveling man, Detective Karras. I think he gets around. But he might live in your territory. It wasn't bad luck that he turned up at that girl's door. You might want to follow up with the neighbors. See if they observed anyone a little strange in the 'hood."

McNally ended the call.

Traveling man. Salesman. Trucker?

Finding a traveling salesman would prove a little tough to follow up on.

But a trucker had to have a rig. And if it were a semi, that kind of vehicle would stand out if it were parked on the street. If he were an independent truck driver, he might own his own vehicle.

Nick took the tour. He circled block after block in the vicinity of Karen's building, but all he spied were standard automobiles parked at the curb. McNally was right. A truck parked on a city street would stand out like a cow's ass in a pasture.

•   •   •   •   •

He couldn't stop telling Nora that he was sorry about taking her to a murder scene, and Nora kept insisting that he forget about it.

Nick was also concerned about coming forth with the declaration of his love for her. Both had insisted there'd be no games. But it wasn't a move on the chessboard when the word had erupted out of his mouth.

He had meant it completely and sincerely. It came out as naturally as any other genuine sentiment is spoken. He did love her. It hadn't been accidental. It really was the way he felt about her.

The time element always seemed to come up in his head. Here he was, falling for someone the way he had with Carole, and he'd paid for his mistake with his first wife. Nick understood he hadn't been mature enough to marry someone at that youthful juncture in his life, but he'd felt that the emotion was real, then. He had loved Carole. He'd simply fallen in love with the wrong woman.

It wasn't his wife's fault. She was who she was. But he paid the weight anyhow. Her moods and her temper. Up and down. She was unpredictable.

Nora seemed far different, so far. They'd been together only a month, and still they hadn't had a single scene he could call a fight or a spat or even a misunderstanding. He just couldn't feature getting into a squabble with Nora about anything. He understood how unlikely it was that they'd never get into marital 'combat'. Nick just couldn't feature they'd turn out the way he and Carole had.

There was only the one big mistake, so far. He brought her to Karen Manski's place, a crime scene. What was he thinking? Nora was an artist. She was a painter. When he asked to see her work, however, she told him she either sold her stuff or she threw it away. She never kept any of her artwork. That was why she had so few belongings when she'd moved in. There was only a trunk with her supplies.

She'd begun a new piece at their place. When she came home from her job, she worked on it for a few hours each night after dinner. But she insisted he not peek over her shoulder, and when she was finished working, she promptly covered it over with a beach blanket. He never tried to sneak a look, either. If she wanted him to see it, Nora would let him know.

When he got in bed after his four to twelve tour, she rolled over to him.

"Maybe we ought to try it again at that girl's apartment. Maybe I can try to help find this animal."

When Nick apologized to her again for bringing her there, she cut him short.

"I want to help you, Nick. Let me try again."

CHAPTER FOUR

Illinois was a desolate state. Great expanses of nothing. He was heading west toward Colorado with a load of lumber. He'd be on the road for several days after dropping his goods off near Denver. Then he'd pick up another load and head back toward St. Louis. There would be a night or two in a motel because there were no sleeping accommodations in his cab. He always preferred to wrack out in a cheap motel rather than pulling alongside the highway somewhere. It was worth the money.

And if he found what he was looking for, he needed somewhere inside to take her. There were always strays in the diners and fast food joints where he stopped to eat.

This one he found in a dive just outside St. Louis on his way back from his last drop-off. She was alone. Looked like a runaway. Runaways were prime targets. No one cared if they disappeared.

The thrill was better with the college kid back in the city. Someone would miss her, and they would eventually call the cops. But with these stragglers, it wasn't much of a problem. They were discards, anyway. Toss-aways. Like the paper wrappers on fast food burgers. They'd never make the papers because no one even remembered them. They tended to be one-parent kids or no-parent street garbage.

He bought her a cheeseburger and fries, and the look on her face gave away her availability. It wouldn't be a task to convince her to hop in the truck and drive to a motel not five miles from this roadside flea-trap. The food was surprisingly good. He was hungry, so he joined her in a burger and fries and a couple of soft drinks. The pop was flat, but he was thirsty. And he never complained to the waitresses in these places because it might help them remember his face and this street bitch's face, too. Waitresses had good recall on faces. They remembered regulars, but they filed away first-timers, as well. There might be a next time with a customer, and they did work on tips.

"What's your name?" he smiled across the booth.

The seater had cuts that made his ass uncomfortable. This joint was on the verge of collapsing. The entire environment wreaked of failure. There was only the one waitress, and she looked like she might very well be aware that she'd be looking for a new job very soon.

Her hair was dirty and stringy, but her face made up for her hygiene. She was bone-thin, the way he liked his targets. Fat girls, fat people, disgusted him, made him almost nauseous. His dick wouldn't function with any mounds of excess flesh. They had to be scrawny, child-like, for him to perform the way he liked.

Her hair was a nameless variation of medium brown, and she looked as if she hadn't had a meal for a long time.

"Could you spring for some ice cream?" she smiled.

At least her teeth were white and even. He couldn't handle missing teeth. Bad breath was a deal-breaker, too, but he hadn't sniffed any problem there, yet. The college girl was clean, well-groomed. He preferred them that way, but you couldn't be too choosy out on the road.

"Sure."

He motioned for the bedraggled waitress.

"She wants a chocolate Sunday. Plenty of syrup."

The waitress trod off toward the counter. There were only four or five customers, and the others all sat at that slab in front of the kitchen. The place wreaked of fried onions, and it appeared as if clean-up was not their forte.

"What's your name?" she smiled again.

"Frank."

It wasn't his name, of course, and it didn't matter if she knew his real given appellation. She wouldn't be able to tell anyone who he was in about two hours.

"You like drivin' a truck?"

"It pays the bills, sweet thing."

"Where you from?"

"North of here...You want to take a ride with me?"

"I really don't know you, Frank."

He liked it when they played coy.

"I was just offering you a lift. No strings."

"That's what they all say."

"I'm not everyone...What's your name, pretty girl?"

"Eva. Eva Watson."

"Where you from, Eva?"

Her face darkened.

"All over the place. I travel a lot."

"And guys give you lifts, here and there."

"Yeah."

"And they buy you food, too."

She tightened, facially.

"Why you askin' me that?"

"Just passing time, pretty lady."

"You said you was heading north?"

"I said I was from up that way. That's what I said."

The waitress brought her sundae, and she attacked it ferociously.

"You better take a breath or you'll get one of those brain freezes."

She smiled but kept right on shoveling the ice cream and syrup into her hungry maw.

Finally, she cleaned the glass bowl completely of all the sugary concoction. A little bit of color invaded her cheeks.

"How old are you, Eva?"

"Eighteen."

He smiled.

"You sure you ain't jail bait, now?"

"I turned eighteen three months ago, and I ain't making it up."

"You wouldn't have a driver's license, would you?"

He smiled, and then he let the subject go.

"Are you married?" she asked.

"Do I look stupid?"

She laughed. Her face brightened back up again.

"I don't think your wife would like it if you picked up girls off the interstate, or from anywhere else."

"You worried about my morals, girl?" he grinned.

He knew she would come along for the ride, then. He knew that she thought he was attractive. He could always tell. If she didn't like the looks of him, she would've bolted after the free meal. She wasn't going anywhere.

"You run away from home, Eva? Is that what it is?"

Her face soured again.

"You child services or some goddam thing?"

He laughed.

"I don't think so. I drive that red truck out there in the parking lot, and I'm just trying to get to know you a little better. Is that all right with you, Eva?"

"I just don't like getting the third degree from anybody, Frank."

He smiled lazily. He was full and he was getting a bit sleepy from the long haul here. He'd been on the highway for five days, and he wanted to get on with it with this little bitch before he became even wearier.

"I'm staying at a little motel just down the road. I gotta crash before I get back on the road tomorrow...You want to come along?"

She studied his face.

"How come a good-looking man like you ain't married, Frank?"

"Haven't found the right one right, yet...Christ, how old you think I am?"

"I can't tell ages very good with men. I figure you're thirty. Most guys, good lookin' guys, are hooked by then."

"I'm only twenty-five, Eva. Prime of life, and I ain't in no hurry."

"I could use a shower, shampoo my hair. Is this motel clean?"

"It's four- star. I been there before."

She sat and watched him.

"Where you headed up north?"

"I-55 all the way to Chicago. You ever been?"

"No. I'm from New Mexico. 'Round Las Cruces. You know it?"

"Never been," he told her.

"It's a shit-hole. I hate it."

"You have family?"

"Not so's you'd notice. My old lady is back in rehab. Never knew a father."

He watched her carefully.

"So you're all alone in this world. Sounds like you could use a friend, little Eva."

She grinned over at him.

"All you want is a friend, Frank?"

"We could start out that way and see which way the wind blows."

He left a twenty- dollar bill on the table. That'd leave about five bucks for the tip. The eats were cheap, at least.

"Let's head off, if you're ready," he told her.

She followed him out the door like a trained puppy.

•   •   •   •   •

He let her take that shower she wanted.

Then he got naked and followed her inside the stall. She didn't seem surprised to see him with her under the warm water. She reached up and threw her arms over his shoulders.

"What's that?"

She pointed to the scar that stretched from his rib cage on the left side to his belly-button.

"It was from the war."

"You were in that Vietnam?"

Her eyes were wide, the droplets running down her cheeks and down her flanks.

He nudged himself against her.

"What do you like, Frank?" she grinned.

"Surprise me."

She got down on her knees.

He thought he might explode, and he couldn't leave anything behind, inside her or outside.

"Let's go out to the bed."

He dried her and himself when they stepped outside the stall.

Then he took her out into the room.

She saw the rope on the bed cover. She turned to him and he could see the terror begin to gather on her face.

"Don't you like it a little freaky?" he smiled.

"You mean you're gonna tie me up?"

"Not exactly, Eva."

The trepidation regathered on her.

He clasped his hands to her throat, and her eyes popped wide. He squeezed, and she tried to claw his eyes. He skull-butted her, and she was dazed and wobbly, and he flung her onto the queen-sized bed. He went into his gym bag and found the rubber. He ripped the package open and fit it on himself, and then he yanked her legs up and onto his forearms and he plunged into her. She was small, and she gasped in pain as he forced himself all the way in.

It didn't take long before he was finished, and she was beginning to regain consciousness. He pulled her up from the mattress by the hair and circled her neck with the thin strand of rope. He crossed the rope in front of her neck and pulled it taut. Eva attempted to tear his hands apart, but she became weaker and weaker, and finally she wasn't breathing.

Her eyes were wide and her tongue lolled out the side of her mouth. He dropped her back onto the bed cover.

He went into the john and flushed the condom and its wrapper, and again he made sure that nothing floated back up. The toilet had strong suction, and everything disappeared.

He took a wash towel and wet it and soaped it, and then he went back to her and cleaned all of her flesh. He hadn't touched her hair, so he scoured her from her face to the bottom of her feet, front and back.

Looking down on her, he felt the desire to do her again. But she was dead, and dead bodies weren't a fascination for him. He wasn't a scavenger; his kills had to be alive when he did what he did to them. There was a need for the dread he saw in their pleading eyes. Creation and destruction—they were God's things. The only power he had was to take their lives from them.

It was enough.

Then he took the small sheers and the pliers from his bag. He used batting gloves when he did the cutting because he'd have to touch her breasts and her toes. First, he removed the pink nubs from the small mounds on her chest.

This time he thought he'd do the big toes on either foot. When he was finished, he placed his trophies in a gallon plastic bag. The big toes took up too much room to use quart bags.

He shoved her body onto the left side of the bed. And then he pulled the covers back and lay down opposite Eva, being careful not to touch the small pools of blood that remained on the bed covering. He threw the covering over her, and he lay down beneath the sheet and blanket. He turned over onto his right side and gave Eva plenty of room.

•   •   •   •   •

He departed from the motel at 4:15. The room was paid for, cash, naturally, and he dropped the key in the drop box. The clerk had seen him only briefly, and he'd parked the truck far away from the office. He'd put down a bogus license plate number on the register, and he was certain the young punk clerk was too lazy to verify his license by dragging his fat ass out into the cold to take a look at the plates.

The road was humming beneath him as he headed back to the city, north on I-55.

•   •   •   •   •

He was beat when he returned to the apartment. He parked the usual three blocks from his building, and he always made certain not to leave the cab on the same side street. Safety first, he figured. Who knew if some cop had figured that he just might be a traveling man, perhaps a truck driver. He never underestimated the opposition.

A lot of guys overestimated how clever they were when it came to the police. Not him. He read about these serial killers. He read a lot about them from the library. He had a card and used the big one downtown. They had all kinds of good stuff about guys who traveled around, about how hard it was to catch them because they were 'prepared'. The ones who were unprepared tended to be caught and caught quicker.

He thought he was fairly meticulous about his *modus operandi*, his method of operation. He was thoughtful, nothing spur- of -the moment about him. Choosing his targets carefully was a strength, he figured.

Crashing on the bed, he didn't even take off his clothes. Not even his high-topped construction boots.

There was another long haul coming in just three days, and he figured he'd sleep and eat and not do much else until he was back on the highway again.

CHAPTER FIVE

Nick got her back into Karen Manski's apartment before everything was removed. The place came furnished, so the furniture remained, but none of Karen's personal possessions. They were downtown in evidence. Hair brushes, toothbrush, cosmetics, jewelry.

"It feels as empty as it looks," she said.

"Take your time. I don't think this place'll be occupied for a while. The whole neighborhood, let alone the city, knows what happened here."

Nora walked through the small flat, from the bedroom to the kitchenette to the bathroom.

"There's nothing left of her here, Nick. Just a kind of sad echo. And him...I don't sense anything of him. He's bloodless. Nothing. Empty."

She looked over at Nick and sighed.

"Sorry. Washout."

·   ·   ·   ·   ·

Karras signed out some of Karen Manski's personal items from evidence. He brought it up to his office on the seventh floor where Nora was waiting for him. She had her visitors pass dangling about her neck, the ID on her chest.

"I got the look when we came here," she smiled.

"They're detectives. They're always inquisitive. Nature of the beast."

"Do they know about us?"

"I haven't told anyone anything. I'm not all that close to my colleagues. Maybe that's why no one wants to partner with me."

"I would, Nick. You'd be my first choice."

When he shut the door of his office, he grabbed hold of her and kissed her.

"They frown on fraternization, don't they?"

"Only between cops. You're not supposed to defecate where you eat. Like that."

She laughed.

"Interesting comparison. Poop and romance."

"I imagine some of these coppers have flouted the laws about mingling with other coppers on the job."

He put the box from evidence on his desk. She sat down opposite him.

"Help yourself."

Nora dug into the items in the container. She took out the hairbrush.

"This might tell me something about her, but not likely anything relevant to the animal who killed her."

"Again, take your time. You're all I've got right now. In a couple of ways," he grinned at her.

She turned the brush over in her hands. He thought it looked as if she'd vacated the office, somehow. It was as if he weren't sitting across from her. Nora had departed.

Nora pulled a thread of hair from the brush. She stared at it as if she were reading text.

"Sad girl. Very lonely. I see her in blue. It was her favorite color. Blue, like an aqua blue. She loved the water. She went to the Lake often. Alone. Sat on the beach. Didn't read or anything. Just watched the water and the way the sun played on the surface with blinks of sunbeams careening off the water. She watched the swimmers out in the water in the summer, watched the women and girls and saw the way they dressed in shorts and tank tops and bathing suits, one-piece and bikinis. Colors of the rainbow.

She watched the young men and wondered if they were in love, if they'd found someone to be with in a real, true way.

"It hadn't happened for her, that closeness to another. She ached for it to happen to her, but it wouldn't come along. She was always an observer, a spectator, but she was never able to connect with anyone.

"Her father and mother were too busy. They were detached, always, even from each other. There was no love between her parents. Just convenience. They were comfortable with each other, but there was no passion, no heat.

"Karen wanted it to be romantic, enflamed, for her. But it just didn't happen.

"And then..."

She finally looked up at Nick. Tears welled in her eyes.

She dropped the hair brush on the floor and it made a quiet thud.

"Then what?" Nick asked her.

"I don't know. This monster came to her door. I still can't see him. All I get is a hollow feeling, Nick. There was nothing human about him, but he didn't appear that way to her. He couldn't have. She would never have let him in if she'd..."

Nora bent over and picked up the brush from the floor.

"The other stuff in there wouldn't help. There's nothing of hers on those things. They won't show me anything.

"I'm sorry, Nick. It wasn't much help, was it."

Karras stared at her intently.

"I don't know what to say, so I'll start with 'are you kidding me?' You saw all that by grabbing a hank of Karen Manski's hair? I'm...stunned. I never knew any of that was for real. I think I'm a little bit frightened of you," he smiled.

"Frightened?"

"How about 'awed', 'impressed'. How's that sound?"

"Maybe I've just got an over-active imagination. Isn't that what science would say?"

"Then why'd you wind up at the University of Chicago? They're no barber's college, Nora."

"I couldn't find him, Nick. I'm sorry. I wanted to help."

"You gave me a lot more than her parents did, or anyone else I interviewed. You gave me a ton of insight into the vic."

"The vic?"

"The victim. Cop talk. Sorry. I won't abbreviate anymore."

"How can you do this, Nick? Doesn't it devastate you?"

"They teach you to be objective and aloof. That's why they insist on calling it 'the job', like it's going to work at a factory or an office. Those guys don't become personally involved with the crap on an assembly line or with reams of paperwork. We're supposed to carry over that attitude to what we do. Don't let it get personal. Stay apart from the messes we encounter. Anybody who can't needs to find another line of work because it will eat you up from the insides if you let it. All that misery, every single time, in varying degrees of savagery."

She watched him and smiled.

"I don't think you've ever let it all hang out like that in front of me."

"It's only been a couple of months, Nora. Give me time. I'll bore the hell out of you yet."

"No chance. You might get tired of me first."

"Oh yeah? When will that occur? When we're both on the beach in Florida, watching ourselves crinkle into crust?"

Her face turned serious again.

"What if it stays the way it is, Nick? What if you can't find him, if no one can, either?"

"It happens."

"You think it'll happen for this...creature?"

"I'm going to try like hell, Nora. You wouldn't like to hear the percentage of cases that go into cold storage."

"Don't let it happen with this one, Nick."

He reached across the table and took her hands.

"Let me return this to evidence, and then we'll go out to eat. I'll take an extended dinner break with my informal new partner."

•　　•　　•　　•　　•

Nick took her to Caz's on Randolph Street in the Loop. It was an expensive Albanian joint, but the food was worth the price, and he figured he owed her something for her efforts back at the Headquarters. Nick noticed the other detectives eye-balling her as they passed their cubicles on the way to the elevator down from the seventh floor. He couldn't be sure if they were interested or amused with the strange face among them. Karras had the reputation for being a loner on the floor. It had been a long time since he lost his partner, and now this strange woman showed up to distract them briefly from their paperwork and their boredom between calls out to the streets.

"This is awfully pricey," she stated after perusing the menu.

"These are the wages of your sins, today," he beamed at her.

"Not necessary. I was a flop as a wanna-be cop."

"You don't really want to be a police."

"No. But some of it is fascinating."

"There are women who hang at cop bars. Groupies. They're like the chicks who stalk ball players at the airport."

She laughed.

"You have babes stalking you?"

"I don't hang at cop bars, or any other watering holes, either."

"But you do drink a little."

"Only a little at dinner or parties, and I don't go to many parties, either."

"Not without me, I hope," she laughed again.

"I'm not a social animal, Nora."

"I got that. I'm good with it, too."

"If I had parents alive, I'd have you meet them."

"We're there already?"

"I was there the first night."

"I don't talk to mine, anymore. I think they were happy when I moved out fifteen years ago."

"Why don't you talk with them?"

The waiter came with the bottle of red wine and two glasses. He took their order. They both chose Italian dishes, in an Albanian restaurant known for Albanian cuisine. But the waiter didn't blink.

"They were both rather exhausted with me, I think. They were never convinced about the reason everyone thought I was 'different'. It got old for them, the things that popped out of my mouth. They never really bought into 'second sight' or 'clairvoyance'. They were practical people. Extra sensory perception wasn't part of their worlds. Normalcy was their karma. I was the odd child, and I think they were relieved when I got a job and a place of my own."

"I don't know how you stayed single. I really don't."

"I went on dates. And I made the mistake of coming forth with an impression, now and then. It spooked them all, Nick. They might've thought I was a witch, something satanic, and there weren't many encore dates. I never learned how to keep it all to myself."

"To my good fortune."

"Yeah...So why didn't you head to the exits, Elvis?"

The waiter brought them their lasagnas.

"You had me in about ten minutes. What could I do?"

"I don't want to frighten you off, too, Nick."

"Frighten me off about what?"

"I think we'll have a lot of history together, and I don't see the ending coming any time soon."

"That's clairvoyance, right? Seeing the future?"

"I wouldn't test it on the tables at Vegas. But yeah. You got some free time to spare?"

"You think we'd get in trouble if we barricaded ourselves in the john after dessert?"

"I think it'll hold until we get home, Nick."

"Every party loves a pooper...You know that one?"

"I'll make up for the delay."

He took a bite out of his meal, and Nora did, as well. Then they each took a hit on the red wine. The place was packed. It was small, but there might have been fifty customers present. He was lucky they didn't require a reservation, but it was a Monday night and it was still jammed.

"We already passed the L word," he told Nora.

She looked up at him.

"The next usual junction is the commitment."

"I'm already committed. Didn't you notice?" Nora grinned.

"I noticed. But I think we should think about doing it up formally. As in a ring. Like that."

"Well, that I didn't see coming."

"My, my. I've surprised you."

"I'm not omniscient, for Christ's sake, Nick."

"That's good because I enjoy coming out of left field on you, occasionally, at least."

"I don't need a ring, Nick. They're expensive."

"I didn't bring one, yet. I just thought I'd let you entertain the idea. It'd give me a chance to prepare for the worst when you'd turn me down. I take disappointment poorly."

"Who says you'd be disappointed?"

"Really?"

"Do I get input on the ring?"

"I'm off tomorrow."

"I hate to be the voice of caution, but it has only been a couple of months, Nick."

"I'm still off tomorrow."

"Do we have a budget?"

Nick rose. He pulled a golden band with a diamond out of his right pocket. Then he walked over to her side and kneeled. The other surrounding customers began to watch the two of them.

"It's my mother's ring. It's just temporary. You're still getting one of your own."

"When'd you plan all this?"

Her eyes were moistening.

There was laughter around them.

"Will you marry me, Nora Papanickolas?"

She didn't hesitate.

"I *see* no reason not to, Nick. Yes. Of course, it's yes."

He slipped the ring on her finger, and then he kissed her.

By the time he sat back down, the lasagna was cold.

Then the waiter brought out a magnum of champagne. It was courtesy of the house, he told them. The crowd erupted as if they were at a ballgame when the home club scored the winning run in a walk-off.

CHAPTER SIX

The call came from McNally on a Thursday morning in early February.

"The cutting is pretty much the same. Breasts, I mean. The big toes were severed, but the nails on the others were intact. I think he's mobile."

"Who was the victim?" Nick asked the federal cop.

"Homeless. A drifter. Made her money to survive at truckers' stops. No one remembers seeing her in any close proximity to where the body was found in a motel. The cops on scene found no prints, no fibers, no body fluid. He's got his act down, Detective. He washed her clean. Not even a partial."

McNally ended the call by saying he'd be in touch.

Nick peered out the window out onto the street.

Maybe this guy wasn't a local who moved about, city to city, town to town. Perhaps he'd run into Karen Manski by accident. There was a chance he might have been laid over in Chicago when he'd happened upon her. Her apartment was walking distance from the Lake...But there were no motels or hotels near her apartment building, and he would have been on foot. He couldn't see the young woman being picked up in a drive-by. They came together when she was walking home from the bus stop on Michigan Avenue. Her father said she used city transport to get to her early evening class at the university.

Somewhere between that stop and her apartment this guy had met her, struck up a conversation, and found his way into her flat. That was the theory, the only one he had.

Unless this prick pulled another killing in the city, it was a pretty feeble idea, Nick thought.

But he put faith in Nora's impressions about Karen. His fiancee was not an act in Vegas or a guest on *The Tonight Show*. Karras had never believed in clairvoyance, in seers, or whatever they were. They were con artists who doubled as fillers on talk shows, nothing more.

Then Nora came around, and he became a believer—at least in his bride-to-be. She was authentic. She had something unusual in her. It was a second sight or a sensitivity. But she got into Karen Manski's head, into her sad life, and her description of the college girl's isolation resonated with the notion that she just might be susceptible to some charming maniac who dropped into her existence and then ended it.

Nick had other cases, plenty of them. And the Captain was becoming insistent on pairing Karras with another detective. Which happened in the second week of February.

It was snowing and the plows were barely able to keep up with the accumulation. The weatherman was calling for six to eight inches. Schools were closed in the city, and the closing was a rare event. Nora took the bus and the El to her job at the art store where she worked. Nick was worried she might be stuck at her place of employment.

Driving was an adventure, all right. Bumper to bumper in a white-out on the expressway and the Outer Drive. He got to the office twenty minutes late, but late arrivers were forgiven due to the storm out of the northeast. Lake Effect, it was called. If it kept up, he might be sleeping in his office. Nick didn't much like the prospect of sleeping alone. He and Nora were a couple, by now.

The new partner was Mara Crosby. She was new to Homicide. She'd moved up from Vice only a month ago. Her first partner had retired only a week ago, and she stood in Nick's doorway with her hair dripping with the snow that had stuck to her crimson locks on the way from the parking lot to the building. There were still flakes turning to water on the top of her head.

"My name is Mara Crosby."

"Nick Karras."

"I know. They filled me in about you."

"Come on in and sit down," he told her.

"I have a cubicle down the hall, not far from here."

She sat down and the flakes turned liquid and dribbled down her face. Mara had red hair, almost orange, like a true redhead. Nick had always found redheads strangely attractive. He had no idea why, other than their color of hair was the rarest hue. Her face was a little bit oval, but not so much that she looked like a moon-face. She might have been a model in that she was tall and lanky. It was hard to tell because she wore a long coat.

Nick reached into a desk drawer and pulled out a hand towel and then tossed it over to her.

"Thanks," she said.

She wiped her forehead and cheeks. He didn't see any residue of makeup when she tossed the towel back to him.

"I hear you're swamped," Mara said.

"I assume that's why the Captain assigned you here."

She looked at him and smiled.

"Is there a problem, Detective Karras?"

"No. It's just that I've been working alone for a while."

"I know I'm new at this, but I'm a fast learner, and I know how to keep my mouth shut and how to observe. I'll catch on quick."

Her pale cheeks colored.

"There isn't a problem, Detective Crosby. You're welcome here. We'll get along."

Her face loosened a bit.

"I hear you've got a cutter," she said.

The snow had melted and her red hair hung a little limp, and even without cosmetics she had a pretty face with just a trace of freckles on her cheekbones.

"Trouble is I don't have him. He may have blown town after doing Karen Manski."

"The Captain told me this guy might be a traveling man."

Karras told her about the phone call from the fed, McNally.

"So, the FBI takes over the case?" she asked.

"Don't they usually take on nation-wide murders?"

"I've heard...You think he'll make a comeback in our jurisdiction?"

Nick looked out the window as he swiveled his desk chair.

"I've got a feeling we're not done with him, yeah."

"You big on intuition, Detective Karras?"

"For crissake, it's Nick."

"Then it's Mara. Are we good on rules and boundaries?"

"Yeah, I think he'll be back, Mara. And yeah, I'm big on intuition, too."

"A lot of cops go by their gut. I tend to follow the evidence."

"Where do you suppose truth comes from?" he asked her. "Out of a book? From some preacher man's lips on a Sunday sermon or homily?"

He smiled at her and she grinned back at him.

"You're telling me it arrives as resonance. Inside. Here."

She pointed to her midsection.

"You can take your coat off. They keep it warm in this building."

Mara removed her long, black overcoat. She draped it over her chair and sat back down again.

"Why don't you give me a little history, you know, so we can get more familiar with each other."

"I worked Vice."

"And?"

She looked at him curiously.

"You want to know if I took money?"

Mara flushed again, this time a little darker red.

"That's a terrible tell. You're such a white girl."

She laughed. He'd apparently caught her off guard.

"Relax," he said. "No one's accusing you of jack shit. You wouldn't have made it here if you took cash. I'm sure you know Vice has a reputation."

"Yeah, and the legend is just that, bullshit. Most Vice coppers are clean. There are exceptions, just like in any other division in our house."

"So, we're clear on all that. I had to get it out of the way," Nick apologized.

"This is a copper ACT test?"

"Something like that. I'm no one's mentor. You're here because you can handle it. Not everyone gets into this club, as I'm sure you understand. It takes some adapting to. The bodies keep piling up. They never stop. They take no breaks or holidays."

"So I'm told," she said with a solemn face.

"Does blood bother you?"

"I was pre-med before I dropped out and went into the Academy. I've seen my share of corpses, Nick. I can deal with it. I'm not squeamish, and I won't hurl up lunch all over our shoes."

"You don't look dainty, no."

She smiled.

"Are you married?" she asked.

"Engaged."

"I'm single. No attachments on the horizon. Except to my mutt. He's a nine- year -old mixed breed. Blind in one eye. Has a bladder like cold steel. Only needs to go out two or three times a day. His name is Bob. I got him out of the pound, but he's the one who saved me."

"Saved you from what?" Nick asked.

"Whatever I needed saving from."

He didn't press her for further details.

She looked over at his white board. There were fourteen outstanding cases lettered in red marker. There was an eraser on the ledge, presumably to remove the solved cases.

"What's your solved percentage?"

"It varies. Between forty and fifty percent, I guess. I'm more concerned about what remains up there," he told her.

"That's pretty lofty. The Captain tells me you're his 'brightest pupil'."

"The Captain was pretty good when he was out on the street...I'll show you the jackets and you can get caught up. I don't think we'll be cruising any streets today. This shit is supposed to quit around midnight."

Karras was on days, this week. Checkout time was around five or five-thirty. It was already 4:00 PM.

He stood, went to his file cabinet and withdrew some manilla folders.

"Happy reading," he grinned.

She took the files and headed out of Karras' cubicle.

•　　　•　　　•　　　•　　　•

When he drove home, the snow had tapered off and the plows were catching up with the dwindling downfall. With any luck, he'd be home in twenty minutes. He was following a plow to his exit off the Stevenson.

As he opened the door, he saw Nora lying on the couch.

"They sent me home sick. I've been crapped out here since noon. Took an hour to get here, mostly because the bus was creeping along."

He sat next to her and felt her forehead.

"You're pretty warm," Nick told her.

"Just a nudge over 100. I took some pills."

"How do you feel?"

"About the way I look," she murmured.

"You should stay home tomorrow, too," he advised.

"Where'd you get your MD?" she cracked.

He didn't answer.

"I'm crabby when I'm sick, but I'm almost never sick."

Her face was paler than it usually appeared. It was easy to tell because she was dark-skinned, about like him.

"Don't let me bark at you, Nick."

"You didn't bark...Did you eat anything today?"

"No. Just a piece of toast. The wages of sin, toast. I hate burned bread."

He palmed her forehead again.

"When's the last time you took some aspirin or whatever?"

"A few hours."

She took hold of his right hand suddenly.

"There something you want to tell me, Nick?"

"Are you sensing something?" he smiled cautiously.

"There's something you want to tell me."

"The snow stopped," he told her.

She waited.

"Oh, yeah. I got a new partner today."

"Really? What's he like?"

"It's a she, Nora."

She smiled slyly.

"You already knew, right?"

"I knew you wanted to tell me something that was on your mind.
That's all I meant."

"She worked Vice."

"Was she undercover, Nick?"

"I don't know. Didn't ask."

"Married?"

He shook his head.

"Do I need to worry?"

"Not about me, you don't. I have this beautiful witch I live with who
sees every move I make, false or not. I figure she'll lay a curse on me if I
even think about going astray."

"Is she worth going astray?"

"No one is worth it. I know when I have a good thing going."

"Is she very pretty?"

"She's attractive. A redhead."

Nora's pale face darkened slightly.

"But I think I'll stick with the swarthy Greek goddess I lucked into."

He bent over and kissed her on the forehead.

"You'll catch my cooties," she warned.

"I don't give a rat's ass if you pass me the black plague. As long as we catch it together."

He kissed her on the lips, but she didn't pull away from him.

"This was almost our first argument," he said.

"I don't want to fight, Nick. I want to get married."

"Name the date."

"As soon as the plague passes. I don't want to puke on our wedding day."

"We need to get invitations, all that crap," he told her. "Didn't you want a church thing with all the candles and shit?"

"I'm no more Orthodox than you are, Nick."

"You mean you want a civil ceremony?"

"I mean I don't want the pomp. I just want you."

"Tomorrow's my day off. The snow's gone, for a while, anyway. Think you'll feel up to it?"

"You can buy some cheap wedding bands at the Venture. We can save up for better ones, more permanent ones."

He kissed Nora again.

"Save it for the honeymoon," she smiled. "I need to recover. I usually get better in a hurry. I've got a great immune system...Are you as sure about this as I am, Nick?"

"I can't remember moving in with any other strange woman and falling in crazy love with her and proposing. Other than that disaster of a first wife. And you ain't anything like her, Nora.

"Yeah, I'm sure."

He sat on the couch next to her and held her until she fell asleep, and then Nora was snoring lightly, like a cat on its back.

CHAPTER SEVEN

His childhood included no abuse by his parents. He hadn't been adopted. No one had slapped him around or beaten him. It seemed to come all too naturally for him to kill small animals—cats and dogs and whatever unfortunate mammals or reptiles he found on his forays into the woods around his luxurious home in a northwestern suburb of the city.

He graduated into killing human beings quite gradually. His first was a teenaged girl he came upon in a forest preserve just outside Chicago. She'd been walking alone, and he'd come upon her on a trail through the nature park. There were no other people on the trail because it was a cold January morning. The trees were leafless and everything seemed appropriately dead.

She came at him from the opposite direction, and he smiled at her and she returned the smile. He was a good- looking young man at eighteen. The girl was not exceptionally pretty, but he had a honed sense for vulnerability. Joining her in her walk, they talked easily about themselves. There was no reason not to tell her his name. Hers was Jane Merrow. It seemed an odd name, Merrow, and she explained she was named after an English actress that her father admired.

They walked toward the parking lot, but he asked if she were cold, and Jane replied she was fine, her parka kept her warm. It was yellow with a hood that had faux fur about it like a halo. She wore leather gloves, and she had hiking boots on, as well.

He wore a navy peacoat and a watch hat. He had seen *The Boston Strangler* film, and Tony Curtis wore the same hat and coat. He wore leather gloves, but they were black, not brown, like Jane's.

They turned around and headed back into the woods. The sun was overhead, but it didn't heat up the frosty air.

Jane was going to college the next year, but she still hadn't decided where. She had several scholarship offers, and she'd have to decide by spring. She thought she'd major in psychology. She wanted to work with kids. She didn't connect well with her peers. It was why she took these solitary walks in the woods by herself.

"Aren't you frightened to walk alone out here?" he asked.

"I don't feel lonely in the woods. I know it's strange, but I feel at peace by myself."

Her face was plain, but it was hard to tell about the rest of her under the bulky parka.

It didn't matter because he wasn't interested in fucking her. He simply wanted to kill her. And he was amazed at his good luck in finding Jane, or anyone, walking alone in a forest preserve. He certainly hadn't planned on his first kill happening here today, but he wasn't going to lose the opportunity.

There was the fear factor, however. Someone might come along, and the visibility was better on account of the denuded trees and shrubs. Someone might spot them from a distance without his being aware of their presence.

"Why are you out by yourself?" she smiled.

Her smile was superior to her overall looks, he decided.

"I guess I'm like you. And I don't mind the cold."

"Are you going to school somewhere this fall?" she asked him.

They were getting farther and farther into the trees. He'd been on this trail several times before. The path wound around a slough, and it was perhaps a mile to fully circle the water.

"I guess," he answered.

"You're not sure? Don't you want to go? I can't wait. I can't wait to get away from home. I want to be on my own. My parents are okay, but I guess I'm too independent for them. They're always giving me this lame advice. It's like I don't have a mind of my own, sometimes."

"I like hunting."

"Really?"

She stopped and looked directly at him for the first time.

"I can't imagine killing anything," she said.

"It isn't the killing so much as it is the hunt. You know, stalking the prey."

"What kinds of animals are you talking about?"

He could sense the growing antipathy from the plain, doughty girl. He wanted to see the sea change in her face when he grabbed her by the throat and squeezed until her face turned darker, deeper shades. The blood would rush to her cheeks, and her eyes would pop wide, and he'd squeeze and squeeze, impervious to any struggle she might retaliate with against him. He knew he could overpower her easily, and throttling her would choke off any screams.

"Small stuff. Just rabbits and squirrels, mostly."

Jane's face darkened.

"I'm getting cold. I think I better go."

"I thought your coat kept you warm." he grinned.

"But I'm getting chilled. I think I better go."

They were halfway around the slough, and there was no noise from the woods. No birds singing, no crawling critters chattering. No rustles from all the fallen leaves around them. It was soundless except for her breathing and his own. And there were the frosty puffs coming out of their mouths. But no sounds. Just the sun rising toward its noon zenith.

"I'll walk you to the lot," he told her.

"I'd rather walk alone."

"I can't let you do that. You can't be alone in places like this."

"It's all right," she explained.

When Jane turned to retreat from him, he took hold of her sleeve. He spun her about and then clutched her throat with his black-gloved hands. She tried to tear his grip from her neck, and then she swung wildly at his face. She was only able to strike one glancing blow off his right cheek before he tightened his grip and cut off her air. Then her swings became feebler, and then she began to go limp, and he laid her down on the path on her back and he found himself on top of her.

He was aroused, but he was aware that he couldn't leave any traces on her or in her. As he looked down at her glazed eyes—they were a strange color, green and brown—he saw her lights were fading.

As he continued to choke her, there were no more billows of frozen breath coming out of her mouth or her nostrils.

He released her, and her head lolled to her right.

The first thing that occurred to him was transporting her body off the path. He needed time to get out of the preserve and time to get back home before anyone came upon her.

She wasn't a heavy girl, he found, after he'd pulled her up and lifted her onto his right shoulder. She seemed almost weightless. It was probably all the adrenalin, he figured.

He labored his way to the dock that jutted out from the slough, and when he got to the end of the tiny pier, he looked all around and saw no one in the vicinity who might be witnessing what he was about to do.

He bent forward and released her from his shoulder, and she made a plopping noise as she hit the surface of the slough. She seemed to float for a few moments, and he began to sense panic gathering inside himself.

Then the water accepted her, and the body disappeared. It was all that heavy clothing, he thought. It became saturated and weighted, and the slough sucked her under. He had no idea how deep the water was out here at the end of the dock, but there wasn't a trace of Jane Merrow, anymore.

He looked up and across the slough. There was no one, and there was still no sound from the preserve. It was frozen and still, but the temperature must have been above freezing because the water hadn't frozen over into a sheet of ice. He'd been fortunate that it hadn't been cold enough to solidify.

He didn't want to leave. He stood at the end of the abbreviated pier and looked down into the murk.

What were the odds there'd be a Jane Merrow walking the same desolate trail he'd trod? It was like hitting all the numbers on some lottery. Astronomical. Impossible. The next time, he'd have to hunt more fertile grounds than this. He'd only figured on a solitary excursion, this morning. When his parents asked him where he was going, he lied and said he was driving out to the beach in Chicago.

"The beach? In this weather?" his father laughed.

He hated it when his old man laughed at him. He always seemed to condescend when he talked to his only offspring. There were times when he lusted to kill his mother and the old man, both. They never laid a hand on him. Never denied him anything. Most people would think they were the perfect duo of parents. But they didn't live with the two of them. They didn't endure all their well-meaning patronage.

He'd stormed out to his car. He didn't care what his father thought of his destination. Rage had brought him to the slough, and he didn't want to leave the scene of his first triumph.

It was far better than shooting a rabbit or a squirrel or a dog or a cat with his BB rifle that he kept hidden in his room. They'd given it to him when he was twelve for Christmas. His father insisted that he only shoot the air rifle when the old man was there to supervise.

His father and mother weren't old. They were in their early forties. He was a divorce lawyer and she was a corporate attorney. Very affluent. They lived in a rich suburb, all white, of course. They claimed to be liberals, but he knew better.

He could go to any school he liked, any Ivy League factory he wanted. But he enjoyed taunting them both by telling the two of them that he thought he'd join the Army after high school graduation. He said he'd like to join some elite corps and find adventure in some strange terrain.

What he didn't tell them was the military would teach him to be more proficient at slaughtering human beings and that they'd provide tools more efficient than his own two hands.

The parents, of course, never heard his reasons, later, for enlisting.

Now he remained on the end of the pier at the slough surrounded by naked trees and dead foliage. But he felt alive in spite of the death around him and just below him in the dark water. Jane was at the bottom by now, and it would take a long while for some fisherman to snag that parka and haul her up to the surface. He'd be long gone by that time, but he couldn't wait to read about it in the paper or see it on TV. It was a pity that no one would ever know it was his handiwork.

Again, what were the chances he'd walk right into his first kill here on this freezing January day? He'd dreamed about it since he was fourteen or so, but mostly he dismissed the possibility of actually accomplishing what he had only minutes ago. He used to figure it was all just fantasy, some dark dream he had that would never really happen. There was the usual trepidation about being caught, about being caged up in a cell for the rest of his life.

But without the danger of incarceration, of execution, even, there couldn't be a rush. Nothing could compare to the reality of what he'd just experienced, no movie, no book. Nothing could compare to this moment.

Something finally happened to me, he felt. It was as if he hadn't been born until this day, this hour, this minute. He never crowned at his mother's opened wound. No one had pulled him from her womb. It was all preface to this day in January.

He knew he couldn't stay in place relishing the moment any longer. Someone would come along and see him standing solitarily at the edge of the dock, looking strangely down into the blackness of the slough. Then someone would become suspicious seeing him lingering here, and perhaps they might call the preserve cops, who'd poke around into the water until they felt the lump of sodden parka below.

He walked quickly but deliberately back toward the parking lot where the VW Bug that his parents bought him for a pre-graduation present for Christmas, last month.

He encountered no one as he turned the motor on and as he slowly drove out of the lot. Traffic was sparse until he got onto the Stevenson Expressway, headed toward the Outer Drive, and then north and west toward home.

•   •   •   •   •

The Army was the proper choice. There were rumblings going on in a place he had never heard of before—Vietnam. They were only sending advisors over, at this point, but the advisors were highly trained special forces. So, he decided to join up with an elite group of warriors. He'd read about the Green Berets and their exploits. They were rather new to the Army, but they were highly trained in combat and weapons and languages.

When he was accepted into the Green Berets—or just the Greenies— he found out to his amazement that he was gifted with a talent to learn exotic languages, like Vietnamese. It was a subtle tongue, but he picked it up rapidly. He was proficient in the language after only ten weeks training. His instructors were amazed by his ability to speak it fluently in less than three months. But it was, as he learned, a gift.

His other gifts had to do with his mastery of firearms and explosives. His instructors thought he was a special student, when it came to killing people. A few of his instructors wondered if he needed a psychological evaluation after observing him on the firing range. It was the odd look on the kid's face as he fed rounds into standing targets. He appeared to enjoy trigger time perhaps a little too much.

But this nineteen-year-old killer was exactly what the Army required at the time, and they were all too happy to unleash him on the insurgents, the Viet Cong.

There were awards. Bronze, silver. One purple heart that left its reminder on him, on the side of his torso. He was a skilled sniper, and he had more than his share of authenticated kills.

He spent two tours in the bush, and it was the wound on his side that sent him home. He came back in 1967. His parents were waiting for him at O'Hare, but he dodged them at the airport, and it was the last time he'd seen them. He met them at the gate and then told them he had to hit the head, but he never came back from the shitter.

He disappeared, thereafter.

·   ·   ·   ·   ·

But he hadn't really left the city. He got a job as a trucker, transcontinental. He hauled everything and anything, and he finally saved enough to buy his own vehicle. It was red and beautiful.

He found an apartment not far from Lake Michigan. It was home when he wasn't on the road, which was most of the time.

There hadn't been much of an urge to seek out another Jane Merrow. All that slaughter in the jungle had sated his previous urges to murder young women. Killing a mark in the bush wasn't nearly the thrill he'd had in closing off Jane's air, watching her become limp, seeing her headlights dim. Dumping her sad ass into the drink at that slough.

He was too busy in the rainforest trying to survive the gooks to try and seek out some civilian to choke out, in some hamlet. The Army frowned on whacking indigenous personnel who were non-combatants.

There were rules, even there. But the real problem was availability and convenience. He was part of a body, a corps, in the shit, and you tended to be surrounded by other troopers, most of the time. There was lone wolf time when he set out toward a villa to pop some honcho's weasel from a distance, but on other ops you were always surrounded by your band of brothers, and most of them weren't into strangling girls.

He had to bide his time to go back home to a different happy hunting ground.

CHAPTER EIGHT

Mara Crosby had her quirks. She was hooked on tomato juice. Unlike any other cop he'd known, Nick watched her top off a can of tomato juice every morning, instead of the requisite, perfunctory coffee. She bought the juice at the cafeteria on the first floor in the cafeteria.

Nick was hooked on soft drinks. Coke, Pepsi, it didn't matter. They both had caffeine, like the bean water did, and they already had the sugar tossed in for the burst he needed in the morning. Nora tried to get him to drink the new sugar-free stuff, but Nick didn't like the sugar-substitute. She told him he would be flirting with diabetes someday if he didn't kick the sweet shit.

Nick and Nora were wed the day after the big snowstorm. Karras didn't know anyone he wanted to be their witness, and Nora had no people in the vicinity to call, so Nick rang up his new partner. He reached her on her home phone. They'd exchanged numbers in case of an emergency.

"Why me?"

He laughed.

"Because I came up empty. It'll only take twenty minutes or so at the JP's, and then you get a free lunch out of it at Terri's."

Terri's was a mid-list joint on Michigan Avenue. Celebrities who were visiting town ate there, once in a while. The food was good and the price was in Nick's neighborhood.

The JP had walked out in his navy-blue robe, and he had extinguished his cigarette before the nuptials took place. Karras had hurriedly purchased two gold bands he bought at some pawn shop on Wacker Drive.

The permanent rings would have to wait until he could figure out the finances. Nick hated credit cards and liked to deal in cash. It didn't always work out for him, but his debts were minimal.

Mara showed up as promised, and for some unfathomable reason, she cried during the ceremony. Nora caught sight of the waterworks, and she felt compelled to join in the boo-hoos. Nick couldn't help suppressing laughter. And his bride shot him an evil eye, and his face sobered up.

It took fourteen minutes, and they were joined in holy matrimony. He took the trio of them to Terri's and they all ordered the steak sandwich. It was worth the drive over there.

It was dry and cold on that mid-January day. The sun was bright, and Nora had recovered as promised. Her fever was gone.

She eye-balled Mara throughout lunch. But she somehow couldn't help but like the new, redheaded partner of her husband. Nick observed the two of them at lunch, and he was relieved to see that they got along fine. He imagined they might talk behind his back, soon enough.

They drank no alcohol because Mara ordered her usual tomato juice, and Nora was still only a little bit wonky from the fever. Champagne was overrated anyway, Karras figured. He ordered a diet soft drink just to please his brand-new wife.

The lunch took thirty minutes. Terri's was a rung or two beneath swank, but it was clean and non-repulsive. It was the kind of joint you might come back to again.

He thanked Mara for witnessing, and Nora hugged her like they were high school besties, and the drama, for the moment, was done.

•　　•　　•　　•　　•

They re-consummated the relationship when they got back to the apartment. The wooze had departed from Nora's eyes. He felt her forehead, and it was cool to the touch. He thought she might have heated up because of the sex, but she'd been enthusiastic enough. The passion for her hadn't disappeared because they were legal, now, and he was hoping it was the same for Nora.

"Is it different?" he queried.

"You mean *that*?" she smiled.

"I mean *that*, yes."

"Married sex is supposed to be strange?" Nora laughed.

"I don't want it to be DDSOS."

"Huh?"

"Different day same old shit," he informed his wife of two hours.

"That's idiotic, Nick. Really."

"I just don't want the boredom to kill us."

"It's called *ennui*. I don't think it's likely, not from my side of the bed."

"I want you to be happy. That's all."

"I'm there, Nick. I'm there for the long haul."

"The average length of a cop's marriage is—"

"Don't you dare."

"I was just trying to say I'll work at this thing, Nora. That's all I meant."

"You're getting all self-conscious, my love. It's all good. Can't you feel it?"

"I can't see my life without you in it."

"I'm here. For the duration, Nick."

"In sickness and in health."

"I'm a fair hand at looking into the future. You want me to read your palms?"

"You have Gypsy in your blood?"

Now his face broke out into a sunnier frame.

"Greek on both sides, just like you."

"Where'd the sight come from? It had to be there in the past from one of your relatives."

"My mother's grandmother. She lived in a village just outside of Athens. The neighbors thought she was a witch, but they left her alone because they were afraid she'd cast a hex on their goats and kill off the whole herd."

"Are you making all that up?"

"Only the part about the goats."

She rolled closer to him and threw her arms around his neck.

Nora was darker than he was, and he loved the deep brown shade of her smooth flesh. She was hairy in only two spots. The stuff on top was lush and thick and so dark brown that it appeared black. The fur south of the border was a lighter brown, but it wasn't too bushy. She was hairless on her arms and legs, and there wasn't even a faint shadow above her lips. Mustaches on women were deal-breakers. She shaved her pits, as well. But then she was thoroughly American in spite of her roots back in the old country in times gone long by.

They joined, and she was on top, astride.

When it was over, she lay her head on his chest.

"We didn't discuss kids," she said.

"You're still on the pill, no?"

"I didn't Pearl Harbor you, Nick."

He laughed loudly.

"Thanks for the tip...You want children?"

"Don't you?" she retorted.

"Only if you do."

"That's no answer, lover," she told him.

"I want kids, yes. But not right away. Is that all right?"

"Of course. But I'm at the tail end of my biological clock, Nick. It becomes iffy after thirty-five, and I slipped past that yard line a couple of years ago."

"Then maybe we ought to go for it. What do you think?"

"I just want one. No Russian roulette for us. Okay?"

He embraced her tightly.

"One healthy one is perfect. Stop taking the pill, then."

"You're sure? You're not just stroking me?"

"I'm sure."

"What about a honeymoon? Can you get a few days off?"

"I've got plenty of leave. And our boy who did Karen Manski has been quiet, lately."

"Let's go someplace close."

"We could spend a few days in St. Louis. It's warmer there. Not much, but better. I'll make a reservation tomorrow."

"I might not get pregnant right away. Or maybe not at all."

"What does your intuition say?" he asked.

"I can't always just dial it up, Nick. It comes when it feels like it...You've already got a daughter."

"Are you afraid we'll have one like her, like Penelope?"

She put a finger to his lips.

"I didn't mean it like that at all. I'm just saying we're older, and that increases the odds that a baby will be exceptional."

"Exceptional how?"

She watched his eyes.

"I still want a baby with you. My intuition says everything will be good."

She kissed him again.

•　　　•　　　•　　　•　　　•

They took three days and stayed at the downtown Holiday Inn. It was only a few blocks from the Mississippi River. Most of the attractions, like the St. Louis Zoo, were closed down until March and spring, but they spent most of the seventy-two hours in the room making full use of the king-sized bed and eating room service. They lounged in the suite in robes, but only when the guy brought their meals to the door.

They wore the white terry cloth robes when they dined.

"I can't eat naked," he told Nora. "I guess I'm too repressed."

"Eating in the raw is unappealing to me, too. Let's save it for mattress time."

She bit into her double cheeseburger. Room service was a plus in the motel by the river.

•   •   •   •   •

It took six and a half hours to drive back to Chicago, and it was clear sailing because the snow had held off for their honeymoon from St. Louis back to the city.

•   •   •   •   •

He did a pass-by in the neighborhood where Karen Manski was murdered. He and Mara drove past her apartment building and hit every side street in a two-mile vicinity near the crime scene location. Nick was still looking for a truck to magically appear at a curb on one of those blocks, but the largest vehicle either of them saw was a pickup, here and there. Nothing a trucker would drive from coast to coast. It seemed to become increasingly clear that his theory about their perp being a bi-coastal visitor was fading.

"I still think you were right," Mara said as they cruised the near-north neighborhood.

"The famous shot in the dark. The odds never favored me."

It was cold and clear for the eighth consecutive day, and February was on its way, the shortest, shittiest month of the annum, as far as Nick was concerned. He hated the twenty-eight days prior to the oncome of March and spring. He wasn't a winter soldier. Wasn't a fan of iceberg season.

"If anyone pinches him, it'll probably be that fed, McNally. Or one of his brethren. I don't see our boy returning for a curtain call. That's what makes these pricks tough to catch."

"They're organized. They prepare. The ones who don't fuck something up and get caught quick."

He looked over at Mara and grinned.

"I love it when you talk dirty."

"You have no idea. I grew up with hooligans."

"You have any ideas of your own about our man?"

"He cuts his kills. Maybe a ritual he's got planted in his soggy noggin? I'm not saying he's nuts. He's very premeditated in the way he did Karen. The victim that McNally told you about was almost the same, no?"

"The toes were the distinction, but he apparently likes to work on breasts and feet."

"I guess the breasts underline his misogyny. Taking trophies isn't unusual, according to the FBI. I took the course at Quantico just before we partnered up," Mara told Karras.

"I don't really understand what a fucking sociopath is, do you?"

"It means they have no clue about right or wrong. They just do their thing because it's their thing. These investigators who interview them in prison come up empty. They have no idea why they do the things they do."

"I like 'asshole' better. An asshole is an asshole because he has no idea he's an asshole. That's why he's an asshole."

She laughed. Nick enjoyed making her laugh. It wasn't easy to provoke chuckles out of Mara Crosby. She was a serious young woman, mostly.

"But, then, I'm no trained psychologist or psychiatrist, you understand."

"I can see why Nora loves you. I'll bet you make her laugh all the time. Men don't seem to get it that we love to laugh."

"I don't tickle her funny-bone often enough, I'm sad to report."

"Make it a point. I'm telling you, Nick, it's like getting to a man through his stomach. With babes, it's making us laugh."

He turned right and drove up another block. They were getting farther and farther away from Manski's building, and they had several follow-ups to take care of before their shift was finished.

"How was the honeymoon?" she asked.

He told her about their room in St. Louis. He recounted their brief visit to the Mississippi River.

"Twain country," she smiled.

"You read him?"

"Yeah. He's funny as hell."

"We skipped over him when I was in high school. I had a black English teacher, and she thought he was a racist."

"Because of that word?" she asked.

"Yeah, I think so. It was rare to have a black teacher in any subject when I was in school. There were only a few black kids in my graduating class, but there were more African-Americans coming into the lower grades. Integration, baby. Things change."

"We need to stop at that scene on the west side, speaking of African-Americans."

"It used to be Negroes. Then blacks. Now it's African-American. Confusing, sometimes."

"You're brown, partner. White, you ain't," she cracked.

"Some people think I'm Hispanic. Some girls I knew in high school wouldn't go out with me because I looked Mexican to them."

"They needed glasses, the silly bitches. You're a brown white guy, partner."

It was Nick's turn to laugh.

She pointed her first finger at him.

"See how it works? You gotta make each other laugh."

"They wouldn't go out with me when they found out I was Greek, sometimes. Not Anglo enough, I suppose."

"It's only rock and roll, Nick."

They took off for the crime scene on the west side. Two very young black children had been torn up on a drive-by shooting. It was being classified as 'collateral damage'. The real targets, two gangbangers, hadn't received a scratch.

CHAPTER NINE

Carl Manski wanted answers. What were the police doing to find the murderer of his daughter Karen? Manski knew people, all the way to the mayor's office and including Hizzoner himself. Manski was a name brand in the Democratic party. He was tight with several big shots in several wards in the more affluent sectors in the city. He was a big-time donor.

The shit trickled downward, courtesy of gravity, as always, and the fecal material landed squarely on the topknot of Captain Magrette. He was ex-military, like most police, and he well knew the truism 'it isn't your fault; it's your problem'. So, Karras and Crosby were hauled onto the carpet for a conversation. It wasn't a very pleasant interview, of course, but Magrette let the two detectives know that the poop was relegated currently to the Captain's desk.

Nick had heard the tale before. Chicago was like most cities and towns—a political circus filled with political animals. Mara had her share of the same kind of lecture ever since she worked patrol, so it was nothing new to her, either.

"Sideshow Dick has been burning my ear for a week, now, courtesy of the bereaved Carl Manski, and I can't say I blame the father. He just happens to have his nose attached to the right anal apertures."

The Captain had an appropriate scowl on his face. He was just the messenger, Nick figured. Nothing personal. He'd been waiting for the Manski family to show its frustration with their lack of results.

'Sideshow Dick' was Magrette's appellation for the Big Man at City Hall. It was the name no one uttered around the hordes of sycophants that attached themselves like sucker fish to sharks.

"Are there any rays of sunshine I can pass on to the mayor's castle?"

Magrette was still clenching his jaws as if he were about to pass a kidney stone.

"Sir, we've canvassed that neighborhood several times a week ever since we started conducting interviews," Mara piped in. "It's not like we've ignored Karen Manski's case."

Karras looked over at his younger partner and wanted to grab her by the shoulders and shake her. He waited for the volcanic response from the bulky boss, but it never arrived.

"I understand, Detective Crosby. I seek an update, not a cheap shot from a first year Homicide."

He wasn't shouting, at least, Nick mused.

"I still think he's peripatetic," Karras interjected.

"He's what the fuck?"

"He moves around, place to place. There hasn't been a similar case since the first one."

"That's all you got?" the Captain smiled wanly.

"I could make shit up, I suppose," Nick offered.

"Another wise guy heard from."

"I'm not trying to be," Nick told him.

Mara and he were standing opposite the seated Captain. It seemed easier to make a quick getaway, standing upright. But there was no chance this meeting was going to be brief.

"We need to expedite. I'm assigning four more detectives to this case. All of you need to hit that neighborhood hard, come up with a witness, anything...You think he travels a lot. Is that correct?"

"Maybe a truck driver. A transcontinental driver would fit my theory."

"Your theory...Knock on doors and get off your asses. You know the drill? Okay, so find out if anybody in the area drives a fucking semi. Exhaust your *theory*, Karras...You buy into his shit, Crosby?"

"I think it's definitely worth looking into. We've been trying to spot a vehicle in the surrounding blocks, but we haven't seen anything yet."

"He might be on the road, out of town. We'll keep looking, and we'll try door-to-door," Nick added.

The Captain finally unclenched.

"I know it's unfair, what I said. But I either let it all go or I take my service weapon and start shooting people and I'm too close to retirement to begin a new career as one of your customers. Do you read me clearly?"

Nick nodded. He couldn't help smiling. Mara had a touch of color in her cheeks.

"The new guys I assign will contact you today. I want the six of you tag-teaming this motherfucker. He can be found. Anyone can be found. Let's see if we can beat the FBI to him. That's all. Go with God."

They turned and left Magrette to think happy thoughts about Sideshow Dick.

·   ·   ·   ·   ·

"I always feel so much lighter after being reamed," Nick told Mara as they headed back to the crime scene vicinity. "It feels so much lighter inside me now."

She laughed. Then she looked over at Karras, behind the wheel of the Crown Victoria, the standard copper ride.

"It could take weeks, months, Nick, to pull a house-to-house. 'Hey, you seen a truck parked out by the curb?' How likely is that? This guy needs to come home. It's the only way we get him."

"It's a high toll, Mara. Someone has to get dead."

She shifted her gaze out the passenger's window.

"You do think he'll come back, don't you?"

"They have a tendency to come back to their territory, yeah," Nick answered.

"By that time, we could be directing traffic in the Loop," she lamented.

"Change is good," he shot back.

She laughed again.

"Funny guy. I just got to Homicide, remember? I just recently arrived."

•   •   •   •   •

They took it a block at a time. Mara worked one side of the street, and Nick did the other. He figured it was faster to split up, and Crosby agreed.

He barely got the first five to open the door, even after he flashed his ID.

On number six, a grandmotherly type opened the portal wide and asked Karras to come inside. The apartment reeked of cat urine or something equally as nasty. He saw three of the furballs lingering in her living room window.

The old woman had to be pushing the century mark, he estimated, but she stood erect, as if a ramrod took the place of her spine. Her hair was white and her neck was appropriately marked by turkey wattle. But her eyes were fierce and blue.

She sat him down on the couch.

"I know. It stinks in here. My daughter hasn't come to clean out their litter boxes, and I can't bend over anymore, and the bags of litter are too heavy for me to lift. I try to spray, but it doesn't do much good, as you can smell."

"It's all right."

"It isn't all right. I'm embarrassed, just so you know I haven't lost my olfactory sense. My name is June Bryant, by the way. You?"

"Nick Karras. I'm a detective."

"I saw that, yes."

"We're investigating a murder that happened not too—"

"That girl in the papers. Karen Manski?"

"Yes," Nick grinned.

"I'm still here inside me, Detective. It's just my outside is betraying me."

"You look fine."

"I look ninety-seven. That's what I look. I haven't been damned with dementia, just yet. I was a college professor, you know. I have my doctorate and several publications, most of them about the Romantic Poets."

"I was taking a few courses in American literature at Northwestern."

"I assume you haven't come to me to talk shop," she smiled.

Her blue eyes were as piercing as shards of jagged ice.

"Have you noticed a truck parked out on the curb, June? A truck like a semi, maybe?"

"The man upstairs has a red truck. But he hasn't been out there for weeks."

Karras felt his pulse quicken.

"He lives upstairs?"

"Yes, right up there."

She pointed at the ceiling.

"Can you describe him?"

She hesitated.

"About your height. Good looking. Brown hair. Lighter skinned than you. I think he told me his name. It was a Scandinavian surname...But I can't remember it, I'm afraid. It's got to be on the mail box downstairs, of course. His first name was Bruce. That's all I recall. You see I only talked to him a few times down at those boxes. He didn't seem all that inclined to be chatty."

"How long has he lived here? Do you know?"

"Less than a year. I've been here for thirty-seven years. I've seen a lot of them come and go."

The stink was beginning to get to Karras. She could see his discomfort.

"Listen, June, show me where the litter boxes are and I'll clean them for you."

Her weathered face brightened. She rose and led him into the kitchen and showed him where she kept the litter and the disinfectants and the trash bags. Nick scoured the three containers and washed them in her small utility room and then scrubbed his hands after he took the trash out to the garbage cans in the alley behind her building.

"When I leave, lock your door and don't go out until I let you know we're done with Bruce, if he's up there."

"He won't be there. I can hear him trod around when he's home."

Nick looked up at her kitchen ceiling.

"Just let me find out if he might be home. This won't take long."

Nick thanked her.

"I should be thanking you...My daughter's in her seventies. She doesn't get around all that well. I don't know who'll take care of these cats when I'm gone. I know Lila, my daughter, hates cats."

"You let me know, and I'll come over and do it again."

He excused himself and rushed toward the old woman's front door. He ran across the street when he saw Mara coming down a flight of stairs about a half block north of him.

She looked at him and her expression turned to concern.

"What's wrong?"

"I think I might have a hit. We need to go back to the car and call in for backup."

"Where?"

He turned and pointed in the direction of June's apartment building.

•   •   •   •   •

His name was on the mailbox, just as the ninety-plus old lady had informed him.

Bruce Swanson.

It took ten minutes before the other four detectives showed up. Detective Jack Petersen and Detective Drew Frank were partners, as were Detective Charlie Swank and Detective Pete Long. Those were the other members of the crew assigned to find Karen Manski's killer.

"Bruce Swanson?" Long asked.

He was a tall cop with Sandy hair and a scar from a knife on his left cheek he'd acquired in a domestic dispute when he was still in uniform.

They ascended the stairs. Nick and Mara and Petersen and Frank. Long and Swank circled the building to cover the back door if this guy Swanson tried to boogie out the back door.

Nick knocked on Swanson's door.

"Police!" he shouted.

No response.

"Now what?" Mara whispered.

Petersen and Frank had their pieces out and the two remained mute.

Karras dug into his pocket.

"What's that? It's not what I think it is, is it?" she whispered again.

"Turn around," he told her. "You two also," he warned the two men behind his partner.

They turned around, their backs to him.

"I didn't see a damn thing," Petersen affirmed.

Nick popped the flimsy lock in a few seconds. He pointed his weapon into the darkened apartment.

"Police!" he shouted again.

They walked in in single file, and then they spread out. "Clear" came from the bedroom and the bathroom and the living room. No one was present except for the four intruding detectives.

They searched the place and came up empty. It took about twenty minutes. The guy's flat was spartan, no extras. No books, no magazines, a cheap 17- inch TV. A few dressers that were almost empty. Only a few pair of Jockeys lay in one of the drawers.

"He must have taken all his shit with him on the road," Nick told the others.

"So now what?" Frank asked.

He was short and stocky. If he were painted red, dogs might be tempted to lift their legs.

"We go out the way we went in. Then we watch the building until Bruce does a homecoming."

They filed out, and Karras relocked the front door on his way out.

•　　　•　　　•　　　•　　　•

There were no arrests or traffic tickets. The man was a ghost. He had a social security number and he worked for Pafco Trucking on the northwest side. His employer could say only that Swanson made his hauls, never had a speeding ticket and that no one knew anything else about the guy because he was made for his job. He was a loner, never associated with anyone at work. He'd say hello when he came in to pick up his paycheck, but that was about it. He was an employee of Pafco, end of story.

He was out on the West Coast for a long haul and he was expected back in a week. Swanson had drop-offs in Colorado and New Mexico on the way back to Chicago.

The owner of Pafco was a bald, skinny white male who reminded Nick of Don Rickles.

"Why are you interested in Bruce?" the bald man asked from behind his desk at the truck outfit.

"We just have some questions for him," Mara answered.

"You said you were detectives? What kind of detectives?"

"Homicide," Nick answered.

"Holy shit," he grinned. "Did he kill somebody?"

CHAPTER TEN

Swanson wasn't supposed to return for a week, but they pulled round the clock shifts waiting for him outside the apartment building where he lived. Nick and Mara did the four to twelve, and the other two pairs of Homicides covered the rest.

It was boring sitting in the cop ride for most of the eight-hour tour, so Karras brought along a paperback novel.

"What's that?" the redheaded detective asked.

"*Notes from Underground,*" Nick replied. "Dostoyevsky," he explained.

"I'm impressed. You don't look like a high-brow kinda guy," she grinned.

"Thanks for the input."

"It wasn't a crack, Nick. You just look like more of a Sunday NFL addict, toking at a beer with a bowl of Fritos on the coffee table. You never told me you liked that literati stuff."

"I hate TV. I don't like going to the movies because I'm afraid I'll cold cock some jerk who talks through the flick or some asshole who likes to kick the seat."

"You don't go to the movies with Nora?"

"She's a reader, also."

"Do you sit there and watch each other poring over the pages?"

"Now you are being a wise ass."

"It's how I pass the time. One of us has to keep the watch, and I doze off if I don't occupy myself."

"You could bring some tapes and a tape player. I like jazz."

"Too hairy for me," the redhead said. "I'm into the world's greatest rock and roll band."

"You mean the Beatles?"

She snorted.

"Oh, *please.*"

"What?" he snorted back at her.

"The Stones, you ancient goof, you."

"Oh, yeah. Them."

"Do I sense disrespect, Nick?"

"No, I like them well enough, but rock is like fluff compared to jazz— That's only my humble opinion, of course."

A red truck pulled up behind them and parked. It was the front end of a semi. His lights were doused, and then he got out of the cab and walked toward the apartment building.

"Is it him?" Mara asked.

"It's dark and the goddam street light is out, but he's the right size and build."

Mara got on the radio and called for back-up. The response said they were on their way.

They waited a beat and then they got out of the unmarked ride.

He was already inside when they got to the door. Nick pushed the bell for June's, the old lady's, apartment, and the cat lady buzzed them in after she asked who it was.

"It's Detective Karras," he told her.

"It's late. What do you want?"

She sounded as if she were half asleep.

"Your neighbor is home upstairs. We didn't want to alert him we were coming."

The buzz startled the two cops, and then they ascended to Swanson's flat.

Nick put his ear to the door. He had his .38 in his right hand, and Mara had unholstered her piece, as well.

He slammed the door with his knuckles three times.

"Police. Open up."

The reinforcements hadn't arrived, but the two detectives were too excited to wait around, and Nick figured they probably should have followed protocol. He pointed to the other side of the door frame in case one of them should take a blast through the door. He knew that Swanson might pull a cute one and pop a cap through the wall on either side of the doorway, but there was no foolproof way to avoid a slug on one of these calls.

The door opened slowly. It was dark inside, and Nick kicked the entry open wide with the heel of his right foot.

"Show me your hands!"

The dark figure flicked on a light, and now they both could see Bruce Swanson clearly.

He threw his hands into the air.

"What'd I do?" he moaned.

"Step back," Nick commanded.

He stepped back three paces. Mara proceeded to frisk him.

"What the hell is going on?"

The man appeared to be genuinely frightened.

Nick flashed his ID.

"Sit down on the couch."

Swanson did as he was told.

"You want to tell me why you're crashing in here?" he asked.

The two cops returned their weapons to their holsters, and they stood in front of Swanson, looming over him.

"I apologize, but this is a homicide investigation."

"Homicide? Are you fucking with me?"

"Let's have a talk."

Nick did the talking. Swanson answered all his questions as if he'd done all this before, but Karras remembered the guy didn't have a sheet.

"Where were you on December 12ᵗʰ of last year?"

Mara remained the mute partner. He was the one with the experience, and she watched him work.

"Don't you need a warrant or something?"

"Do I need one? We can always come back," he told Swanson.

Swanson peered out at both of them.

"We're just here to ask you a few things," Mara interjected.

She was surprised that she entered the interview, but the interruption just seemed to come natural to her.

"That was a hell of a way to start the proceedings, what with the two guns aimed at me, I mean."

"Where were you on that date in December?" Nick repeated.

He was a handsome young man of about twenty-five, just the way June the cat lady had described him.

"I don't recall."

"Would your memory return if we took you downtown?" Nick asked.

"Don't I get a lawyer or something?"

"You need an attorney, Bruce?" Mara asked.

He hesitated with a glance at her.

"I mean I really don't recall where I was...What day of the week was the twelfth?"

The four patrolmen suddenly appeared behind them at the doorway.

"It's all right. You can just hang there outside the door," Nick told them.

"What the fuck is this? What do you think I'm supposed to have done?"

Nick took out the photo. It was in color and it was a recent picture of Karen Manski.

"Know her?"

Swanson peered at the picture.

"Am I supposed to know her?"

"Let me ask you one last time. Where were you on the twelfth of December, last year?"

He sat and looked down at his feet.

Then he jerked his head upright.

"I was in Tulsa, Oklahoma. I didn't get back here until Christmas Eve."

"Can you verify all that?" Mara queried.

"As a matter of fact, I can," he retorted angrily. "What *is* all this bullshit?"

"You're going to need to, Bruce," Nick explained. "Verify all that, I mean."

"I can call the terminals where I dropped my hauls. They can tell you the same goddam thing I just told you. I was in Tulsa, then Austin, Texas, and finally I made a drop in Corpus Christi. They can tell you where I was. I told you, I didn't get back here until the twenty-fourth."

Nick turned around.

"You guys can take off," he told the uniforms. "We're good, here."

The quartet thumped back down the flight of stairs.

"We're going to need to confirmation as soon as possible," he told the man sitting on the couch.

"I'm going to file a complaint about the way you two stormed into here."

"Absolutely. You do that...Don't leave town until we've heard from you, Bruce," Nick told him. "We're going to be around until you confirm all of your stops."

"What the hell does that mean—'we'll be around'?"

"Just stick around until you send us the information."

"Sorry about the inconvenience. We're just doing what we have to do," Mara told him.

It didn't sound like an apology to Nick. He was proud of his partner.

"You're going to hear from my lawyer. This isn't right."

Nick stepped forward aggressively at the now-erect man.

Swanson tumbled back onto his couch.

"You just take care of all those alibis, Bruce. If we were rude, I'm real sorry."

He took out Karen Manski's photo again.

"Someone strangled this twenty-year-old girl and then he sliced her up with great prejudice. She was someone's daughter, Bruce, so excuse me for coming at you the way I did. You call that lawyer, and do your worst, but if we don't hear from you immediately, we'll be back, and then I'll show you some downright discourtesy."

Karras turned and walked out the door, and Mara followed him and closed Swanson's door behind her.

•   •   •   •   •

"Who was that guy up there?" Mara smiled. "I don't mean Swanson. I mean you, partner."

He started up the motor on the Crown Vic.

"You wouldn't be taking it out on this guy, I mean with what happened to Penelope? What if he was just where he said he was, back in December?"

He pulled out onto the side street with a squeal.

"I have to learn how to play nice, yeah. The times they are a changing."

"I thought you didn't like rock. Bob Dylan, really?" she laughed.

"I have to give him his civil rights. I understand."

"It's not like the fifties, anymore, is it."

"How would you know, Mara? You were still attached to momma."

"Cheap shot, Nick. Unworthy of you."

He drove toward the Stevenson quietly.

"I apologize," he told her. "I was out of line."

"Accepted. You know you can't get all personal with this shit, is all I'm trying to say."

He looked over at his partner. She wasn't a lot older than his daughter Penelope, sitting or lying somewhere in a vegetative state at Elgin.

"You're absolutely right. I stand corrected."

She watched the traffic bobbing and weaving about them on their drive toward the Lake.

"I don't think he's our guy, Nick."

"I don't think so, either, goddammit."

His voice wasn't angry, Mara heard. It sounded defeated.

•　　•　　•　　•　　•

Everything Bruce Swanson told them was verified by the middle of the next week. FAXs were received, and Swanson had been checked in on his stops in the Southwest. They had to let him go.

The real perpetrator was still out in the wind. Nick started to think he was going to stay out in the breeze, too.

"I want to go with you," Nora told him.

"You don't have to. There's really nothing to say or do. She won't recognize me or respond to you, either."

"I'm going with you, Nick."

There was no arguing with her. So, they drove off to Elgin on a chilly, late February Sunday morning. Visiting hours were from 11:00 AM to 3:00 PM.

•　　•　　•　　•　　•

The psychiatric nurse escorted them to Penelope's single room. Nick paid extra for her to be by herself. She wouldn't know she had a roommate anyway, so she might as well sleep alone.

"I'll be right outside the door," she told Nick and Nora.

She closed the door behind them.

Penelope assumed the fetal position beneath the covers of her single bed. At least she wasn't hooked up to oxygen, Nick observed. Penelope could breathe on her own, but she had to be hand-fed.

"This is Nora, honey. She's my wife, now."

There was no response to the introduction, but by now Karras was not surprised at his daughter's silence.

"We were married a few weeks ago, Penelope. You'll like her. She's very nice."

They sat down next to the bed on folding chairs that were provided by the nurse outside the door.

They were only allowed thirty minutes for the visit, but the half hour always seemed interminable to Nick. He did the talking and Penelope just lay there in silence, every time.

"Can I touch her?" Nora asked.

Karras looked over at her with surprise on his countenance.

"I...I guess you could."

Nora reached out and touched the outstretched hand that dangled over the side of the bed. Penelope's hand to seemed to quiver almost imperceptibly.

"Jesus," Nick blurted. "Did she move?"

"She's in there," Nora turned and said to Nick.

"She's in there? What's that mean?"

Nora turned back to Penelope, but the young woman's hand hadn't moved again.

"Your dad's here, Penelope."

Nora kept her grip on the girl's limp hand.

"He loves you very much," she told the prone figure. "We'll come and see you often. I know you're going to get better."

"Nora," Nick protested.

"We'll be back soon," his wife told Penelope.

The half hour was over, and the nurse entered the room.

CHAPTER ELEVEN

Mara and Karras were summoned onto the carpet of Hizzoner shortly after Bruce Swanson turned out to be a wrong-way street. It was the first time in City Hall, at least in the Mayor's Office, for the two detectives.

He was just the way Nick had pictured him in Karras's mind's eye. He pretty much looked the same as his photos in the city newspapers. The Mayor didn't appear very often on TV because word was that he was uncomfortable with live interviews. The turkey wattle neck and the cheap off the rack suits didn't come off well in the media, so he limited his exposure to hand-picked newsmen who didn't give him a pain in the ass.

Hizzoner sat them down in front of his spacious desk.

"Why haven't you got this guy yet?"

He went right for the throat.

"We had a lead on someone, but it didn't work out. The guy had solid alibis," Nick explained.

Mara's face was a bit red and she looked overheated even though it was early March. Nick stole a quick glance at his partner, but he'd have to inquire about her health later.

"Magrette tells me you're one of his best detectives. Is he overrating you, Karras?"

"We're doing all that we can."

Nick wanted badly to tell the Mayor to go piss up a rope, but he declined the compulsive response. He was too far from retirement to tell him to go fornicate with a very compliant bulldog.

"They have the FBI in on this, Magrette tells me. The feds seem to think this guy might be crossing state lines. I'm hoping we can catch this prick by ourselves. You're not handing this off to the federals, are you?

"Do you have the capacity for speech or is this guy doing all the talking?" he tossed at Crosby.

"I can talk, but he's told you the facts, Mr. Mayor. We have no intention of letting the FBI piss on our territory, if that's what you meant."

Hizzoner smiled.

"Spunk, that's what I like in a woman."

Karras looked over and saw Mara clenching her fists.

He placed his right hand on her left forearm and gave her a stern look that told her to clam up and save herself. Everyone understood what a dick with ears this politician was. He was a party hack who kept himself clean while picking the pockets of several million Chicagoans. They guy was a douche bag. It was common knowledge.

But he ruled with an iron hand, and Machiavelli himself would've been proud. His system of sycophants and lackeys was the mark of his hog's head reign of terror. It was a one-party town, and he had chosen the right side to rule over.

Hizzoner was a night school law graduate, and as far as Nick knew, the man never litigated a case in his life. His genius was running rough shod over anyone who challenged him, and anyone who opposed him disappeared into the miasma of vaguely remembered failures. You had to give him credit for acquiring the clout that slammed his fat ass into that leather swivel chair where he was perched like some baronial big shot.

"We are sweeping the neighborhood where Karen Manski was murdered. We think he was a truck driver who's been killing as he goes. We're not confident that he'll try it again in the city, because these kinds of killers are too smart to go to the same well more than once, but they do hit the same territories in multiples on occasion."

"So, you been to the FBI school at Quantico, huh?"

He sat back in his imposing chair.

"We've both been there. It's standard for Homicides ever since the term 'serial killer' or 'series killer' became popular in the media. The prepared ones are sometimes difficult to apprehend. They're clever and they plan and they get better at what they do every new time out."

"He picked a wrong number with Karen Manski. Her old man isn't going to let go. He knows people, including yours truly, and he has designs on taking my job away from me. Did Magrette tell you that?"

"No, he didn't," Mara finally offered.

Hizzoner smiled at the redhead.

"How much time have you had in Homicide, young lady?"

"A couple months."

"I find that interesting. Normally, Magrette would put someone more experienced on what they call a high-profile case like this, wouldn't he?"

Nick could feel his own fists clenching, all by themselves.

"Now you, Karras, I can understand. You have a track record. So do the other four cops your Captain assigned. Isn't that right?"

"Detective Crosby is very much qualified to work this thing. She's got all the tools and smarts it takes, and I've worked with other detectives with much greater experience who were less able than she is. I have complete confidence in her," Nick retorted.

"I'm glad to hear that, Karras, but I don't give a shit about your opinion. Results are the only fucking thing that matters. You're on notice that you better come up with the piece of shit who killed Carl Manski's daughter. You and the whole Police Department are going to make me look good on this thing. I don't give a good goddam if the two of you were Rhodes Scholars. Catch him or you'll be blowing a goddam whistle on traffic control on fucking State and Lake. I assume I'm being clear?"

Karras rose before Mara had the chance.

"You can do what you like. Now, if there's nothing else."

"You don't have proper respect, Detective. I heard what a hard-ass you think you are. The only reason you're not waving your arms in traffic in the Loop is because you have a track record of arrests...You don't like having partners, I was informed. Why was that?"

"I have a partner, as you can see. Is there anything else?"

Mara stood.

"Get the hell out of here. No one likes a wise-ass, Karras."

The two cops turned and left the office.

•   •   •   •   •

"We're doomed," the redhead grinned widely.

They sat in a booth at the White Castle on Mannheim Road. They were just outside the city boundary. Mara wasn't a fan, but it was fast food and Nick said he felt like taking a brief ride to clear his head in order to keep himself from going back downtown and bitch-slapping the fat-faced Mayor of Chicago all over his cavernous official office.

"Fuck him," Nick said. "If he really wanted us shit-canned, we'd be standing outside in the cold waving our arms with traffic detail. If he talked to Magrette, he knows better than to tell him his job. Our Captain has zero tolerance for interference from that tub of guts. He knows how effective our Captain is and how Homicide is one of the few gears in the city mechanism that actually functions.

"He must really fear this Carl Manski as a threat. The election is next November, and chubby can't flash the success of his new street lights anymore. The Machine is faltering, or he wouldn't have dragged us into his domain. The polls must be lousy, and he's running scared. Manski's got his daughter's murder in all the papers almost every day. And the news guys have no great love for Hizzoner, either, especially one columnist from the *Sun Times*, that guy Royko. He wrote a book on the fat fuck. It wasn't complimentary, either."

She took a hit on her Coke. She didn't want to partake in the sliders, as Karras did. It was two in the afternoon, and the Castle wasn't exactly bustling with customers.

Nick inhaled three of his cheesesliders.

"How can you eat that crap?"

"You get to choose, tomorrow," Nick promised. "Fru-fru salads, whatever you like. Then I get to bitch about your choice. We've got to come to an understanding about dinner break, Mara."

She broke into a dynamic, wide smile.

"I didn't sign on to play politics, Nick."

"I don't know of anyone in Homicide who did, but I'm sure we've got our pols, also."

"I just wanted to smash that bastard in the teeth."

"Self-control is the operative term. I don't think Mrs. Hizzoner likes him much, either. Just thank sweet Jesus you don't have to wake up to that puss every morning."

"They have a son?"

Nick nodded as he put away the other three miniature burgers.

"You're going to make Nora sick when she gets a whiff of those nasty onions."

"I told her to eat garlic for lunch today."

Mara chuckled again.

Then her face went sober.

"What do we do next, Nick? Swanson bust our bubble. Now what?"

He drained his glass of the soft drink.

"I still think he lives somewhere close to where Karen Manski lived. We keep looking for another guy with a truck parked on the street. Maybe he's leaving it away from where his crib is. Maybe he's being cute and walking a few blocks from the truck to where he crashes. If he does live in the vicinity, it can't be too far from the crime scene.

"Otherwise, I'll work traffic until I've got my twenty years in. You're going to be a bright star, Mara. Don't worry about it. Hizzoner doesn't blame you. He thinks you're the sweet young thing who's just along for the ride. He'll lower the boom on me, not you. He won't fuck with Magrette, either, like I said. Our Captain is a scary guy. And the rank and file love him. There'd be walkouts if Sideways Dick tried to screw with him. No, it'll be me, Mara. I never learned how to pucker up and close my eyes and my nose."

Mara peered out the window and watched the traffic on Mannheim Road.

"The feds have the resources and they've got the whole country to roam in," she said. "We have to deal with the likelihood he won't return to our turf and do his thing again. And maybe he'll change up his MO, if he does come back."

"He already has. He let Penelope live."

•   •   •   •   •

Nora washed the dishes. Nick made his not-world-famous spaghetti and meatballs.

"I don't know how to cook Greek. My mother preferred American. Meat and potatoes, nothing too swank. The old man liked the home cuisine, too."

Nick sat at their tiny kitchen table. It only sat the two of them comfortably.

He looked up at his wife.

"Why'd you tell me that she was still inside herself?"

Nora looked at him, away from the sink with the soapy, hot water. She let the dish she was scrubbing sink into the water.

"I felt her inside. That's why."

"You know how many times I expected the call from Elgin and some shrink tells me she's come out of it? She's lucid and aware and she asks to talk to me."

"I didn't say it to upset you, Nick."

"I know that. That's not what I meant...I've been learning to put it into a compartment. Penelope, I mean. I'm trying to live with her loss. She's gone, and she's not coming back. It's like she's dead and I'm visiting her grave, not a body on a bed in some hospital. It's the way I've been living with it, Nora. I didn't know what else to do.

"And then you said that, and I started to think she's in there trying to escape, trying to get out."

"I didn't mean to hurt you, Nick. I didn't mean to—"

He got up off the kitchen chair and took hold of her. Her wet hands pressed against his shoulder blades.

"You didn't hurt me. You couldn't. I knew that from the beginning. That's why I was so sure about you. It's just that you jolted me and reminded me that she's still here and that she always will be. Maybe it was exactly what I needed. I was making myself numb. Sometimes it takes a pop in the skull to remind yourself that nobody lives in a protective bubble. You'd think a cop would already know that, wouldn't you?"

There was nothing new on the baby-making front. They were still trying, but her period came along like clockwork. Nora was nothing if she wasn't regular.

They thought about visiting one of those fertility clinics, but they were adamant about doing it the old-fashioned way.

"Maybe it's me. I could go get checked out," he'd told Nora after a few weeks of vigorous attempts at murdering the bunny.

"It might just as well be me. You've already got the job done. It's me who hasn't attempted to add one to the population."

They held off on doctors' appointments and decided to give it time.

"Maybe I waited too long, Nick," she lamented, a few weeks earlier. "Maybe you have to try when you're younger. It's supposed to be better when you're younger."

"Don't give up so easy. Maybe we're both trying too hard. Just keep going and see what happens. Worst case scenario, we adopt."

"You'd do that?"

"If you went along with the notion, of course I would."

"Let's keep trying. There's plenty of time before we go to an agency."

It wasn't long after the discussion that they were both back in bed.

When they disengaged, Nick looked over at her. They were both trying to catch their wind.

"You know a kid would change things. I mean with this."

"With the sex?"

"I'd be cut off for six weeks until the birth and then six weeks after it pops out. That's three months we can't have this," he laughed.

"It's only three months."

"Yeah, and then you'll be too tired because the critter'll wake us both up all night, probably. When it gets bigger, it'll come wailing to us that it can't sleep."

"Stop referring to it as it, dammit."

He laughed and bent down and kissed her.

"I'm getting kind of used to getting it regular, was all I meant."

She slapped his cheek lightly.

"The baby will not cut either of us off, you idiot. Is that what happened with your first wife?"

He laid his head back down on the pillow, his left hand resting on her wet belly.

"She never liked it much before or after. She had other shit to contend with in her own head."

"That was then. This is us, just us, and the other thing is gone. Right?"

He rolled over to her.

"It is most definitely over with. You and I together are totally different. There're no ghosts in this place, Nora. No spooks. No shadows from another life. You and I are all that there is. Don't ever think otherwise...Where the hell were you when I got back from that shit hole in Korea?"

"I was waiting. It was worth the wait, Detective. It was most certainly worth the wait."

CHAPTER TWELVE

It may have all begun when his mother's cats kept disappearing. He didn't like cats. He didn't like any pets, as a matter of fact, but his mother was partial to felines and they kept on disappearing, five in all.

They were outdoor animals, so he never came under his mother's suspicions, and their bodies were never found. He made sure to bury them where she'd never find them. The methods he employed to dispatch them varied. Sometimes it was strangulation, but the creatures fought back and laid stripes down his arms. His mother never asked why he wore long sleeved shirts and sweatshirts in the heat of summer.

Neither of his parents paid all that much attention to him at all, and if they had, they certainly wouldn't be aware of the symptoms that marked him from his youth.

He'd read all the literature he could find about sociopaths who became bent on murder. Serial killers or series killers was the term used currently. Jack the Ripper was likely the most notorious of the breed, back in 19th Century England. But he had not much similarity to the infamous and phantom-like slice and dice killer. Other than the mutilations, which weren't all that similar to the Whitechapel monster's.

Monster. He never thought of himself as one. He was unique and he was not what his mother would have hoped he'd grow up to be, but he wasn't *that*. He was human, like everyone else. He wasn't some perversion of nature like all those factual and fictional characters who planted horror in the public's mind. There was no doubt he didn't fit in with any typical notion of morality, with the standard person's view of right and wrong.

You would have to fall under the umbrella of common or ordinary to judge him as some sort of aberration, and common and ordinary he was not. All you had to do was study Darwin. The duality of predator and prey was the key, he thought. Human beings had somehow erased the fact that homo erectus could himself be as predatory as the other mammals and reptiles that roamed the earth. They'd denied what Nietzsche created when he came up with the 'Overman'. He was the prototype of all the creatures with their eyes on the front of their faces—the hunters. Civilization demanded that these alpha types be subjugated under the norms of law and order. Laws protected the weak from the strong, but it was not the way Nature intended it to be. It was false doctrine.

He'd been reading Nietzsche since he was in the twelfth grade. He understood the existentialist philosopher only gradually, but he kept reading him during his time in the military until the present, and the 'Overman' made more sense as he matured into the man he was now.

Defiance was titillating. It had begun when he started killing the household pets, and the rush came as he kept on getting away with it. When his mother became saddened by the loss of her cats, her sorrow didn't affect him. He figured his lack of empathy was a manifestation of strength. If he'd been weak, he never would have been able to do away with the damned things.

Vietnam gave him the opportunity to move up the chain of living species, but since it was a war, the killings were somehow justified. It was self-defense, and the blessings of the government negated the adrenalin release that he had experienced with the secret slayings in his teenaged years and the current rush he experienced with his human quarry. No, what he did in the war satiated him not at all. It was only when he went on the road and began finding the source of his true satisfaction.

He had never gone to college. It was the Army right after graduation, and then he began his career as a transcontinental truck driver. And serial killer. He gained his education outside the ivy-covered walls of some university that had no connection to the way the world really was. Predator and prey.

The theory was that Jack the Ripper might have been a doctor. Or he might have been a very skilled butcher. Or both. But the rules and governance that protected the herd hadn't stopped him from becoming.

He was becoming. He was on the path to self-realization.

Would they catch him? He thought not.

When he returned to Chicago in mid-March, he read the newspapers and their accounts of the killing of Karen Manski. Karen Manski, the demure young woman who had opened her door for him all those months ago. He had gained her confidence and then she'd let him in her door.

Why would the papers still be concerned about one dead woman?

He read the accounts. They detailed the ineptitude of the Chicago Police Department, and in particular, one homicide investigator named Karras. The journalists came down particularly hard on this single cop. They railed at his inability to arrest even one potential suspect in the case.

One article wrote about his rookie partner, some female named Mara Crosby. The writer wondered why such an inexperienced detective would be paired with Karras, who had a pretty fair track record on the murder squad. There was a lone picture of the two, but Karras's face was blurred. Crosby's countenance, however, came out very clearly.

Karras wasn't the only policeman who was looking for him, he understood. The FBI would surely have become involved by now since the killings had crossed state lines, and certainly the federal profilers would have noticed similarities in the double-digit slayings. He'd left his signature on their bodies, after all. Saucy Jack had done the same, back in the Victorian era. But his stamp on those corpses was much messier. The removal of organs wasn't something he wasn't interested in. The simpler you kept it, the easier it was to stay hidden.

When he got back to his apartment, he took the usual precaution to park his vehicle a few blocks from where he resided. He had also read an account of a truck driver who had been interrogated for the Karen Manski murder. His name was not published because it wound up that they'd nabbed the wrong man, who was now considering a lawsuit against Karras and the CPD. It wasn't likely that innocent trucker would collect damages, he thought. But it was a sobering idea that they were searching the neighborhood for him. Karras must have come up with the idea that the killer was a local, perhaps someone in walking distance from the dearly departed's building.

This homicide detective might not be as inept as the newspapers made him out to be. 'Chicago's Worst Detective' was the headline of one of the articles he'd read. Maybe they underestimated this cop. At least Karras had one correct assumption about him, and perhaps it was time to relocate.

Moving was an expense, however. And Karras had come up empty handed on his local killer theory, so maybe he'd look elsewhere for this current series killer. As long as he distanced the truck from his actual location, he felt safe. For the moment. It was entirely possible that this Greek detective might be shit-canned for his lack of success.

It had to be that Karen Manski's family had some kind of political clout in order that the accounts kept appearing in the papers. If she'd been a nobody, the press would have abandoned her the way they did the murders of whores. Karen must have come from a powerful family, then, powerful enough to sustain interest in her case.

He didn't like the sustained interest. Maybe it really was time to move. Maybe even get rid of the truck. Perhaps become a salesman who traveled in a much more conventional vehicle. The truck did stand out on these streets.

He remembered Darwin's thoughts toward adaptation.

He was putting his rig up for sale tomorrow.

·　　·　　·　　·　　·

He had a buyer within two weeks. He figured it was time to move on from hauling goods coast to coast, and he had enough money to tide him over until he could find new employment.

•　　•　　•　　•　　•

There was an ad for a mechanic in the paper. He'd worked on his own truck, but he was also conversant with automobiles and their inner workings. The interview came on a Tuesday morning and he was hired before noon. The owner liked his military background and his experience with automotive machinery. He started his new job on the following Monday. The shop was distant from his apartment, so he would begin a search for new lodgings. The change might as well be complete. It had to happen before Karras got luckier or before the cops selected someone smarter and more fortunate than the Greek.

•　　•　　•　　•　　•

He moved into a new building on the far northwest side. No more walks to the Lake on wintry evenings, or any other evenings. He settled into a neighborhood that wasn't far from the border of a close-by suburb. It was, however, located nearer to his new job.

The first thing he encountered when he moved in was one of his new neighbors. She lived in the apartment just beneath him. He was perched on the top of a three-flat.

She was attractive, thin, just the way he liked them. Her location seemed to remove her as a possibility, though. The proximity was far too dangerous.

But she began flirting with him almost immediately. He encountered her several times when he moved his belongings into the building. She had a willing smile on her face, and she introduced herself by name, as well. He told her his name and smiled back. It would be rude not to appear friendly, and his first impression would likely stay with her. He had to be civil, at least.

He imagined her body. The slight breasts, the long torso, the well-formed but lanky, lean legs. A perfect match for his list of traits.

It was hands off, and he knew he had to avoid her. You didn't do the neighbors. You searched in more remote spots to find targets.

He thought he might just try to have a more traditional relationship with her. He wasn't adverse to simply fucking them instead of cutting them. What was the harm? It would make him seem 'normal', and his normalcy would reduce the likelihood that anyone might find him odd or suspicious.

It didn't take him long to connect with her. Her name was Ellen Prentice. She worked as a paralegal downtown, was twenty-six years old, and had just broken up with a boyfriend of eight months. Perfect. Unattached and looking for a replacement for the void her ex-boyfriend had recently created. Emotionally, she be looking for what she'd lost.

He asked her out the next time he saw her in the entry of their building. She was retrieving her mail.

"Would you be interested in going out for dinner with me?"

"If it isn't pizza or fast food, yeah," she chirped.

•   •   •   •   •

They returned after dinner to her place. She wasn't a slow study, and they wound up in her bed twenty minutes after bolting down two white wines. Her choice, not his.

Her frame was just as he imagined. Long and tight. No excess.

He could feel his hands on her throat, but his hands were occupied elsewhere. He floated his palms over her breasts. The nipples were perfect, round, pink buttons. He pictured the knife or the scissors cutting into them. The toes and the feet were simply afterthoughts. He found no great satisfaction in removing the nails or the toes. They were just a flourish to his signature. The breasts, the nipples, were the focal point. They had always fascinated him.

Ellen asked him to stay the night, but he begged off because he had to be at work at 7:30 AM, promptly. It was a new job, he explained.

"Maybe I could stay on a weekend night?" he proffered.

She smiled. Staying the night wasn't off the table, then. Ellen Prentice looked pleased with his promise of a more sustained relationship. She was looking for something long lasting, and it didn't matter. There was no question he'd disappoint her, but until then he figured he'd play this hand out.

They lay in bed together for long enough that his departure didn't seem rude to her. They talked about their work. Ellen was going to night school and wanted to become an attorney.

"I might need one. You never know," he smiled at her.

He found himself aroused, and they went to round two. She was more animated and aggressive, this time, and the coupling took much longer to climax. When it came, she became vocal about it. He was concerned her neighbors downstairs were listening to a play by play.

If they were listening in, it would only make the new tenant seem like any other healthy male on the make. So be it, he thought.

He left at 2:00 AM, later than he'd planned. She walked to the door with him and grabbed his crotch and sucked on his neck. Ellen hadn't bothered to throw a robe on. He brushed her left breast with his palm just to show his appreciation.

Then he departed and headed upstairs.

· · · · ·

There were two more 'dates' within the next week. But he was pleasantly surprised that Ellen had said nothing about making their situation more permanent. It was good that she required only a meal and sex and seemed uninterested in anything more concrete between them. She was going to school to become a lawyer, so perhaps her profession was more important to her than engaging in anything that required any kind of commitment.

She was the perfect woman. She had only one downside.

He couldn't very well kill her. He'd be the first visit the police made after her unfortunate demise. And he'd only just recently moved in here. It'd be a pain in the ass to find new lodgings at this point.

•　　•　　•　　•　　•

His new ride was a Chevy Impala, a popular choice of automobile, so his car wouldn't stick out the way his truck had. He could park the Chevy on the street because it would fit in with the other autos out at the curb.

He'd miss the swings from Chicago to either coast, but he could live with it. It didn't pay to become predictable. He might even just enjoy fucking the downstairs neighbor for a while, lay off the hunt, make Karras and friends think he'd died or gone into retirement or been pinched for some crime or other and was rotting in some municipal cage somewhere in the lower forty-eight—He'd never trekked to Alaska, and he had no interest in flying to Hawaii or to Europe or any other foreign destination.

Ellen had her virtues, her attractions.

But when time passed, he understood his old compulsions, his own urges, would return, and he'd be back in business. If it weren't here in the city, he'd find jobs elsewhere. He enjoyed his nomadic life, back when he had the rig. If he saved the money from the sale of the semi, he could buy a new one if his wanderlust returned.

•　　•　　•　　•　　•

Ellen liked to be tied up. She told him she wasn't into pain, however. No whipping or slapping or choking into an orgasm were her things. She just liked being lightly bound to the headboard. She wanted her legs unbound so she could wrap them around his middle when he entered her.

He tried to tell her that it might be precarious, that he might become carried away, but she laughed and told him to wrap her scarves around her wrists and to tie her to the bedposts.

When he did so, the fantasy came back to him. He didn't have his tools with him, but he pictured her gasping beneath his hands. He would do it slowly, almost lovingly, throttling her gradually until her eyes betrayed her absence.

Ellen looked up at him, and he could see the growing fear in her.

Then he smiled down, instead, and they began again.

CHAPTER THIRTEEN

Everyone had babies. It wasn't difficult, so why was there a problem for Nora and Nick? She'd always been healthy, but there had never been an opportunity for Nora to conceive since none of her previous relationships had placed her close enough for a long-term commitment. She'd never become seriously attached to anyone in all those years, but she wasn't a virgin by any definition of the word before they'd married. Nora had problems with her period when she passed puberty, and in her late teens the doctor had put her on birth control to regulate her monthly arrivals. There had been a lot of pains and excruciating cramps before she'd started the medication, and she kept on taking the pill thereafter.

She went to the doctor without telling Nick. He was a fertility specialist, and the result was that Nora had a clean bill of health. There was no reason she couldn't become pregnant. But she didn't want to tell Nick because she knew he'd start having doubts about himself, even though he had helped bring forth a daughter, all those years back.

So, if it wasn't Nora and if Nick obviously was able to get the job done at least once, what was the obstacle to their plan?

Maybe there was a stop sign for them somewhere cosmic. Maybe it was just fate, and perhaps they were both too old to get it done. Nick was forty and she was thirty-eight, but people that age seemed to be able to spring forth with infant after infant.

If it were a cosmic conspiracy, what had she ever done to deserve it?

Everyone had babies, so why couldn't she? Nora never got into the mindset of thinking it wasn't fair. Fair had no place in this world. Why could a few singers hit the high C and the rest could only warble somewhere below? Why did some actors become superstars and the rest wound up waiting tables or driving taxis? It just wasn't fair across the board. If you were born white, you didn't get stuck in the back of the bus until the Civil Rights thing came along. If you weren't white, you couldn't get into a university, especially in the South.

Things weren't fair everywhere you looked.

Some received a bounty of talent, and the majority wound up waiting to collect Social Security and living on a fixed income.

It just wasn't fair.

But she figured they'd keep on trying. They were only a few months into the marriage, so it was a bit premature to stop going for it. It wasn't like the relationship hinged on a child coming forth.

And she thought about Penelope, Nick's kid. Look at the way she turned out. There was always a chance their child might wind up as tragic as that poor soul in Elgin. What if Nick passed on the psychological issues that his daughter inherited? It was possible it was he, not his ex. Nora couldn't buy into the idea that it was her husband. He showed no signs of depression, the way it had been for Penelope.

A kid could have developmental disabilities, all different kinds of them, and at Nora's age, the chances for something like the above were increased. It was also possible that their baby could be born into that minority of geniuses or gifted people. Who knew?

It didn't lessen her anxiety to tread over all that ground, but you had to consider the possibilities.

She was sure she wanted to buck the odds and keep on trying to get pregnant, however. Nora couldn't see a real downside to creating a life with Nick Karras. It just didn't seem likely to her that their offspring would grow up going sideways.

Nora didn't tell him everything she sensed when she touched Penelope. She didn't want to exacerbate an already anxiety ridden situation for her husband. She could sense that Nick was very uncomfortable visiting Penelope. She knew he likely blamed himself for her condition. Nick probably thought he could have somehow prevented Penelope from running away and being caught in an alley by some monstrous creature who raped and mutilated her. Then she became this poor human being stretched out, paralyzed mentally, on a bed in a mental institution.

Nora felt her struggling to emerge in spite of her catatonic life. She could only touch Nick's girl briefly because the pain shot out of her in waves. She could only tell her husband that she was still in there, waiting to emerge back into the light from the dark place where she was imprisoned.

•　　　•　　　•　　　•　　　•

Nora was disappointed that she couldn't pick up anything in the murdered girl's apartment after Nick took her there. There was only the heartbreaking sensation of a young woman alone, a young woman being brutalized out of her young life. There was no one to save her, just like Penelope. Nick wasn't there to stop it, and Karen Manski's father wasn't there to save his daughter, either.

If only she could've sensed something that would've helped Nick find this terrible killer, she would have been glad to have whatever this thing was that she'd been fated to own. She had never felt fortunate to see things others couldn't. It had marked her as 'different' all her life, and all Nora longed for was to be like anyone else. It was fine to have talent, and she thought of herself as a reasonably skilled visual artist. Her paintings sold pretty well at the gallery where she was employed, but her art sales would never make her a living by themselves. She didn't fancy herself in the league of the French Impressionists or the Romantics or the Surrealists or any of the various schools who had paintings in the world's art museums. She had talent, but she followed the dictums of the multitudes of also-rans in the art world. Nora knew her limitations.

The second sight thing was harder to take. Especially when she couldn't get an image of that bastard who tore up Karen Manski. What was the point of her 'gift' if it had no practical application?

Perhaps she should convince Nick to take them to some gambling casino and try out her luck on the gaming tables. Who knew? Maybe she could out-win the card counters. She'd never tried to beat the gambling palaces in Las Vegas, but at least she might make them both comfortable financially, and then Nick could retire early and not have to pursue animals who destroyed father's and mother's daughters.

How could he take looking at the bodies, year after year? He'd already been doing it for a long time, and he was only forty. Didn't it get to him? All those bloody crime scenes. And then there were the cases he didn't solve. Nick told her that no one in Homicide had ever solved all their cases. No one. How did he or any detective process all those failures?

And now they had failed to get pregnant. Everything seemed to be land-sliding on top of them both.

•　　•　　•　　•　　•

They lay on their backs, trying to catch their breaths.

"If this one doesn't take—"

"Don't say that," she told him.

"I was joking. Take it easy."

She rolled over and faced him. Her cheeks were glistening from effort.

"Maybe we should try to adopt, Nick."

"Aren't you giving up a little soon?"

"This might be a sign that it's just not going to happen."

"Is that your *impression*?" he grinned.

"It's just a hard fact. It doesn't seem like it's going to happen, and maybe that's not a bad thing."

"You're worried the kid might be a bad seed."

"No. I'm just thinking about the likelihood that it'll be different, like me, or different, like Penelope."

"Who says that kind of thing has to happen again? It's like lightning striking twice in the same spot."

"If we adopted, we'd have a ready-made healthy child, Nick."

"No one knows what they'll become. You take your chances either way...If you want to stop, it's okay with me. You can go back on the pill. We can adopt. You figure it out. All I want is for you to be happy. You're my mission in life, Nora."

Her eyes teared up.

"What the hell is that?" he laughed.

She moved to him and kissed him hard and long.

"Jesus, Nora, you overestimate my resiliency. Give me a few minutes, huh?"

Tears began to trickle onto her cheeks.

"No one ever made me their mission."

He kissed her back the same as she had done.

"All I do at work is try to find killers, Nora. That's not a mission. That's a job. That's a shot at justice. Making you happy is the most important thing I've got left to do. This prick I'm after might very well get away with it. It might wind up being out of my control. But with you, I can make it happen and I'm going to. See, you're my second chance, and second chances don't happen. They just don't. You get a single shot, one opportunity, and most of the time if you blow that chance it never comes round again."

She looked up at him. She was dry-eyed, now.

"Me? I spent all my time trying to keep everybody away. All I had was my paint brushes. I thought the work was enough. Then you show up all those years later, and I think I'll keep you away, too. What was I thinking?"

He held her crushingly close, but she didn't protest. She gave as good as she got.

• • • • •

Her easel stood by the bay window in their apartment. It looked out onto the busy street below, and she was trying to capture the scene on her canvas. The picture might sell or it might hang on a wall at the gallery where she worked for a few months. If it didn't sell, she could take it home, framed, and try to find a space on their living room wall. It was dark. The colors were dark. But there were bright shades on the coffee shop across the street. It was an all-night café, and the neighborhood denizens went there late at night when nothing else was opened and when they likely suffered from insomnia or when they worked the late shift and didn't want to go home, yet.

It had been inspired by a story by Hemingway, "A Clean, Well-Lighted Place". Nora had read it in college, and she had re-read it a few weeks ago. A lonely, deaf, old man frequented such a place in Spain somewhere, and he had no other place to go, late at night. It struck her as poetically sad, and she wanted to recreate her own feeling about the story by drawing the real café across the street. Nick and she had gone in for coffee several times since she moved in with him, and the place fairly reeked with atmosphere. It was run by an old Albanian man. He'd been there for forty-six years, he'd explained late one evening.

It struck her deep, so she had to paint the exterior. She planned on doing a picture of the inside, as well.

It had no name, outside, but everyone in the vicinity knew what kind of place it was, and it was usually crowded.

Her art saved her. There were times when she considered walking off a pier into the Lake, but the work kept her going.

Then Nick finally showed up and she became angry at what might have happened to her.

• • • • •

Nick and Mara continued the search. They canvased block after block.

Until a middle-aged woman who lived alone on the first- floor apartment of a building told them she recalled seeing a red rig parked outside at the curb.

Her name was Mary Malloy. She told them she was a school teacher at a primary, not five blocks from where they sat.

"I only saw him a few times. It was strange. I watched him walk down the block, but I never saw him go in anywhere. He just kept going."

"Which way?" Nick asked her.

Mara sat next to Karras on the couch, across from Mary Malloy.

The word 'spinster' popped into Mara's head as she observed the school teacher. It was an old-fashioned word, but she seemed to fit the term. She was closing in on fifty, Mara thought, and she wore no ring on her left hand.

"He headed north, and then he turned left at the corner. That's all I know. I wasn't about to follow him."

She smiled demurely.

"Can you describe him?" Nick asked.

Mary's hair was highlighted with small wisps of silver.

"He was a good-looking young man. About six feet or a little under...I remember he smiled at me once. He had a space between his two front teeth."

"You've got quite a memory, Mary," Mara told her.

"I remember faces. It comes with the job of keeping little hooligans in line."

"Have you seen him lately?" Nick queried.

"No. That's what I was going to tell you. That truck has been gone for almost a month."

"So you last saw him in early February?"

Mary looked at Nick's partner.

"That sounds about right...What was this about?" she asked.

"It's about a homicide. You might have read about it. Karen Manski?"

"Yes! Wasn't that horrible? Such a young girl. I can't imagine why her parents allowed her to live alone. Can you?"

"Is there anything else you can recall about him?" Nick asked her.

She paused.

"Oh, yes. He had a slight limp. His left leg, I think. He must have been injured, I guess."

"A limp," Mara repeated.

"Yes," Mary told her.

"Pronounced?" Nick asked.

"Not bad. Slight, I'd say, but noticeable."

•　　•　　•　•　　•

They drove to the end of the block and then they turned left. At the first block, they got out of the Ford.

"We begin again," he informed his redheaded partner. "I'll take the other side of the street."

"How far are we going to go?" Mara groaned. "It's cold."

It was spring, but you couldn't tell by the frosty cold of the northeast wind off the Lake. It was called The Hawk for a very good reason.

"He can't have gone all that far. When you get frozen, let me know," he grinned.

•　　•　　•　•　　•

They made three blocks west that day, and then it became dark and they met back at the vehicle.

"Nothing," she informed him.

"Same. We can go a few more blocks west tomorrow, and if we come up empty, fuck it."

They headed back to headquarters, and their shift was over and they both went home.

• • • • •

"Sounds like him. But he's been gone a while. I think he moved. Haven't seen him in a few weeks," the elderly man said. "He lived right above me. I think they've already rented his place to someone else."

"You ever talk to him at all?" Nick offered.

"Once in a while. He said he was a truck driver. Funny, I never saw a truck."

"Did he have a limp?" Mara added.

"As a matter of fact, yes. I asked him and he said he was wounded in the war."

"Anything else?" Nick asked.

The old man had sparse gray hair on either side, but the top knot was barren of follicles.

"Yeah, he had a little gap between his teeth. Sort of gave him character."

"You think you could describe him to a sketch artist?" Nick asked.

"Maybe. Yes, I think I could give it a shot."

"Do you recall his name?" Mara queried.

"Sure. It used to be on the mailbox...It was a strange kind of moniker."

They waited for the old man.

"Darren Kakos, it was. Never heard the like before. Have either of you?"

CHAPTER FOURTEEN

They talked to every transport outfit on the north side. They asked if they had a trucker fitting Darren Kakos' description, and Manley Trucking on Western Avenue told Nick and Mara that they indeed had a private contractor by that name doing some of the hauls for them.

Karras had gone to the department's artist to get a rendering of Kakos from the accounts given by the two witnesses who'd IDed him from the neighborhood where Karen Manski lived. The picture depicted a handsome young man of about twenty-five with a marked gap between his two front teeth.

Fred Collins, the owner of Manley Trucking, recognized the face immediately.

"He did a lot of hauls to the West Coast for us. Yeah, that's him. Hard to forget a name like his. Think he said he was Greek or Albanian, I can't remember. I just recall how odd the name was. Good worker. Always showed up, did the jobs."

"Did you notice if he had a limp?" Mara asked as they sat in Collins' office.

It was noisy even inside Collins' cubicle with the door shut. The rumble of trucks flying by outside on the heavily trafficked Western Avenue couldn't help but be a distraction if you were trying to have a conversation.

"Yeah. Now that you mention it, he did. Left leg, I think. I asked him about it and he said he got it in that fucked war."

Nick was surprised to hear anti-war sentiment from a blue-collar guy like Fred Collins. But people could surprise you with their politics, now and then.

"Is he still working for you?" Nick asked.

"Haven't seen him in weeks, maybe two months, by now. Funny, I called him, but his phone had been disconnected and he never got in touch with me since then."

•   •   •   •   •

They found two other trucking firms who had hired Kakos, but they received the same answer: the guy had sounded, the last two months. His phone had been unplugged and they couldn't get a hold of him.

The second outfit, Garski's, had his plate numbers, and Nick checked them out and found them registered with Darren Kakos. He put out an all-points on the semi, and a week later they traced the vehicle to an address in Oak Lawn, on the southwest edge of the city.

They brought two other sets of Homicides with them in two other cars. If they hit the right number, this time, they wanted to come prepared for a hostile suspect.

The address was on Oak Way Boulevard, just off 95th Street. Two detectives drove around to the alley and parked behind the three-flat building.

The red semi was parked right in front of the brown brick address.

"He's not hiding by parking remote," Mara said.

They got out of the Ford. The other two detectives, Jack Calloway and Vince Giulli, got out simultaneously and followed Nick and Mara toward the entrance.

There was no Darren Kakos on any of the three mailboxes.

Karras rang the first- floor apartment. The male voice asked:

"Yeah?"

"Police," Nick replied.

"What do you want?"

"Open the fucking door."

"Jesus, don't have a seizure."

"Open the fucking door, please."

He buzzed them in. The four police walking up one flight, and the door was already cracked open.

It wasn't Kakos.

"You have a roommate?"

"No," the sixty-something man replied.

"You know this guy?" Nick queried.

He showed him the artist's rendition.

"No...What's this about?"

"The other tenants look anything like this?" Mara threw in.

"Not that I know. Are we done?"

"One of the occupants drive that red rig out front?" Nick demanded.

"The guy on the third floor drives a truck, I think."

Nick glanced at Mara and at Calloway and Giulli. He pointed up the flight of stairs. They walked right up to the upper flat on the third floor.

"Shit," Karras muttered as they ascended.

Nick slapped knuckles on the third-floor apartment.

The door opened right away.

The occupant was six-three and looked like a pro wrestler—bulky and tall, wide at the shoulders. He had a buzz cut, military style, and he was no handsome young man of twenty-five. More like forty-five, his peak years well behind him. They could see the drooping muscles beneath his white dago tee.

"You own the red truck outside?" Nick wanted to know.

"Yeah...Who the hell are all of you?"

Nick displayed his shield.

"Detectives?" he asked.

"Can we come in?" Karras said.

The bulky man studied the four of them.

"What if I say no?"

"I take rejection badly," Nick responded.

The man in the doorway hesitated.

"Am I in the shit, somehow?"

"Would you like to be?" Nick shot back.

"Shit."

Then he waved them inside. The apartment wasn't the picture of tidiness. Newspapers were scattered on the carpet of the living room just inside the entry, and there were several beer cans jutting out of the garbage can in the tiny kitchenette next to where they all stood.

"You live alone?" Nick inquired.

"What do *you* think?"

"What's your name?"

"Al Terrio."

"When'd you buy the truck?" Mara asked.

"A female Homicide?" Terrio smirked.

"Would you like to relocate this little chat downtown?" Nick interrupted.

"I didn't mean nothin'."

"Let's try it again," Nick warned him.

"I live alone."

"I meant when did you buy the goddamned truck," Karras reminded him.

"About three weeks ago. From a lot on Kedzie, couple miles from here."

"You can prove that purchase? You wouldn't want us to have to go down there and find out you're lying to me."

"I got the paperwork in my drawer."

He walked toward the bedroom. He came back with the title.

"I paid cash...I'm not trying to hassle you, but what the hell's going on?"

"The name Darren Kakos mean anything to you?"

"What's that? A disease?" he grinned.

"You never heard the name."

"No. Never," he told Karras.

Nick breathed out slowly.

•   •   •   •   •

"He sold the fucking truck. How much you want to bet that he put a phony address on the papers when he sold the goddam rig?"

"Bad odds. No thanks," Mara said as they drove back downtown.

They looked into Al Terrio. Nick made a few calls to Headquarters. A few speeding tickets, but otherwise he was a solid citizen. He was a Marine in Korea, they found out when they heard the details about his background. But his physical appearance was the clincher. It just didn't fit the picture with this guy Kakos.

"What are the odds that it's not his real name?" Nick asked her.

They were headed east on the Eisenhower. It was getting toward the end of shift and they hadn't taken a dinner break, and it was already 4:35 PM.

They went for pizza at Marty's Pizza on Pulaski Road. It was famous for its thin crust Neapolitan pie.

It took twenty minutes for their order to arrive to them on the red and white checkered table cloth. Marty's was old-school, across the board.

"He's still in the wind, Kakos or whoever the hell he is."

Nick took a bite into his dinner. They went with soft drinks since they were still on the clock.

"We have the picture, anyway. It's all over town, by now," Mara consoled.

"What if he boogied out of the environs?"

"Then we're in the shit, I guess."

"If Magrette caves and puts us on traffic, at least we'll get a lot of fresh air."

"There's always that."

Her cheeks were slightly blushed.

"Don't take it so hard. They'll just throw us off the case, worst case scenario."

She nibbled at her piece of thin crust.

"No wonder you're so goddam lean."

She looked up at her partner, across the booth. Marty's was quiet because it was a week night and because it was only a little before 5:00 PM.

"You don't think he's really flown the coop, do you."

Karras stared at the redhead. He was starting to feel as if he was adopting her as a replacement for Penelope. But the family resemblance just didn't cut it. She was a portrait of the Irish lass on St. Patrick's Day. Erin Go Bragh.

"He made changes. He's screwing with us. Sells the truck. Maybe changes jobs. We'll come up with zero on his name. Nobody's fucking name is Kakos. The prick is a chameleon. He blends in with the wall paper. No, I think he's still among us. And he'll vary his MO from here on out. That's my theory, Mara. He won't leave a paper trail. He'll just leave a few more bodies. They'll be slightly different when we find them, but he'll keep a piece of his signature on them."

"That's a happy thought," she groused.

"Just saying."

"Too bad we can't use Nora's gift to find him."

"Her talents are limited. Yeah, too bad."

The pizza was gone. Nick had scarfed the majority of the rectangular squares. Mara ate a piece or two, but she ordered ante pasta as well.

"How can you eat lettuce with no dressing?" he demanded.

She laughed.

"The dressing is where all the calories are."

"We just came up empty and cold on a multiple murderer, and we're talking salads. Jesus Christ."

"It ain't over until it's over. You know that one, Nick?"

"One of my favorite bromides."

"We better head back to HQ."

"The mayor will not be happy."

"The mayor seems to be perpetually unhappy. Screw him if he can't take a joke."

Nick stared at her.

"What if he does go local?"

"You mean Kakos," Mara replied.

He kept watching her.

"It's to our advantage if he stays close to home. And we can keep looking for the guy with the toothy gap and the limp on the left side," she said.

•   •   •   •   •

The artist's picture was circulated throughout Cook County. There had been several bogus tips about a man fitting the description, but Nick and Mara came up empty on each occasion. There were also nut jobs who copped to being the subject of the police artist's rendition, but none of them fit the bill, either.

"Everyone wants their moment of glory," she told Nick as they drove out to the current crime scene on the near north side.

Some seven-year-old boy had found his father's .32 and had put a hole in a nine- year-old male who'd called the shooter a twat. There were two slugs in the victim's chest, both dead-center. It was no picnic informing the mother, a single mom, that her boy was dead. Mara handled it. Nick thought she'd be better at being the bearer of bad tidings because of her sex. She'd relate better to a twenty-four-year-old with an only child who had suddenly become childless.

They left the near north two hours later.

• • • • •

The phone calls continued, but no success. The papers kept Karen Manski relevant by publishing human interest stories about the cut-short life of a talented young woman who was going to make her mark. They played up the 'what might have been' angle quite well, Nick thought.

They were both brought to the carpet by Magrette, once more.

"I know what you're thinking," Magrette told them as they sat across from him.

"You're supposing you're here for yet another rag session. You think I'm going to tell you that Sideways Dick is back on a rampage against the two of you. But I haven't heard from the mayor or his good buddy, Carl Manski. The newspapers are doing enough to slander us, so I won't go there.

"You kill a white girl with affluent parents, and this is how it goes down. Nick, you know how the game is played in this city, and this is your apprenticeship, young lady. Are you following me?

"I'm here to help. I'm assigning four more detectives to Karen Manski's case. You got enough for a baseball team, now. But it's not going to be forever. There are lots of other murders out there, as you know. And I'm understaffing those investigations because I take orders, like everyone else around here. I don't like it, but there it is.

"Is there anything other than that picture going on? Anything at all?"

Nick and Mara didn't answer him.

"Do you want a reassignment, either of you?"

"No, I do not," Nick told Magrette.

The blood was rising toward his ears with a good measure of heat.

"Absolutely not," Crosby agreed.

Her face showed a bit of blush, as well.

"You caught a rotten situation," Magrette told them. "And the federal presence is gathering. Latest word is they think this guy has twenty scalps across the country, give or take. They like the headlines, as everyone is well aware, even though they'll deny their lust for publicity. The Director loves to see his name in print, so our cousins in the FBI are feeling the avalanche of shit flowing down on them, too, so you're not alone with the fragrance of fecal matter.

"I know all this information helps you not at all, but I'm trying to explain that misery sure as fuck loves company.

"Look, I'm on your side, but Christ, we're all most definitely in a world of hurt, so try and make me happy as soon as possible. That's my prescribed threat. Or it's my motivational speech to buoy your spirits. Morale, and that kind of bullshit.

"So, off you go to pinch this miserable motherfucker. End of lecture. Adios."

CHAPTER FIFTEEN

They got the warrant to search Al Terrio's truck, and the only prints they came up with were Al Terrio's.

"The guy with the gappy teeth wiped it clean. You sort of knew he would," Nick told Mara after they received the report from forensics.

The partners sat together in Karras' office overlooking the bustling traffic of the street below.

"We have another problem. Or maybe you might call it a challenge, if you like a positive spin," Nick told the redhead.

Mara wore a .32 snub-nose in a holster on her left hip. Somehow it just didn't fit, seeing her with the weapon on her trim waist. She ought to be a model wearing something fashionable from Paris, and she ought to be walking a runway in some fashion show. She had that *look*, Nick decided.

"What?"

"A visitor will be arriving in a half hour."

•   •   •   •   •

The visitor was an African-American federal agent, courtesy of the FBI. The FBI was setting up task forces to arrest the transcontinental series killer who had again evaded Nick Karras and Mara Crosby. It was never a comfortable conversation with a fed, Nick knew. He'd been there done that. By and large they were overly-competitive cops who liked to mark their territories regardless of who owned the case. Once they dug in, it was very difficult to keep out of their way. It was a cliché of police work, the competition between the local constabulary and the federal agents. They had greater resources and manpower.

In this case, female power. The Bureau was now beginning to integrate their special agents with people of color, as well as diversifying gender.

Special Agent Abigail Adams could've given Mara a run as a model candidate. Adams was tall and angular with high cheekbones that displayed her pure African roots. She didn't seem to be a multi-race production. Karras was quite taken by her outstanding presence. She was the kind of beauty that only Hollywood could produce. Abigail Adams had a singular appearance that made him hesitate to reply to her.

"You're Detective Karras, and you must be Detective Crosby."

She held out her hand to Mara first. Nick could see the surprise on his partner's face. You didn't see all that many black detectives on the CPD, and an African-American FBI agent was rather rare, as well.

"Please, sit down," Nick mumbled.

He had an extra folding chair in front of his desk. Mara sat next to her.

"I'm just here as a courtesy call," Adams explained to them.

Bullshit, Nick thought. You're here to piss on our property.

Marking their territory as hers, now.

"We've created some task forces across the country to catch the killer who's been traveling coast to coast."

"We think he's living here as his base," Mara told her.

"I know. The name you came up with was Darren Kakos, correct?"

Her cheekbones gleamed in an ebony hue, Karras noticed.

"That's his alias, we presume," Nick replied. "There's no such person we can find record of."

"So, he bought himself some false ID," the FBI Special Agent said.

"Looks like it," Mara added.

"And you found a vehicle you think he might have been using to travel to his crime scenes."

"A red semi-truck. We dusted it and only found prints from the new owner. He's careful, this guy. Wiped the cab clean."

"The new owner has an alibi, I'm sure."

Nick nodded.

"You think he's still here, in Chicago?" Adams asked them both.

"That's the notion we're working on, but the son of a bitch could be in Canada or Mexico or parts unknown. We have to start somewhere," Karras told her.

He wanted to ask her how tall she was. He figured six-three, at least.

"That's why I'm here. I'd like to work in concert with the Chicago Police Department. I know we have some bad history behind us."

"That sounds refreshing," Nick had to smile.

"I'm sincere, Detective Karras. I'm not snowing you."

"Time will tell," Nick shot back.

"Indeed," Abigail Adams returned.

"What can we do to help you?" Mara interjected.

His partner was playing good cop, the politician. The role surprised Nick a bit.

"Take my calls, first. We've had communication problems previously. That's history, too."

Her teeth were white, perfect, and large. She flashed them a wide smile. It reaffirmed her photogenic profile, Karras decided. If she caught this current killer, she could do the role of hero cop on film.

"We'll try to play nice...Look, his signature, as I'm sure you're already aware, is that he removes the nipples and does some cutting on the feet. Either toes or toenails. We figure they're his trophies, and I have the idea he doesn't dispose of them.

"We've got his picture from our department artist posted all over the city and Cook and DuPage County. The State Police have his likeness, and still we haven't got a single solid sighting. Either the picture is flawed or he's taken off for those parts unknown. I still think he's around, and the only way we'll find out is if he does his deed again," Nick informed her.

"We think he might have been in the military, and we've sent out the likeness to all the branches. But it'll take time for their cops to match his face to one of their vets. Vietnam is winding down, but they've still got a war to wage," Mara added. "We're not a priority, I don't think. But they said they'd look into it."

"I think I might be able to help expedite matters," Adams smiled again with a full portrait of gleaming white teeth.

"I'm sure you can," Mara answered.

Her smile looked lethal, suddenly. She was catching on to how this game was played. Like chess, perhaps. Moves and countermoves. Political horseshit, Nick figured.

"I'm going to be set up at HQ, not far from here. You know where we are, I assume."

"We know," Mara volleyed back at her.

Adams gave the redhead a piercing stare of her own, but Nick's partner kept contact eyeball to eyeball with the Special Agent. Nick had to stifle laughter.

"Is there anything else we can do for you?" Karras said after he'd restrained himself from an outburst.

"Here's my card."

Adams handed it to Nick and avoided looking at Mara.

She exited the cubicle as quickly as she entered it.

"Think she's a basketball player?" Karras mused.

"Is that a racial observation?" Mara grinned.

"No, it's a height observation."

Crosby chuckled.

"You looked as if you were rather taken with Special Agent Adams."

"She was beautiful. But she has to have six inches on me. Can you imagine her with high heels?"

"She was wearing flats. Probably doesn't want to loom over her male counterparts."

"I think it was nice seeing something other than a white guy in a suit for a change. A lot of girls in high school thought I was Hispanic. Cut me out on a lot of women. The Bureau needs to get into Latinas."

"Now that we've solved racial inequalities…What's her game, Nick?"

"Like she said. They're sending out task forces. They've got a little wider jurisdiction than we do. I told her. We're not going to pinch this guy unless he does it again, close to home."

"You think he bought another truck?" she mused.

"If he's as organized as we think he is, I figure he's out of the hauling racket. He knows we'll be looking for a man in a rig. The FBI's profile has him picking off strays in fast food joints and diners, mostly. At least eight of the victims fit that picture. He's not hitting expensive hookers from hotels. None of them have been married women. The physical stuff is the same, too. Like Karen Manski, tall and thin and young. She wasn't one of his strays, but he apparently seeks a certain body appearance."

"Sort of like you."

She gave him a sardonic look.

"Thanks. I feel safer, now."

"You're armed and dangerous, though. He picks the 'poor souls' types. Helpless, lonely, like that."

"I only fit one of those categories."

"How can you be lonely? You have me."

"Tell that to your wife."

She grinned maliciously at her partner.

"She knows we're purely professional."

"You're too old for me. And too married. I have a code, you know."

"You look at me and you think 'grandpa'."

"Thanks. I needed that. Puts me in my place."

She lowered her eyes to her lap.

"Someone's really got to die for us to stop him."

Nick was all out of repartee.

"Maybe we'll get lucky with the artist's rendering."

"Maybe."

They sat in silence for a few moments.

"I thought she was more like six-five," Mara looked up at him.

•   •   •   •   •

The State Police brought him in. The gap between the teeth was there, but they couldn't see a limp when they brought him into the interview room on the first floor. They watched him through the one-way window where they observed their suspects before they engaged them face to face.

"He's the right age. Good looking. But I didn't catch the limp," Mara confided.

"Maybe he had surgery. Maybe he's been to therapy."

"What's the name on the sheet?"

"Jack Madsen. He has ID that matches. Driver's license, social security. And a library card."

"They found him where?"

"Hitting on a homeless girl who was trying to hitch a ride near a McDonald's on Route 55 near Pontiac."

"That's a fur piece from here. What? Fifty miles?" she asked Nick.

"Out of our province, yes. At least the Staties respect our jurisdiction, unlike Special Agent Abigail Adams and friends."

"Let's hear it for cooperation on the professional level."

"I don't like it."

"What?" she asked.

"He's nervous. Doesn't fit the profile. A well-oiled sociopath wouldn't fidget. He'd be getting his story together, coolly and calmly. He might even put his head down and go to sleep. This guy looks like he might be getting ready to irrigate his Jockeys."

They watched him for five more minutes. Jack Madsen looked as though he might become hysterical and try to bolt the interview room.

"You like Coke?" Nick asked as they walked in together.

He had a cold can in his right hand and he laid it in front of Madsen. Nick and Mara sat opposite the young man at a long, rectangular slab of wood that sported a dull, aged surface.

"Why am I here? I didn't do anything."

Nick laid the artist's picture in front of the young man.

"What's that?"

"You mean you don't think it looks like you?" Mara threw out at him.

"Looks like a dead ringer to me," Nick added. "Drink your Coke. You must be dry by now. Do you need to use the bathroom? We can have you escorted to the head, if you need to pee."

"Why am I *here?*" he repeated.

"You don't recognize the pic?" Mara smiled warmly.

"I don't know what you're talking about."

"You were chatting up a young girl at that fast food place near Pontiac. Why were you there?" Nick asked.

"I live in Dwight. It's only a few miles. I was looking for a job in Pontiac, but they already filled the slot. I was stopping there to get something to eat before I went home, that's all. What is this?"

Jack Madsen's driver's license had a Dwight address. So far, it was looking bad, Nick estimated. And the kid was hyper. Their guy would be cool to the point you wanted to strangle the prick. This young man was one degree away from 212 degrees. He was bubbling up to an explosion.

"What'd you have in mind for the young girl, Jack?"

"Nothing. I was just talking to her, for crissake. Why'd I get dragged all the way here—"

"Look at the picture again, Jack. Is that your double or what?" Nick smiled.

"Who *is* that?"

"A guy we're looking for."

"And those State Police thought I was that guy?"

"You gotta admit there's a resemblance," Mara told the young man.

"Do something for me, Jack," Nick asked.

"What?"

The young fellow was close to tears, Karras observed.

"Just walk around the room for me."

"Huh?"

"You heard me."

It was a demand, this time.

"Jesus."

He rose and walked around the interview room.

No hitch in his giddyup.

Nick looked over at Nora. He shrugged at her.

The ID was genuine. They put in a call to the Dwight Police, and the sergeant actually knew the kid. Confirmed his story about job hunting in Pontiac.

The sergeant was a friend of the family. He asked Karras what the hell was going on, and Nick explained the State cops thought he was the guy in the rendition.

"Those Staties need to get their fucking eyes checked."

And the Dwight policeman hung up on him.

They returned to the interview room. Neither of them sat down.

"We'll give you a lift home," Nick told him. "You have our sincere apologies for carting you in here. Just an honest mistake."

"I have to pee," Jack Madsen told them.

He didn't look even a little bit relieved or happy.

CHAPTER SIXTEEN

Hiding in place.

They knew by now that they had a traveler. He'd been obvious enough about his calling card. The deviations were only slight, and he'd read about the FBI and its profilers. They'd have him sketched out by now. The police artist would have his face transmitted across the country, and the federals would have put a full court press on him cross country, at this point.

So, the best thing for him to do was take his chances with the Chicago Police Department's Homicide Division. The newspapers had shredded this guy Karras' efforts already, and perhaps the media was correct in assuming they had little or no chance of apprehending him.

The false IDs had been valuable, but he had been fingerprinted in the Army, and sooner or later someone would recognize his widely circulated likeness. He'd seen the sketch in the newspapers and it was a reasonable facsimile. Getting a hold of his prints wasn't likely. He wiped his old apartment clean.

But there was always the possibility that he'd missed something, so it was a good idea to lie low for the time being. He could make a few changes. Grow facial hair or color his mop on top. There were always glasses. Or he could shave his head. There were a few options to alter his appearance, and he knew he had to blend in or be caught. Karras might not be as dumb as the papers made him out to be, and if he really was any good, the bad publicity would spur him on until he proved them all wrong.

He thought it was more probable that the vicious stories in the papers about the detective who couldn't bring Karen Manski's killer to justice would serve as motivation for the detective to vindicate himself. Never underestimate the force of humiliation, he reckoned. It had worked on him, after all.

By this time, he should have forgotten her. It was high school. Only a juvenile romance. But it lingered in him all these years later. It seemed that he had finally felt something for another human being, but after a few months she'd confronted him and let him know she wanted to see other people.

"I don't feel the way I did, anymore," was her parting shot, back around the tail end of twelfth grade, right before graduation.

It was strange how badly he felt, how badly he had been betrayed. But it all happened long before he settled his frustrations with his hands and his knife. There were times he thought he'd like to look her up and redeem his pride with the technique he'd employed all over the country.

Certainly, she would recognize the artist's version of him. That goddam gap in his two front teeth that shamed him all his life. His parents wouldn't pay for orthodontia to close that space in his teeth. They told him it displayed character. What it did was make him self-conscious about smiling, so he kept his 'mark' hidden by tightly closed lips.

He had to make changes. It was apparent, now. And he could not keep traveling the highways in search of targets. The FBI had too much manpower for him to remain elusive. Only a handful of serial killers were able to evade the federals. They just kept on coming.

The city police were riddled with corruption, however. It was his ace in the hole that a lot of cops were more interested in bribes than they were in solving crimes. Homicide was a bit different, though. They tended to be more success-oriented. It was as if they took murders personally. The other breeds of policemen were more laid back about statistical triumphs. It was more just a job with a lot of them. The murder police tended to be a little more dedicated to removing outstanding names from their case lists.

Which was why he didn't dismiss Karras as the incompetent that he was described as in the newspapers. Unfortunately, Karen Manski kept him in the spotlight longer because it was obvious that her father, perhaps both parents, had clout, and clout was the way it was played in Chicago. You didn't have to be a politician to figure it all out.

●   ●   ●   ●   ●

The urge to hunt was still as strong as it had ever been. He understood the psychology. You always wanted most what you could not have. When he choked the life out of them it was all a grand release, orgasmic. In fact, it was better than the climaxes he experienced in the carnal aspect of the killings. The strangling and the cutting were far more intense than the release of his seed into a condom.

Perhaps it was because he did them wearing condoms that blunted the power of his cums. It was far too dangerous to go into them bare. Too many ways to be caught, that way. He never would have arrived where he was if he had been that blatantly bold.

No, the fucking, the rape, was simply an afterthought. The killing was godlike. It was the buzz by itself. Sex was profoundly mundane, pedestrian.

It was gathering inside him like a painful infection, and there was only one remedy. If he killed again, it was at maximum risk. You could never tell if one of his targets recognized him as he appeared now, without adaptation. He needed time to make the necessary changes, and he needed time to suggest to Karras and the other armies of cops that maybe he'd disappeared off their radars altogether. He could be dead, killed in a car accident, or he could have succumbed to cancer or a thousand other maladies that fit into any number of natural categories. If he waited long enough, they would tire of the chase.

When the time was right, he could find another one, and this time he could cross them up by cutting off her head or by dismembering her and floating her body parts in Lake Michigan or the Chicago River. Proving he was smarter than they were was part of the rush, being superior to ordinary drones, worker bees, who went off to perform a task for a wage until they reached retirement or were able to go to Tampa/St. Pete and wear white pants with a white belt and to seek the early bird at cut-rate restaurants. Take up golf or fishing and wither away under a semi-tropical sun in some gated community that catered to the old and soon-to-die.

He hated them for their low bars of accomplishment. He was famous, notorious, even though he was to the world anonymous. Anonymity was the way you stayed active and free from their boring, automaton existences. He despised them for their easy pleasures, their dull drive.

He changed apartments. Dumped Ellen Prentice. She didn't seem hurt.

Then the hair was the first step. He colored it auburn red, distinct from the blond-brown he'd been born with. He grew a beard and mustache and dyed it the same color as his top knot.

The final step was to make an appointment with an orthodontist. By the time of the appointment he sported full facial hair along with the new hue of the hair on his head. Braces were applied after the second appointment. The cost was steep, but he figured that it was worth his liberty.

His new employment was salesman for a nationally known insurance outfit. He set up an office on the northwest side, but most of his time was spent going door-to-door to sign up new clients. Apparently, his changes only enhanced his ability to convince a lot of stay-at-home housewives to buy a policy or two. They were inclined to buy life insurance, mainly. God bless their paranoia about losing the hubby and trying to raise children as a single mommy. He provided them peace of mind that came with six digits.

The new gig was far more lucrative than driving his red truck from coast to coast, and it was not nearly as exhausting. The money came pouring in, and his list of customers kept growing. He was a natural at schmoozing housewives out of their vacation money or out of whatever they could have been squirreling their cash away for. He was convincing them they were being long-term smart instead of short-term stupid. Insurance was the Great Con, and he fell deeply in love with it.

•　　•　　•　　•　　•

Some of his potential clients were single women. Office workers, nurses, teachers. And a few of them looked like potential candidates for something far more pleasurable than signing on the dotted line. They were in their early or mid-twenties, mainly. Just his type. He eliminated the obese types. Just not his thing. But youth kept most of them in his do-able list. Tall, thin, lithe, athletic, lean.

A number of them went bra-less during his appointments—always in the comfort of their own homes. They were more relaxed on their home fields. More confident. The phone was right there, and the neighbors could hear through paper-thin walls in their apartments. They lived in cheap buildings that catered to women who were out in the world alone for the first time. Independent, young women. Still in the mating hunt at bars in Old Town or Rush Street nightclubs that catered to cunts on the make. They all seemed the same.

•　　•　　•　　•　　•

The front teeth gradually came together after a few months with the braces. When he looked in the mirror, he almost didn't recognize himself. The hair had grown long, a fashionable style in the early '70s. Discos were popular, and the Travolta movie had spurred bars with rotating globes on the ceilings. He went out to several clubs and he even dressed in mod leisure suits. His body type wore the stylish clothing well, and it wasn't a problem coming back to his new apartment in Oak Park with a young, impressed woman in tow.

Fucking was a natural conclusion to the evenings, and he brought several young women to his bed.

It was hardly satisfying to see them all depart in the early hours after their encounters. Killing them would have been ever so much better, but he was maintaining his self-control. His appearance had evolved into something brand new. There was nothing about him that resembled that cop's sketch from all those months ago.

It was late summer. Six months had burned away, and the articles about poor Karen Manski had begun to evaporate from news print and the media in general. She was simply a sad statistic, nothing more. Her wealthy, connected parents had run out of the public's attention span. There were other issues in the headlines, and one unfortunate, young, mutilated female was no longer of interest. Karen Manski wasn't news any longer.

When he peered down into their glazed eyes, it was the sex not the power of his gripping fingers that sent them into an orgasmic throe. It was just coupling, what any pair of mammals could achieve with a few, well-placed thrusts.

It began to bore him, so he put his leisure suits on hangers and placed them at the back of the line in the closet. He refrained from going to the discos and the clubs where he'd always managed to snare a bed partner for the night. Some of them seemed interested in encores, but he never called them back. He never gave out his home phone, so they weren't able to bother him with their tiresome callbacks.

He knew he'd weaken, give in, and then he'd have messes to clean up in the morning. All his other kills had been in motels or in the cab of his truck. He had a permanent place, now, and he couldn't afford to leave their traces here. He was meticulous in clean-up, but it was too risky to do them where he lived. It had always been at their residences or in some twenty-dollar-a-night flop.

It had gone quiet with Karras and his colleagues, but he remained wary of the FBI. He didn't read a name or see a photo of one of them—it wasn't their style to show themselves in public. Only the big shots in the Bureau allowed themselves to be photographed. They preferred to toil in anonymity, just as he did, and it was their ghost-like habit that frightened him the most. He never knew if they were still out there after all these months still searching for the killer of twenty women.

•　　　•　　　•　　　•　　　•

There were times he thought he should retire altogether, get married, have children, melt into the surroundings forever. The only problem was that the compulsion was getting even greater rather than receding.

He wasn't normal. He wasn't like everyone else. The herd.

It wasn't his genetic structure. He wondered where his inheritance had come from. There were no signs of similar instincts from his parents or grandparents, maternal or paternal. Perhaps it had skipped several generations. There was no way of knowing.

He knew the primal urges were still inside, and all the trappings of normalcy, the job, the apartment, the new appearance, were simply façade, false. He was who he was. He'd never give up his hands and his knives. Killing was his reason for being. Hunting, capturing the prey, and then relieving them of everything they truly owned—it was his reason for being. He could never fit into the bovine herd that his parents raised him to become part of.

How long could he tolerate the way he was living? The money was great. His list was ever-expanding on the paranoia of young house slaves. They all had that bleary-eyed look to them. Trapped in marriage. Handcuffed to a house full of noisy urchins that they regretted more than they loved. They'd never be free again, but they had to buy a policy just to keep eating and existing. It was his profession, now. Relieving their anxiety about the possibility of becoming alone once more, the way they were before they sold themselves into a soft bondage.

He almost felt sorry for them, but feeling anything was not one of his strong suits. It was for them to suffer with cheap emotion. That was why they were eternally unhappy and unfulfilled. Feeling was their Achilles heel, their weakness. He used to be able to permanently separate his kills from all that weight.

He feared he was becoming more like them daily. He was terrified he was leaving his best self behind and that their world-weary lives were spilling over him like a tidal wave that would cover him and obliterate him forever.

• • • • •

In the fall, he decided it was time. He picked up a young brunette in a bar close to O'Hare. It was a young twenties, college punk club that attracted singles. She sat with a table of four other young women, so he was careful not to attempt to approach her in front of her friends.

It was nickel beer night. For one hour the beers were five cents, so you stood in line and drank and then refilled your glass mug as soon as you got to the front of the line again. The brunette was suitably sloshed about fifty minutes into the discount beer hour. She was apart from her companions and he was right behind her. Beer didn't have much effect on him. His Army buddies told him he had a wooden leg. It was simply a matter of tolerance to alcohol. It never seemed to faze him, even in great quantities.

"They refer to this as a cattle call in Hollywood."

She turned and giggled. She was another nickel beer from collapse. He had to grab onto her now.

"You okay?" he smiled.

His looks had been altered, but women still liked what they saw.

"I think I need some air," she burbled.

"Me, too," he grinned again. "Want to take a break outside?"

She looked him over again.

"What's your name?" she asked.

He could barely hear her from the blasting of the jukebox.

"Say what?"

"What's your name?" she bleated.

"Ron. What's yours?"

"Funny. They call me Ronnie...For Rhonda."

"You want to get some fresh air, Ronnie? Rhonda?"

She wore a bit too much blush and lipstick. Her lips were a garish red.

She nodded woozily. He looked over his shoulder at the table where her companions sat. They were engaged with some other male nighthawks, at the moment.

He led her out the door, away from the rumbling of the music in the packed club.

Nickel beer hour had come to an end.

But when he had her outside, Rhonda began to puke on the parking lot. A few of her girlfriends from back in the bar appeared and swept her up and threw her in one of their cars.

They gave him glares as they pulled out onto the street, and he stood in place, watching them depart.

•   •   •   •   •

He thought he might look up Ellen Prentice again and show her his new look—the beard and the hair color. It was always good to change. Ellen might just be impressed.

CHAPTER SEVENTEEN

Abigail Adams graduated summa cum laude from Georgetown, went on to law school at Yale, and promptly spent four years in the United States Army as a member of Intelligence. Which was appropriate in regard to her academic achievements. She ran track in college, as well as competed in cross country. After her stint in the military, she went directly to the Academy at Quantico where she earned her spurs as a top-notch profiler. She rose in the ranks until she received her current assignment as Special Agent in charge of a task force aimed at pinching the Coast to Coast Killer, as he was known in the FBI. The media had yet to pick up on the killer's moniker.

Abigail was aware that the Bureau's new attitude on diversity gave her a boost a black woman would not have been offered a decade earlier. She had high hopes that her ascension would not be impeded by her race, and her abilities would be a plus in her rise, now that a chunk of the systemic racism had been carved away, but there were still old-school bureaucrats that became very nervous when Adams made any appearances in their offices. Still, things were improving, although not quickly enough. 1863 was more than a century behind her and every African-American in the country, and still the playing field was not level.

She had to work twice as hard as her white co-workers, and she was aware of the injustice. But she figured if she could apprehend the murderer of twenty women, her odds at rising with the tide were in her favor. Abigail even had secret ambitions of getting into politics someday. She could picture Representative or Senator in front her name in the future, even though black females in Congress were about as rare as the dodo bird.

She made an appointment to see Karras and his partner, Crosby, at the CPD's Headquarters on Michigan Avenue, but when she arrived, she was rerouted to a crime scene on the far northwest side.

Abigail flashed her ID, and the uniform grudgingly let her in the door of the apartment.

Karras was bent over the body, and Crosby stood opposite the corpse.

Nick stood erect and turned to the Special Agent.

"Hello there," he said evenly.

"What have we got?" Adams retorted smartly.

"Ellen Prentice. Or she used to be."

"Cause of death?"

"Strangulation," Mara shot back. "You can see the ligature marks on her throat."

"Yes, thank you."

"The mutilation was done post mortem," Nick told the FBI agent. "Or so the ME tells us. He's already been and gone."

"Why didn't you notify my office?" she demanded.

"We've only been on scene ninety minutes," Crosby informed her.

"Do you think it's our person of interest?" Adams continued.

"You mean the Coast to Coast Killer?"

"Where'd you hear that?" Adams wanted to know.

"Leaks. Where else?"

"You didn't hear that from my task force."

"If you insist," Mara said.

"I thought we were going to cooperate, Detective Karras."

"Let me know when your side starts sharing the wealth. I was going to call you as soon as we wrapped, here."

Adams knelt toward Ellen Prentice.

"The strangling fits. But the eyelids don't."

The eyelids were cut away, and Ellen Prentice seemed to be staring bug-eyed.

"And the X cut on the abdomen is new, different. Nothing on the toes or the toenails," the Special Agent observed.

"We're not giving out details to the media, naturally," Mara interjected.

"We never do, Detective," Adams rejoined with an attempt at a withering stare.

"Yes, of course," Crosby shot back.

"In the spirit of cooperation, we'll send you the report as soon as we have it ready."

She looked at Karras. The withering stare didn't seem to work on either Homicide.

"I'll send my forensics people over here immediately," she told both of them.

Neither detective rose to the insult.

"Have at it," Nick smiled. "Our people are pretty proficient."

"This is a federal case, Detective."

"You're in Chicago, Ms. Adams. We have first dibs."

Mara let out a muffled laugh.

"And it's still a federal case."

"Until it isn't," Nick explained. "The MO isn't the same, as you can see."

"And you don't think it's the same perpetrator?" Adams said.

"Could be a copy-cat. Our boy has been dormant for months. Maybe the original gave it up and moved on or got himself whacked or found a new hobby."

"There's nothing funny about all this, Detective."

"You see any grins around here?" Mara said.

Adams tried another glare at Crosby, but the redhead wasn't impressed.

Nick looked over at his partner and wanted to give her a bearhug, but he refrained from anything unprofessional, especial in front of a fed.

"He could be throwing a new pitch, adding to his repertoire, but I'm betting he didn't leave any evidence for us to hook him up. So, we'll have to hope that someone caught a glimpse of him, our Coast to Coast guy. But I have a feeling he did something about his appearance. The guy's organized, one of those. He won't make anything easy," Nick told the fed.

"But you think it's the same killer," Adams threw back at him.

Nick didn't answer, and Mara was walking about the apartment, looking for anything remotely evidentiary.

"I'll send you the complete report, as soon as I have it."

"My techs'll be here in thirty minutes. Don't remove anything, please, including the body. When everyone's done, we'll give you a call and you can send her to the morgue."

"Her name was Ellen Prentice," Nick reminded Adams.

The Special Agent looked down at the torn body.

"Yes," she concluded.

And she walked away from Karras.

• • • • •

There were six apartments in the brownstone building on the northwest side, and Nick and Mara split up and knocked on doors.

Nick came up dry until he rapped on the third door, the one directly above Ellen Prentice's flat.

"Chicago Police," he said as the female inside the cracked-open door restricted by a chain peered out.

"What is it?"

"I'd like to ask you a few questions. May I come in?"

She took a close look at his ID, and then she unlatched the door and let Karras enter.

The woman was middle-aged, dressed in an ankle-length robe and wearing child-like bunny slippers with pink fluff.

"Your name is?" he asked.

"Frances Buranski."

"Did you know Ellen Prentice, one floor below?"

"What's wrong? What happened?"

Fear took hold of her face. She wasn't wearing makeup, and her fourth decade hadn't been kind to her.

"There's been a murder, it appears."

Her hand shot to her mouth.

"Ellen, you mean?"

He nodded.

"Oh, my—"

"Did you hear anything, last night?"

"No, I—"

"Or see anything?"

"I...I looked out the window there, about midnight. I heard two people talking. One of them was Ellen. They were laughing, and then they went inside and I couldn't hear them anymore."

"Did you see the man with her?"

"Only for a second...He wore a beard, I think."

"You see anything else?"

"The lighting isn't great out there. They only stood in front until Ellen unlocked the door."

"The parking lot is right in front of the entrance. Did you see them coming in? Did you see a car?"

"Ellen drives an old Chevy. I saw it parked out there this morning, but I never saw the two of them coming from the parking lot...Sorry."

"Don't be sorry, Frances."

She looked sad and plain, Nick thought. There was no ring on her finger and he had the impression there never was. He took her for a career woman. She had a job and that was about it. But it was only an impression. He'd been wrong before. People tend to surprise you, he knew.

"If you can think of anything else, here's my card. Please call me, day or night."

He handed her the card and he walked out just when the flood erupted out of Frances Buranski's eyes.

"Who'd do a thing like that to Ellen?" she bleated as the door was shut behind him.

•　　•　　•　　•　　•

"There's been another one," Nora told him right when he walked in the door.

"How'd you know? It hasn't been released to anyone yet."

She watched his eyes as he flopped onto the couch.

"It just popped into my head," she said as she sat next to him.

"I never know what you're going to spring on me."

He leaned into her and kissed her.

"Was I right?" she asked.

"You were right."

"What happened?"

"You certain you want to know?"

She waited for him.

"Strangulation and some cutting."

"Is it like Karen Manski?"

"Not exactly."

"What does that mean?" she asked.

"You don't really need details, do you, Nora?"

She waited.

"Was it the same as the other girl?"

"Not the same. But I think it was the same guy trying to fuck with us. I think he's been hunkered down, waiting, and I think the son of a bitch is back. He reads the papers, Nora, and he's screwing with us, changing things just slightly. The cutting was different, but the choking was the same. He's telling us how clever he is. And the FBI is pissing on our territory because *they can*."

"What's that mean?"

He explained to her about Special Agent Adams.

"I thought you handled cases in the city."

"This guy has gone national. They call him the Coast to Coast Killer. We didn't make it up. The Federal Bureau of Incompetence did."

"I take it you don't get along with them."

"Can't pull one over on your intuition, can I."

She leaned over and kissed him, this time.

"You're going to catch him, you and Mara."

"Your second sight see that one?"

"I have faith in you, Nick. You'll get him."

"Tell that to Captain Magrette and the Mayor and to Karen Manski's parents."

"Never mind them. They don't see what I see."

"What do you see, Nora?"

"I see that it's Wednesday night and that the calendar says it's prime baby-making night. That's what I see."

"Do you feel like Fertile Fanny, today?"

"What the hell is that?"

"Never mind. First we feed and then we fertilize your garden. All right?"

"Was it bad? I mean, was it worse than the Manski girl?"

He was pressed against Nora, and they lay on their sides facing one another.

"Bad enough."

"You need to stop worrying about pleasing everybody, Nick. I know how good you are."

"I value your opinion above all others, lady love."

"Don't let them get to you, Nick. I think you care too much what other people say and think about you."

"Is that in your second sight, too?"

"I knew all about you the first time we were together," she replied.

"I wish I could hot-wire into your brain."

"You'll get this man. I know it."

"If it's laughing boy, he's changed his appearance. A witness thought he had a beard."

"Someone saw him?"

"She saw him walk in the building with Ellen Prentice. He was fur-bound."

"I remember the sketch you showed me."

"He might have done other things."

"I remember he had something with his teeth."

"He had a gap, yeah," Nick said.

She waited and looked at him.

"Maybe he fixed the gap."

•   •   •   •   •

Nick and Mara canvased virtually every orthodontist on the north half of the city. The new sketch had him with a beard.

There was a legion of orthodontists, and they had only covered twelve on the upper portion of Chicago. There were hundreds in the city in total and in the 'burbs.

Maybe he stayed with the split front teeth. The first tooth fairies didn't recognize the bearded picture.

"Now what?" Mara asked as they took their dinner break at a pizza joint in Cicero, a western suburb.

"We need to eat smarter. I've put on six pounds," he lamented.

CHAPTER EIGHTEEN

They had exhausted the orthodontists on the north side, and the list on the southern half of the city was extensive.

"There must be a lot of crooked teeth around town," Mara complained.

"Not any more, obviously," Nick cracked back.

"I hear the Brits have lousy teeth," she rejoined.

"It must be their diet."

"Yeah, look who's talking," his partner smiled.

"Is it that obvious?""

They were heading out to the southwest side to check out Dr. Teeth and company. They took the Dan Ryan out to 95th Street and then headed west. Most of the orthodontists were located in malls or mini malls near the southwest border. The inner city didn't seem to have many locations, and Nick figured the Coast to Coast strangler wouldn't fit in in a black venue.

They hit three doctors before they headed back to the north side to deal with three cases on their home turf. The outstandings needed to be cleared before Magrette had yet another hemorrhage courtesy of Sideways Dick, the Mayor.

The Manskis must have run out of connections in city hall and in interested journalists at the tabloids because the stories about Karen had dwindled to zero.

Nick drove the Ford on the Stevenson heading toward the Lake.

"Kids aren't the only ones who have short attention spans," Karras said to Mara.

"I have a short span of concentration."

"Life goes on, and shit like that," Nick said.

"If she was your family or mine, would we let her drift off?"

"I don't suppose we would. It's just in the nature of the job to hang on with your teeth until the bad guy gets dropped.

"They're called 'bulldogs', darlin'," Nick smiled.

"Darlin'? That's harassment, grandpa."

"I could have said toots or sweetie pie," he grinned.

"I'm armed. Remember?"

"Yeah, do me a favor."

"You're not the depressed type, Nick."

"Look again. Every fucking time I go for a doctor's appointment, the nurse invariably asks me if I've been depressed."

"What do you tell her?"

"If anybody is never depressed, they're fucking idiots."

The radio buzzed a call for Karras. The message was that he had an important call from the United States Army.

•   •   •   •   •

They rushed up to Nick's cubicle. There was a phone number on a piece of paper resting on the middle of his desk. Mara sat down wearily opposite her partner.

They put Nick on hold for twelve minutes.

"This is Sergeant Blane, CID."

"You left a message for me. Karras from Chicago Homicide."

He shot a stare at Mara and shrugged his shoulders.

"Oh, yeah. We have a match on that photo you sent us. And the sketch fits the guy on the picture, looks like."

Nick raised his hand toward Crosby.

She sat up.

"Guy's name is Randall Murphy. From your town, Chicago."

Nick's call came from Fort Leavenworth.

"You have a location, an address, on him?"

"Last known address was in Gary, Indiana. That's where his disability checks were mailed, but that was back in 1968. When he enlisted, he was from the north end of your town."

Blane rattled off the Chicago address. It was the same spot where they originally located him. No luck with a new location.

"Is this fellow a stone in your shoe, Detective?"

"We like him for a number of homicides."

"I read the papers. It's this Coast to Coast asshole, no?"

"Could be."

"I looked at his file. The guy was a semi-war hero. A few decorations, including a bronze star. Fought several major ops. I guess he got used to trigger time."

"Without the trigger," Nick replied.

"Yeah, like I said, I read the stories. He likes to touch his kills...I hope I've been some help, Detective Karras. It's no joy hearing one of our ex-troopers is a murdering son of a bitch. I hope you nail his sorry ass."

Blane promised to FAX Karras all the information about Randall Murphy to Chicago. Then they broke the call.

So, Kakos was Randall Murphy. It was fairly certain that Murphy was his actual name since the Gov looked at his credentials, and there would be no motive to use an alias when this man was eighteen. But you never knew. He and Mara had to operate under the assumption that they had Coast to Coast's real identity.

•　　　•　　　•　　　•　　　•

The paperwork came through FAX the same afternoon. The photo was several years old, but it was far more precise than the artist's sketch. This time a beard would be added to the picture and it had to be more accurate than the drawing they had.

The altered photo with the facial hair was spread all over northern Illinois by the next morning. Out of courtesy, the FBI was notified immediately about Murphy. Their agents received copies of his likeness.

Abigail Adams seemed a little less hostile when Nick phoned her about the find.

"The Army contacted me an hour before they talked to you," she said over the telephone.

Gotcha, Nick thought. She was ultra-competitive, but he already knew that.

"But thanks for the call."

She hung up abruptly.

"Miss Congeniality," Nick said to his partner, sitting in her usual spot across Karras' desk.

"We wait until there's a new sighting?"

"We'll exhaust the dentists' list. And we still have two outstandings on that white board behind you."

There were two names in red marker on that board. One was a teenager who was stabbed sixteen times in a west side street fight, and the other was a seventy-three-year -old black woman who was killed with a single sucker punch while she waited at a bus stop.

They took off from Headquarters toward the scene of the old woman's demise. They went from store to store asking if anyone saw anything. 'Nobody knew nothing.' It was a black neighborhood, and the victim was also African-American. Nick had thoughts of calling in a black detective to help them canvas, but it was summer and the homicide calls were hot and heavy, just like the weather now in August.

•　　　•　　　•　　　•　　　•

They hit the G-spot on the southwest side. They finally found the right orthodontist.

His name was Frank Gerber—like the baby food. He was a tall, lanky, middle-aged man with a few pathetic wisps of hair combed over a primarily bald head.

147

"I did work on him a few months ago. You know, I saw the sketch of him on the news. He's this Coast to Coast killer, right?" Gerber smiled enthusiastically.

Mara and Karras met with him in his office.

"That's what we're looking into," Mara told the dentist.

"Yeah, I've got his records."

He paid cash and he used the Kakos alias, and Nick was certain the address listed was bogus. But he took everything down and he understood that it all had to be checked out. Thoroughness had been rule number one ever since he received the detective's shield.

• • • • •

The address was false, just like the name he liked to use.

They checked the DMV, and there was no one listed under Kakos. There were several listings of a Randall Murphy, however, and the two cops checked everyone out, and none of them was the man in the Army photo.

"His name is Randall Murphy," Nick told Magrette.

They were standing on his carpet after declining to take a seat.

"That's all we have, a name," he told the pair.

Nick nodded.

"We have his picture, sans the facial hair, and we had the artist do a rendering with a beard. It's much better than the old drawing," Mara explained.

"He's had his teeth fixed. We found the orthodontist who closed the hole in his choppers."

"And you've spread the word across the countryside?" he shot back at Nick.

"Everywhere," Karras affirmed. "All points."

"And still Randall Murphy roams the countryside."

There was no pleasing Magrette unless the three of them stood witness at Murphy's execution.

"We're closer than we were, Captain."

"Tell that to the blimp in City Hall."

Nick had to let loose with a snort.

"Funny, Karras?"

"Absolutely not," Nick said with a suddenly sober face.

Mara was gnawing on her lip.

"The FBI was on the horn to me."

"They have the same information we do," Nick said.

"Special Agent Adams is a pain in my aching ass."

"I concur, Captain," Nick told him.

"You sense the discomfort in my rectal area?" Magrette asked.

"I sense your pain, Captain. I mean I have empathy for you."

"I can't tell you two how much that sentiment means to me. I really cannot."

Nick sensed it was time to shut his mouth before the Boss in front of him went off like Vesuvius.

"I'm tired of fucking with this cocksucker, this Coast to Coast bitch. I want him off the board. Karen Manski and at least nineteen other young women need him out of action, too. I'm sure you sense my stress and anxiety over this nickel-dick murdering piece of flotsam and jetsam. Am I correct in my assessment?"

"Abundantly clear, sir," Nick answered.

"No one likes a wiseguy, Karras."

"I meant no offense, sir."

Magrette took the new, enhanced picture of Murphy in his hands.

"This guy squats when he pisses. I don't like his looks. Looks like one of those sensitive little flower petals who didn't get laid after the prom. So now he's seeking revenge. You think Quantico would agree with my profile?"

"He hates women, sir. That's fairly obvious," Mara chimed in.

"Would you date this needle dick, Detective Crosby?"

Mara blushed and smiled.

"I'm trying not to be gender insensitive, Detective Crosby."

"No offense taken, sir."

"I can't relay how much these little talks we share are as uplifting as I find them to be. I really can't. Perhaps we'll require fewer interviews like this in the very near future. Do you share my high hopes, Detectives Karras and Crosby?"

"We are in full accord, sir," Nick said, straight-faced.

"You don't get any impressions from a photograph, do you?" he asked Nora as they ate at the dinette table.

"I need something more personal."

"Something of Randall Murphy's. Something he's touched."

"It works that way occasionally."

He bit into his sirloin steak. Nora was becoming too good a cook. But he couldn't blame her for his new paunch. It was all that fast food crap at dinner break on shift. He needed to model Mara and start eating fruits and salads instead of pizza and burgers and calory-loaded fat-boy food.

"You look like you're in full bloom, lady-love."

She tended to blush when Karras complimented her looks.

"Is there something you wanted to tell me?"

She began to well up in her eyes.

"We won't know for sure until I see the doctor."

He dropped his knife and fork on the plate with a clang.

"Won't know what?" he asked.

She smiled widely.

"I passed the in-home test. It came out the right color. But we have to confirm it with a guy with a medical diploma."

He reached across the table and took Nora's hands.

"How many times did you do the in-home test?"

"Twice...I didn't try again because I was too scared."

He scanned her dark countenance.

"You think you really are?"

She nodded, and then the droplets began to course down her brown cheeks.

"I'm going with you to the appointment."

"I don't want you to be disappointed if he doesn't go along with the tests."

"I'm still going with you."

"Eat your steak. You have any idea about the price of sirloin?"

"The 'I love you' seems insufficient."

"Say it anyway."

He did.

•   •   •   •   •

She walked out of the exam room beaming. He didn't need any more information on the subject.

"How far along?" Nick asked her on the drive home.

"Early. Six to eight weeks. I knew it might be good news when I missed my period longer than three weeks."

He wanted to kiss her, but the traffic on the Stevenson was brutal. They got out of the appointment at 3:30, right at the beginning of rush hour. He had the air on in the car, but it was oppressive enough that the AC was having trouble keeping up with the tropical heat and humidity. It was 94, currently, one of the billboards off-road read.

When they arrived at the apartment, Nick took hold of her arm on the way up the stairs.

"I'm not disabled," she laughed.

"Oh. Yeah...It's been a while since I..."

"I know. Relax, Nick. Everything is fine. The doc said I'm a fine breeder."

"He didn't say—"

"No. He did not. But fragile I am not."

They got to the door, and Nick let them in.

He kissed his wife just as the door was shut behind them.

He looked at Nora with some trepidation in his eyes.

"I will not break. I promise," Nora told him.

CHAPTER NINETEEN

The posters went up, and then the FBI put out a $25,000 reward for information leading to the capture of Randall Murphy. With the reward came the nutcases, and they didn't relegate themselves to the feds. The Mayor upped the ante when Carl Manski put up $50,000 for someone to shoot Liberty Valance.

"Who's Liberty Valance?" Mara queried after Karras made the crack about Sideways Dick's reward offer.

"John Wayne movie...Never mind."

Mara was a teen when the flick came out, and she made it clear she wasn't a John Wayne groupie.

"I hate westerns."

"That's because you're a commie."

She slapped his shoulder playfully.

They were in Nick's office taking call after call about sightings of Randall Murphy. The one certainty was that Murphy wasn't using Kakos or his given name at the moment. There were the other Randall Murphys, but they'd been cleared weeks ago.

Someone had to be supplying his false IDs.

Nick tried a few contacts from the Chicago Outfit, the city's version of the Mafia. The Outfit didn't make a habit out of talking to cops, but there were occasional trades to be made. Someone's soldier got pinched for illegal gambling or for running whores, and there was a chance for a sentence reduction if the information was good enough.

Still, wiseguys were hesitant to ask favors or do any for cops. It had to be a special kind of situation for them to talk, especially to Homicides.

Carl Manfredi had a relationship with Karras since Nick arrested the killer of Manfredi's sister's daughter. Usually, the Outfit might try to take things like the murder of one of their own into their own hands, but Nick caught the guy before they could stuff him in a barrel of acid. Carl was appreciative of the work on Nick's part, and he had a soft spot for the detective ever since. The dead girl belonged to Carl's favorite sibling.

Manfredi wasn't known for hits. Gambling and girls were his strong suits. If he had to push a button on anyone, he was discrete. Blood was a big investment, and he was more interested in making money than whacking people, and if there was killing to be done it was almost always another wiseguy to be buttoned. Civilians were usually off limits. They drew too much attention to Manfredi's crew.

Mara was back in the office fielding calls from the cash hounds who thought they sighted Murphy. And Nick didn't want her to see he was using underworld guys to try and locate the Coast to Coast killer. She was young, and her hands weren't dirty, yet. It didn't give Nick any satisfaction to deal with Manfredi, no matter how much gratitude the Outfit Capo showed Karras after his niece's murderer got hauled to the clink for life.

The detective met Carl Manfredi at one of the titty bars he ran in Berwyn, just west of the city. Capone did a lot of trade in Berwyn and Cicero in the thirties, and things hadn't changed all that much.

Carl had a booth in the back. He didn't like to sit close to the front door, even though he always had two gorillas working as bodyguards, and they were both legally heeled, licensed to carry firearms.

Nick walked toward Manfredi, but his two primates stepped in front of Karras.

"He's good," Carl told them, and they reluctantly stepped aside.

Carl Manfredi looked like the male lead in an afternoon soap opera. Just a little too pretty. But he was masculine enough when you saw him stand up and stretch to six-five. He had broad shoulders and a thin waist. He watched his pasta, Nick figured. Manfredi had played college football and might have gone pro if he hadn't screwed up both knees at the University of Illinois. Carl didn't bemoan his fate about going pro because he never intended to be a paid athlete. The money was far better where he was. Titty bars, massages with a happy ending in one of the back rooms. High priced hookers in the Loop's pricey hotels. That kind of thing.

"You're looking good, Nick."

He stretched out a hand and took Karras' hand in a crushing grip.

The only thing that belied his occupation was that cosmetically perfect face with a full crop of wavy brown hair on the top. His face was almost as swarthy as Nick's. The guy could've done aftershave commercials, Karras thought.

They sat opposite each other, Nick's back to the entrance. Carl's eyes kept flicking to the front door.

"You expecting someone?" the detective smiled.

"Nah. What'll you have to drink?"

"Just a Coke."

"You're on duty."

"Something like that."

Manfredi waved at the female bartender. It was just after noon, and the dancers didn't start bobbling their wares until eight or nine.

Carl ordered a Coke, and nothing for himself.

The buxom brunette brought Nick his drink and made certain to bend over so he could get a full shot of her cleavage.

"Her name is Candy."

"Of course it is."

Nick took a pull at his soft drink.

"What can I do you for?" Manfredi said.

"You know some people who specialize in forged IDs?"

"Whoa. I don't do anything illegal."

Carl smiled slyly.

"We're looking for that series killer. You know, the one who's made the front page."

"You mean that Coast to Coast cocksucker."

Anger crossed over Manfredi's visage like a quick-hitting squall.

"Yes."

"I got no use for the type. After Sally's girl…"

Sally was Manfredi's sister. The daughter's name was Carrie. Pretty girl. Had a college scholarship, an academic ride, to Northwestern.

Nick nodded his sympathy. His niece had been badly beaten and raped.

"I'm looking for a guy who might do bogus IDs. This Randall Murphy has used at least a few aliases. You know someone that might help Murphy hide behind some paper?"

"I don't break the law, Nick…But I can ask around."

The two bodyguards sat at the bar, but they kept scanning the front and the back, just as Carl kept doing.

"Something up?" Nick asked again.

"Always. You gotta be wary, Detective. There are a lot of bad people out in the sunlight. You'd think they would only come out at night when it's dark."

A weak smile passed on Manfredi's handsome face.

"This guy has done twenty young women that we know about."

Carl's wandering gaze suddenly vanished.

"Twenty? Jesus Christ."

He crossed himself and touched the gold cross that hung on his neck. His shirt was opened at the throat. He wore a periwinkle short-sleeved shirt. It was refreshingly frosty inside the bar.

"I think I know a few people. Let me give them a call. I owe you, Nick. I don't forget, either."

"You owe me nothing. This guy is in the same ballpark with the piece of shit who killed your niece."

"I hear you."

"Anything you can do, let me know," Nick told Manfredi.

He placed his card in front of the Capo.

Nick stood up.

"Keep healthy, Carl."

"Hey, waddayougonnado?" Manfredi grinned.

"Dangerous world," Nick smiled.

"You might say."

Karras headed for the exit.

•　　　•　　　•　　　•　　　•

He got a call from Manfredi two days later.

"Guido Farnacci. World class. And of course you didn't hear it from me, Nick. Right?"

"Goes without saying."

He placed the receiver back down. Mara sat opposite him, as usual.

They headed down to the parking lot. The address was in Old Town, where all the college kids scored their finest drugs.

Traffic was light on a Wednesday afternoon. It was late August and the city was scorched earth. The temperature hit 100 six days in a row and the electric company was living in fear of a black out if the heat didn't die down. It hadn't rained in three weeks, and any sparse grass was brown and dead. People were trying to conserve water, and the heavens weren't offering any respite from the drought.

They arrived at a storefront on Claire Avenue. The sign in the window read Farnacci Printing: Announcements and More.

Nick opened the door for his partner.

"Chivalry ain't dead," Mara cracked.

"I'm ancient."

There was no one at the counter, but there was a bell you were supposed to push.

A short, squat, simian creature approached the two detectives.

"What can I do for you?"

"Carl Manfredi," Nick uttered.

He violated his promise to keep the Capo's name out of it.

Then Nick showed him the ID and the shield.

"Shit," the short man spat.

"You have some place more private?" Karras asked.

Farnacci peered over at Mara as if he were begging her to intercede.

"No sale," Crosby grinned.

He led them into the back where he kept his office. It looked like a one-man operation to Karras.

He sat them down opposite his small, rectangular desk.

"Is there a problem?" Farnacci asked.

"Maybe," Nick replied.

"What about Carl?"

"He sends his regards. He knows you won't repeat anything you hear or say here today."

He raised his hands and shook his head.

"We hear you do some nice paperwork," Nick continued.

"All I do is wedding announcements and graduation and—"

"Creative IDs," Mara smiled at him.

"I don't break the—"

"This is not a roust. It's a fact-finding mission, and I know you want to help."

Karras spread their newest picture of Randall Murphy before the mini-man.

Nick saw the other man's eyes flicker.

"The name Kakos mean anything to you?"

Farnacci stared at the altered photo. He breathed out in a groan. Nick had the feeling they struck a gusher on the first try, for a change.

"You remember Carl losing his niece to one of these pieces of shit?" Nick pressed on.

"Yeah, seems like I recall."

"Carl would take it as a favor if you didn't fuck around and lie to us. Did you do a piece of work for this man?"

Farnacci shot Mara a pleading look.

"I'm lucky this dirtbag didn't kill me. I kept my .45 on the table when he came in looking for ID. It's a dangerous profession, you know."

He was imploring Mara to intercede, but she remained mute.

"When?"

Nick's abrupt question startled the diminutive forger.

"Six months ago. Maybe."

"And I'm sure he never left you a forwarding address," Nick smiled.

"All I know was he pulled up in front with some big-assed red truck. And a month ago he came back looking for a new set of IDs—driver's license, social security. The whole fucking portfolio. This time he was driving a Buick. Blue or black, I couldn't tell. I never saw the plates. I'm sure they were hot. He probably changes them regularly, and he likely replaces his ride all the time.

"His new ID was for 'Bill Blakely'. He ditched 'Darren Kakos' a while ago, maybe three, four months."

"Bill Blakely?" Mara asked.

Farnacci nodded.

"Yeah, Bill fucking Blakely."

Nick let him sit and squirm for several beats.

"Want to keep your business, Guido?"

"Huh?"

"You call me the second this guy tries to flip his ID."

"You'll leave me alone?"

"We work homicides, not forgery."

"And you won't pass information on about me?"

"Make the call, Guido," Mara told him. "Make the fucking call."

Nick looked over at the redhead.

"What?" she asked her partner.

"I think it was you who shot Liberty Valance."

"That makes no sense."

He laughed and rose.

"You better slap that .45 canon on the table if Randall Murphy comes in again, Guido."

Farnacci gulped but didn't retort.

·　　·　　·　　·　　·

"You think he'll try Farnacci again?" Mara asked as they rode by the Lake on the Outer Drive.

"No. I think Murphy's too slick. He'll figure we looked into his change of name. He probably knows we contacted the Army and know his real name. But he'll have to flash this Bill Blakely moniker somewhere. We need to get out the word before he goes chameleon again."

"What about the lovely Abigail Adams? Do we ring in with the latest?" Mara asked.

"Fuck her and the federal horse she road in on."

"And you complain about my potty mouth."

"I'm a bad influence, I guess."

"The worst. And me, a good Catholic girl who never had a foul-mouth rap when I went to confession."

"When are you going to get a boyfriend? Maybe everything's getting all pent up inside you, Irish."

"A boyfriend is no cure. It's a symptom."

"Ah, there you are mistaken. Without Nora you'd be looking at an empty shell, a mere shadow of a man."

"And you're gonna be a daddy."

"There's that. Yes."

Mara looked out the passenger's window of the Crown Vic and observed the hordes that were gathered on the Oak Street Beach.

The temperature was ascending with no relief in sight.

CHAPTER TWENTY

The calls always seemed to come in the middle of a dinner break. They were eating Italian beefs at Pal Joey's on 111th on the southside just after investigating a murder scene a few miles north of the restaurant.

They'd been called to an apartment on Kedzie on the far southwest side and they encountered a thirty-six-year-old woman who had been bludgeoned to death with a barbell. Her live-in boyfriend was holed up in the apartment until a Tactical Team blew open the door with a swinging sledge. The killer surrendered immediately, and Karras and Crosby had him hauled downtown while the Forensics Unit went over the scene.

They finally had an opportunity to eat before they returned downtown to interview the twenty-eight-year-old male in the interview room at HQ.

They were barely into their meals when the summons arrived over the hand-held Karras carried with him.

"We think we've spotted Randall Murphy in a bar on Rush Street," Sergeant Pat Kelly informed Nick.

Mara looked at her partner quizzically.

"We're on our way," Karras said after he got the address.

"We're getting doggie bags. This beef is great, and it's too expensive to dump."

Nick placed a bill on the table, and after Crosby got the take-away bags from the waiter, they bolted Pal Joey's, got into the Ford, and turned on the rotating lights on the dashboard.

It was 10:22 PM on the four to twelve tour, only ninety minutes before their shift was finished.

They didn't use Murphy's aliases to hunt him. The cover name of Bill Blakely hadn't hit their radar, to date. Nick wondered if Guido had passed them bogus information. If he had, Karras figured he'd go visit the forger all by himself in the very near future. The sawed-off printer looked slimy enough to be dubious.

It took twenty-eight minutes to get to Grandma's on Rush. By the time they arrived, the troops had surrounded the club that catered to suits and college kids and sweethearts who were looking for a duckett, a sugar daddy or a meal ticket. The place had a rep as a branch where the vultures came to roost, so it was no surprise to Karras that Randall Murphy might favor the place as a happy hunting ground. There was usually plenty of prey shaking whatever they had on the dance floor at Grandma's. A lot of big-name rock bands got their starts in the saloon/nightclub.

They pulled to a stop at the curb. Traffic had been blocked on either end of Rush Street, and the back alley was covered for any retreat—if it really was Murphy inside.

Sergeant Kelly of Major Crimes waited for Nick and Mara at the door.

"No way out, back or front," Kelly informed the two.

"I assume Tactical is about to charge inside?" Nick asked.

"When you give the okay, yeah."

"See if we can't take him alive and not shoot the place to shit while we're doing it," Nick offered.

"That's the plan," Pat Kelly said.

He was a heavy-set hulk of an Irishman, but he didn't look like there was any soft stuff covering the muscle.

Kelly signaled the Tacticals, about twelve of them, that it was showtime. They led the way inside. The bouncers were already moved out of the building by a few of the plainclothesmen inside where the sighting had happened. Two detectives were in there off-duty, and one of them made the call to Kelly.

They kept their pistols at their sides until one of the Assault cops managed to pull the plug on the band performing onstage. The place was mobbed, and the sudden silence caused mumblings and murmurs.

"Stay right where you are, please," Kelly boomed.

The patrons were startled into silence. A detective approached Kelly.

"He's back there, in the corner, at a table with a woman."

Kelly led Karras and Crosby and a half dozen Tactical coppers toward the table. They weaved their way toward the man who the detectives thought was the Coast to Coast killer.

There was still a hush among the packed house at Grandma's.

There he sat, Karras observed. The face, the beard. He fit the bill completely.

"Stand up," Karras ordered him.

The redheaded woman sitting next to him began to bleat.

"Oh my God!" she cried.

"What the hell is this?" the beard demanded.

"Up, asshole," Nick repeated.

"With the hands up," Crosby said.

They pointed their weapons at their target.

He finally stood.

Right height. Approximate poundage. He looked solid. Randall Murphy or his twin.

The Tac people raised their rifles, and a few female bystanders screamed.

"Walk to me with your hands up," Nick commanded.

He did as he was told.

"On your knees, hands behind your head," Karras said.

Down he went in front of Nick and Mara.

Karras cuffed him, and they walked him out the door. The crowd separated for them like the Red Sea.

As soon as he showed them valid identification, the party was over. His name was Paul Smith. His phone number was real. They called the number and got his wife Vera on the line. Karras could hear the voices of young children in the background.

"What's this about?" Vera asked angrily.

"Your husband's name is Paul?" Nick asked. "Is he home?"

"No. He's working late tonight."

Paul was fucked in the un-fun way.

"Who is this?" she demanded.

"I must have the wrong number," he told her.

Paul Smith had already had a bad enough night. Now he could go home and duck flying silverware and dishes.

"He looked just like him, except for the withered left hand," Mara said.

"The detectives couldn't see his bum fist from where they stood. They made the right call. No harm no foul. No one got shot, anyway."

"The band sounded cool, until we interrupted them," she grinned morosely.

"You ought to check them out. Lots of prospects floating around inside Grandma's. Must be the place to be."

"I don't do bars or discos."

"Why?" Nick shot back at her.

"Because the people at bars are people who go to bars."

"You have to meet Prince Charming somewhere."

"Not with a load on and a bulge in his Jockeys."

"How are you ever going to meet anybody, Mara?"

"What are you? My dad?"

"I already have a daughter."

Nick's face went somber.

"It's okay. You can be all paternal with me. Maybe I need a father figure," she soothed.

They sat quietly in Mara's cubicle, down the hall from Karras' office. Mara had no view at all. Just a wall and a bank of overhead fluorescent lights that were hard on the eyes.

"I thought we had a shot," she said.

This time, Nick was sitting opposite her.

He nodded.

"Let's go down to the café and finish our food. Then we can get the fuck out of here."

●　　　●　　　●　　　●　　　●

There were no more sightings. Two weeks went by. There was a nasty phone call from Magrette who received a nasty phone call from the manager of Grandma's.

"I asked them if they renewed their liquor license, and he hung up," Magrette told Nick during the call.

At least they hadn't been dragged onto his carpet again.

"I know you two are doing your best," Magrette told Karras. "I expect you'll pop Murphy's weasel shortly."

The Captain disengaged and the communique was finished.

●　　　●　　　●　　　●　　　●

The psychos kept ringing Karras' and Crosby's phone at work, but nothing came of the calls. They looked into each one, and not one bore fruit.

Karras went back to Guido's print shop.

This time he went alone.

No one was in the shop. He wondered if Farnacci's sole business was forgery. Guido came loping out to the front after Nick hit the buzzer, and the short man's face fell as soon as he recognized the Homicide.

Before Guido could cop any pleas, Karras had him by the throat and shoved him back into his office.

"You gave me a bogus alias, motherfucker. You want a shitstorm on your fucking head? We came up empty with Bill fucking Blakely, you piece of shit!"

Nick didn't raise his voice, but he tightened his grip.

Farnacci's face went scarlet, and then Karras let go.

"I'll have this dump shuttered by this afternoon, asshole."

Guido huffed out and then staggered around his desk and flopped in his swivel chair.

"Don't fuck with me, Farnacci."

Guido tried to gather some oxygen. Finally, the red subsided into a more natural hue on his cheeks.

"I will dump you into a world of hurt, Guido. What name did you give that son of a bitch?"

"He will kill me, and it'll be on you, Karras."

"Who would you prefer, Guido? Me or the Coast to Coast killer? Maybe he'll broaden his kill zone with a nickel-dicked forger."

Farnacci put his palms down on his desk top.

"You didn't see the look in this cocksucker's face. The prick is evil. He's one of those horsemen, the fucking guy on the fucking pale horse."

"He can't hurt you if I get to him first."

"How's that been working for you, *Detective* Karras?"

Nick lunged and grabbed him by the neck again.

"I don't enjoy the rough stuff, Guido, but you try my patience."

He let go of Farnacci once more, and Guido gasped for air.

"What's it going to be? You got a name for me? And if it's not the right one, guess what happens the next time you see me."

"You close me down."

"The next time you see me, you won't see me coming."

He grasped his own throat.

"I think you broke something."

"I'll send you a sympathy card. Too bad you won't be here to read it. I'll pass it around that you gave his name up, but I'll make sure the word gets out that you can't keep your mouth shut, and the next voice you hear won't be mine."

"This guy is no one to fuck with. I could see it in his eyes," Guido whined.

"You're tiring me out, fuckhead."

Nick thought he might break out into tears.

"You better protect me, Karras. He told me what would happen if I turned him."

Nick waited.

"Parker. Stephen Parker."

Karras leaned across the desk toward him.

"Please! It's the name, I swear to God. I gave him a driver's license, Social Security...Even a fucking credit card!"

"Guido, buddy. Look me in the eyes."

"I'm not lying, I swear."

"That's what you told us the first time, you needle-dick."

"It's the truth. I'm telling you, it's for real."

Karras watched the sweat bead on his forehead. It began to drizzle onto his cheeks and chin. A few droplets hung from his salt and pepper goatee.

"You got somewhere you can go on a short vacation?"

Farnacci nodded.

"Go there. Go there the minute I leave."

Nick waved at Farnacci, smiled, and departed.

•   •   •   •   •

They ran a search on a credit card for Stephen Parker. They came up with sixteen Stephen Parkers in the city alone. The suburbs boasted twelve more, so they tried all twenty-eight cards to see what the most recent purchases were. And they had twenty-eight addresses to visit, as well.

•   •   •   •   •

Nick visited the markers for Karen Manski and Ellen Prentice. They were in two different cemeteries, but they were only a few miles apart on the northwest side. He visited the plot for Ellen Prentice first. There were no flowers on the grave, so he placed a yellow rose underneath her stone.

A little more than two decades. That was all the time either victim had been given. Karras had never been raised in the Greek Orthodox tradition as his grandparents had. He skipped the church altogether, throughout his life. He figured there might very well be a God or god, but he wasn't much impressed with him or his handiwork. Some people got a good chunk of happiness, and others received a more meagre portion. Some people found love, and a lot of others found companionship in front of a TV or at a bar with a lot of strangers.

There were those who lived it out, eighty years or so, and there were some who disappeared too soon to meet the current mortality rate. If you hadn't suffered loss and despair, you could count yourself fortunate, but there was no equity between the haves and the have nots.

He dropped another yellow rose on Karen Manski's grave near her headstone, which was far larger and more ornate than Ellen Prentice's modest marker. Then Nick heard footfalls behind him.

It was Carl Manski. The husky man approached Karras aggressively, as if he were on the attack. But Nick didn't retreat or back off.

"What the hell are *you* doing here?" Manski demanded.

"Dropping off a flower."

"You have a lot of balls, Detective."

"I won't intrude on your visit. I was just leaving."

"Maybe you ought to spend more time looking for the bastard who put Karen here."

"Maybe you're right," Nick replied.

Manski's face softened, and the grief took over, and Nick walked away from the plot and the grieving father of Karen Manski.

CHAPTER TWENTY-ONE

Guido Farnacci was bad at taking advice. The cop had been unsuccessful at warning him to take off for a while, but the creative paperwork business was too lucrative. Guido was in his mid-sixties, and he had quite the portfolio of investments. He'd been astute with where he put his money, and a few of the wiseguys gave him solid tips on betting the nags at Arlington, and his winnings weren't squandered. He put them into real estate gradually over the years.

His retirement wasn't far off, and he was planning on moving to San Antonio. Guido loved the River Walk. He loved the diversity of the town. Mexican food was his weakness, and he suffered indigestion from all the fried food, but he weathered the pain to quench his hunger for tacos and enchiladas and chimichangas. The refried beans gave him gas, but he lived alone except for the rare interludes with pros who hauled his ashes when he got backed up.

Farnacci thought he'd buy a condo in a development he had his eye on in San Antonio. It was on the edge of the city, so it wasn't noisy or crowded. It had a pool which he figured he could lounge at with a few daquiris in tow. Just a few more months of this shit and he figured he'd have enough to last him until the Reaper came around.

The bad news walked in the door at closing, around 8:00 PM.

He'd lost the beard, and when he smiled the gap had been closed. The face was the same as he'd first seen it.

"Hello, Randall."

"Long time, wop.'

"You know I don't like that word."

"But you like the cash, right?" Murphy sneered.

"You're a very hot item, right about now."

"Yeah, you know how it is."

"What do you want?"

"Guess."

"I'm taking a big risk by doing work for you. Homicide guys have been spreading your picture all over the city, and the feds have been looking for you for a while, now."

"But you're very discrete. Right, Guido? That's the word on the street. You know how to keep your mouth shut."

"There's big money for anyone who spots you, you know."

"I read the papers, too. You're not developing a fucking conscience suddenly, are you, wop?"

"I told you not to use that word."

Murphy stood opposite the short man at Farnacci's counter at the front of the 'print shop.'

"You're sensitive for a guy in your business, Guido. You must be paying off pretty well to keep making bogus papers. Aren't you getting a little old for this shit? How many years would you get if those cops and feds found out about you?"

"I can take care of myself."

"You seem nervous, Guido. Why's that?"

The smile emerged again from Murphy. He had that toothsome expression that must have been killer on women.

"You look a little shaky, Farnacci. You wouldn't have been talking to those Homicides or feds about me, would you?"

The short Italian felt his fingers gripping the counter fiercely.

"I haven't stayed in business all these years by running my mouth. I've dealt with some pretty nasty customers, Murphy."

Murphy walked back to the entry and flipped the 'Open' sign to 'Closed'.

Then he found the light switch and flipped off the bank of fluorescents overhead.

"What're you doing?"

"It's after hours. You're closed, aren't you?"

"Come in my office and we'll do business," Farnacci urged.

"Business? You sure you haven't already done business on my account, Guido?"

Murphy walked around the counter and pointed to Farnacci's small office.

"Go ahead. We can talk more privately."

Guido walked toward the office, ahead of Murphy.

When they were inside, Murphy closed the door. Guido walked around his desk, pulled out his chair and sat down.

Randall Murphy stood, looming over Guido's desk.

"This is your last order, wop."

"You leaving town?"

"No. I like Chicago. I'm a home boy. Why would I leave?"

Perspiration began to bead on Farnacci's forehead.

"You look very uncomfortable, little man."

"Let's do business. Okay?"

"You never behaved this way before. I come in to throw you some more cash and you act strange. Like you're afraid of me. You worked with unsavory characters before, like you said. Remember?"

"I keep my mouth shut. That's why I been around as long as I have. And I made some close associates with some very scary guys, Murphy. They wouldn't be happy if anything happened to me."

"Let's start over again, Guido. I trust you. You don't have to sic your gangster buddies after me. Like you said, I already have enough people who want to make my acquaintance. And you're not my type, Farnacci. You're an old, crusty guinea. Why would I want to waste time on you? You're ready to roll over soon enough as it is."

Murphy laughed and showed his dental work once more.

Guido opened the top desk drawer slowly, almost imperceptibly.

He reached inside, and Murphy came around the desk like a leopard and was on top of Farnacci on the floor before Guido could grip the .45 just inside his desk. The chair was turned upside down by the attack, and Murphy was on top of the little man and was throttling him with both hands.

It didn't take long for Guido to lose consciousness. The taller man rose and then reached inside the drawer and withdrew the handgun. Farnacci was barely breathing as Murphy stood over him with the piece gripped in his right hand.

"These things are dangerous, wop. You have to be very careful with them. Someone could get hurt. Then where'd you be? Huh, greaseball?"

Farnacci's eyes began to open. Murphy pulled his prone body upright, and then he righted the upside-down chair and flopped Guido back onto it.

As the shorter man regained consciousness, Randall put the barrel onto the Italian's left temple.

He cocked the piece. Farnacci began to squirm in his seat, but he wasn't all the way back, yet.

"You shot your mouth off, didn't you, you DP cocksucker."

Guido tried to focus his eyes.

"Who was it?" Murphy demanded.

"What?"

"Who was it? Last chance."

"I didn't say nothing."

Murphy pressed the barrel harder against his head.

"Tell me who you talked to."

Farnacci's eyes widened and he gripped the arms of his swivel chair.

"I'll blow your brains on that floor. Tell me, you immigrant piece of shit!"

"It was some cop from the city."

"Who? Which one?"

"That Greek. Karras."

Murphy released the barrel slightly and held the .45 six inches from Guido's noggin.

"I'll do new papers. I swear. Free. Just don't do it. They won't catch you, I swear to God. The IDs will be perfect, my best work. I swear—"

Murphy pulled the trigger and Farnacci was flung off his chair to the floor. The pool of blood gathered beneath the right side of what was left of his face.

Randall took out a handkerchief from his back right pocket and wiped the gun and then placed it in Farnacci's left hand lying atop his left flank. There was no blood splatter on Randall's clothing or on his face or hands. The blood had burst out of the right side of the Italian's head and had splashed on the floor where the dead man lay.

Murphy rifled through Guido's several file cabinets. He finally found a file in the second cabinet. The ID didn't fit him identically, but the photo's likeness on the credentials were close enough that a casual perusal wouldn't notice the difference between Pat Stillman and Randall Murphy. It would have to do.

Guido Farnacci was hardly in any condition to do his usual meticulous work.

•   •   •   •   •

"It just doesn't copy," Karras told Mara.

"You don't like this as a do-yourself job," she replied.

Farnacci's office was crowded with the two Homicides, several Forensic techs, and the ME and his assistant.

"He certainly didn't seem the type to yank his own plug."

"You think someone did the forger and made it look like suicide," Mara said.

Nick squatted down, closer to the corpse.

"Look at his throat."

Mara bent over.

"Well shit."

"Striations. Ligature marks. I can't buy that he tried to choke himself out and then finished the job with that *pistola.* You feature it happened like that?"

"Who wanted him dead? Unhappy customer?"

"Murphy was one of his patrons, remember?"

"So you said. Why would he kill him? He likely needed new ID."

"Maybe he thought Guido talked to me, to the po-lice. The marks on Guido's neck might suggest that Murphy reverted to form. Guns aren't his thing. We might get a print off the throat. If he was in a hurry, he might have neglected the neck or the .45. Maybe we'll get lucky."

Karras eyed the file cabinets.

"Maybe he helped himself to a new identification from those. Someone who looks a little like him, maybe."

"Maybe it was just an unhappy customer, like we thought."

"That's what a terrorist might do to a forger. Happens in all the movies," Nick smiled wanly.

•   •   •   •   •

Murphy's partial on Farnacci's throat made it unanimous. The Forensic boss, Bill Thompson, broke the news to them in Nick's office. Mara peered at the prints.

"He broke the sex barrier, yeah?" Thompson asked.

He was a short, wiry guy who'd been an elite trooper in the Army's Rangers in Vietnam. He was barely five-eight and might have gone 150 pounds. He wore the usual crew cut favored by the military, as well.

"This guy piss him off or something?" Thompson asked.

"Apparently. He responded with extreme prejudice," Nick said.

"Waste of a fine talent," Mara added.

"He should have stuck to wedding and graduation announcements. Good money, there," the Forensics chief told them as he departed.

"He's nervous about his ID. I don't think he intended to kill the little prick. Guido must have dropped his poker face. Something happened and it went sideways for Farnacci. Maybe Murphy's fuse is getting shorter. Ellen Prentice was a while ago."

It was March, and the summer had burned away a long time ago. The roses Nick had placed on the women's graves were certainly dust by now.

The baby was getting closer to arrival, also, and Nora was becoming bulbous and uncomfortable with the bloating of the final weeks.

"I'll bet the beard is gone by now. No way of knowing which ID he helped himself to. He might color his hair or cut it all off. Who knows?" Mara ventured. "Maybe he'll try plastic surgery next...Your buddy in the mob know any good swashbucklers?"

"I could ask."

"I can't have this, Karras. You managed to get my man, Guido, popped in the head, and now you want medical advice?"

The same two goons sat at the bar watching the front and the back. They weren't happy to see Nick again, that was for sure. Karras sensed their displeasure.

"Dangerous profession, Carl. You run into lots of bad actors, right?"

"Thanks for the advice."

Nick sat with his back to the front door, and again the place was vacant because it was just thirty minutes before noon. Only a few devoted barflies sat at the slab, not far away from the bodyguards.

"You must know someone who does discrete alterations for the underbelly of society."

Nick smiled at the good-looking Outfit Capo.

"It's bad for business having a detective showing up here all the time."

"I promise. I'll ask you no more favors. And if you need a huss, if it's reasonable, I'll reciprocate."

"Reasonable? Shit."

Karras watched his eyes.

"Twenty-one women, Carl. Twenty-one. You're a fan of the gentler sex, no?"

Manfredi looked over at his two soldiers at the bar. The front door opened and the sunlight burst inside with a glare that nearly blinded him. He put his hand up to block the intrusion.

"Why don't you tap your FBI buddies?" Manfredi asked.

"Why don't you deal with the Russian mob or the Chinese Tong?"

Carl glared at Karras.

"This is the last time. I have your promise."

"I ever lied to you before?"

Manfredi looked the Greek over.

"There won't be a repeat of good will if you ever do, Detective."

•   •   •   •   •

Manfredi called Karras two days later.

"Dr. Josh Kramer on the far southwest side. He's in the book, but the matronly types don't travel to that part of town. They use the guys on the Gold fucking Coast," Carl told him.

Karras looked up at his partner, sitting across from him.

"He isn't particular about the character of his clients, I hear."

Manfredi ended the call.

"Why didn't you take me to see this creep?"

"I told you. He's a lowlife."

"Don't save me from the big bad world, Nick. We both work in Homicide, remember?"

She looked a bit perturbed, Karras thought.

"All right, Red. If I ever have to get dirty again, you can wade into the muck with me."

She smiled a bit wickedly, Nick thought.

CHAPTER TWENTY-TWO

"She seems to respond to us a little more," the nurse told Karras and Nora.

It was the beginning of April, and the buds were threatening to pop on the trees out on the rolling lawns around the hospital.

"Respond?" Nick asked, his eyes widening a bit.

The nurse's name read Arlene Chapman. She was a tall, willowy black woman with very angular facial features. She appeared to be a half-head taller than Karras.

"Her eyes flicker, sometimes. She seems to notice me when I come in to care for her. It's not like she's suddenly returned. I don't want you to get too excited, but it's looking like she's trying to surface from wherever she is."

The nurse smiled warmly and left Nick and Nora in the room with Penelope.

"Talk to her, Nick. Sit close to her and tell her something."

Karras looked at his extremely pregnant wife.

"Tell her what?"

"That you're here. That you'll always be here."

Karras' eyes suddenly stung. But he went over to the bed next to his inert daughter.

"It's Dad, honey. I'm here with Nora...The nurse says you're doing better. I miss you, Penelope. I want you to come back to me, honey. Nora wants you back, too...We're going to have a baby, soon. You're going to have a baby brother or sister. We don't know which, but we told the doctor not to tell us.

"We'll bring the baby when he's old enough. They'll want to see their big sister."

Nick looked over at his wife again. Nora's face was damp. She smiled at her husband.

"Keep going," she told him.

Nick took Penelope's hand as it dangled over the edge of the bed.

He gripped it firmly, and when he did, he felt a very slight response. It was almost unnoticeable, but it was there.

"Nora," he smiled.

She watched his eyes.

"You were right. She's there."

Nora walked over to the bed, and Karras released his hold and let Nora take Penelope's hand.

"Come on out, Penelope. It's time. You can come out, now."

Nora's mouth opened, and a quiet sob escaped.

"I can feel her, too, Nick."

•　　　•　　　•　　　•　　　•

They sat in the Chevy in the parking lot for several minutes.

"She's getting better. She wants to come back," Nora told him.

"It was just a little pressure, but I felt it. Maybe it's just a muscle reaction."

"I know. They told you it wasn't going to happen, that she'd stay paralyzed for the rest of her life. But they're wrong, Nick. She heard you. She heard us. She's there."

They looked out at the blooming trees and the blossoming flowers. Easter was close. It was the holiest day of the year for the Greeks. They roasted lamb and celebrated. Christmas was more commercial, Nick thought, and he wasn't devout Orthodox and neither was his wife, but there was a feel about Easter. Maybe it was simply the time of year, spring. Everything that seemed dead came back, came back to life.

He wondered if it really were possible for his daughter to return to life. She wasn't in hell or heaven. She was somewhere in between. But she was trying to move toward them. He could feel it in the hospital room with her timid touch. But he could feel it. It hadn't been his imagination or his false hope for Penelope's improvement. Up until Nora told him during the previous visit that Penelope was making an effort to revive, there seemed to be no chance he'd ever see his daughter again. There was simply a body on a cot, nothing more.

•   •   •   •   •

Mara and Karras paid a visit to Dr. Josh Kramer, cosmetic surgeon. His office was on the far southwest side, adjacent to Oak Lawn. The neighborhood was predominately white, but things were changing. Blacks were headed out of the city looking for safer neighborhoods and better schools, so the color line was becoming blurred. Black professionals had had enough with the gangbangers, and the Civil Rights laws had a decade behind them.

Kramer's office was worn and needed a facelift of its own, but the surgeon had only recently got out of medical school and had broken off from a group of plastic surgeons.

He had sandy-colored hair and was going bald prematurely. Dr. Kramer was lanky and a bit over six feet tall.

They met with him in his miniature, cramped office.

Karras wasted no time and showed him the well-worn photograph with the beard and also without the beard.

"Seen him?" Nick asked.

They'd flashed their IDs on arrival.

Kramer studied both pictures.

"Yeah. I've seen this photograph in the papers. Never seen him in person."

"Then you know why we're here," Mara told him.

"He's that serial killer. The Coast to Coast killer."

Nick waited a beat. If Kramer were doing work on criminals as Manfredi led Nick to believe, the doctor would hardly be cooperative.

"I hear you work on guys who want to disappear," Nick said flatly.

Kramer turned a shade whiter.

"I have it on very reliable sources," Nick warned him.

"I don't know where you heard that, but—"

"You know what aiding and abetting means? And this is a homicide. Very bad business to lie to us," Mara threw in.

Kramer squirmed in his chair. Nick and Mara sat on straight-backed wooden chairs opposite him. There was little room for anything but the three of them in his sparse cubicle.

"Why'd you leave that group of cutters in Oak Park?" Nick asked.

"I wanted to be on my own."

"Not what I heard. I heard you were taking on iffy clients. By iffy I mean you were working on guys who badly needed to change their looks, and not for cosmetic reasons," Mara said.

Kramer squirmed a little more.

"It'd be too bad if you lost your license," Nick told the surgeon.

"I told you I never met this man. I only saw him on the television and in the newspapers."

Nick watched him as he rotated his ass on his swivel chair.

"You feeling all right?" Karras queried.

"If there's nothing else, I have patients to see."

Nick smiled. Mara sat back against her unyielding chair.

"If you should ever contact this man, be sure to get hold of us."

Nick dropped his card on Kramer's desk as the two detectives stood up.

"Twenty-one," Nick told Kramer.

There was a question on the doctor's visage.

"Twenty-one women. One man. That we know of."

The Homicides left him sitting alone.

•　　•　　•　　•　　•

"Did he already fix Murphy?" Mara asked as they drove toward their dinner break on Pulaski Road on the south side.

It was pizza again, since they both liked thin crust. Mario's was a legend in the neighborhood. Nick was off his diet, and Mara indulged him. She never ate much, and Nick always took leftovers home to Nora. She had a particular craving for Italian food, lately.

"He didn't have much of a façade for a plastic surgeon. If Murphy hasn't been there, he's made contact. We'll have some uniforms keep an eye on the office. Dr. Kramer doesn't seem to be too particular about his patients. Got him bounced from a prosperous group of swashbucklers already."

"I wouldn't let him do me...I mean professionally."

Nick laughed.

"I know what you meant. You don't need any work."

"Well thank you."

The waitress laid the platter of Neapolitan thin crust between them on the booth's table. The table cloth was the requisite red and white checkered style that showed up in any authentic Italian restaurant.

"How's your love life?" Nick grinned with a half-rectangle of pizza in his mouth.

"Non-existent," Mara said.

His partner always nibbled on her meal. It was amusing to watch her. It was like watching a squirrel sampling a nut in his forepaws while sitting up. All she was missing was a bushy tail.

"You have to make yourself available, kid."

"I don't do bars. I told you."

"You have to go where the money is, like bank robbers."

THOMAS LAIRD

"I'll keep that in mind if I feel like becoming a booster, Nick."

He sipped at his soft drink.

"I was alone for a while. Nothing I'd want to do again," he explained.

"You'll have plenty of company pretty soon," she said as she nibbled the crust of the lone piece she'd been working for several minutes.

"You gotta eat, too," he told the redhead.

"I eat."

"Not so's you'd notice. I'm not complaining because Nora has a taste for this, lately. She used to be heavy on fruits and vegetables."

"It's touching you're concerned about my health," she grinned.

"You're my partner."

She didn't shoot back with any repartee. Mara appeared genuinely touched.

"We saw Penelope a few days ago."

Mara watched him.

"I think she might be improving. Just a little bit. But improving. She squeezed my hand. It wasn't much of a grip, but I felt her there. I thought she was lost, but then Nora touched her and then told me she was inside there trying to get out."

"My God. I mean Christ, Nick. That's great. Did you talk to the doctor?"

"They don't want us to become too hopeful and then nosedive again. He says they're cautiously optimistic."

Mara reached over and took his hand. She rarely saw him this emotional, unless it was to become pissed off with a perp or a witness.

They ate the rest of their meal in silence. Nick asked for a doggie bag because the nibbler had put away exactly two pieces.

•　　•　　•　　•　　•

Two uniforms in one squad made passes on Dr. Kramer's office three times a day. No sightings were reported after one week.

Nick did a few drive-bys with Mara in the late afternoons, but they didn't spot Murphy coming in for an appointment, either.

They decided to check the facial surgeon's phone records, and they traced the calls in and out, but they came up empty on the phone records. Karras decided Murphy already had the surgery or that Kramer had warned him away.

No more visits to Carl Manfredi. That well was dry, now. There had been no new murders in Murphy's signature style, and the FBI had gone silent, lately. It wasn't like Abigail Adams to go quietly into that good night on the Coast to Coast killer, Nick figured. So, the age of cooperation had come to a halt, as if it had ever existed in the first place. Nick expected no help from the feds, but it was the way it had always been. It was like the National League and the American League—you didn't fraternize with the opposition.

•　　•　　•　　•　　•

Nora broke her water one week later on a Saturday morning at 4:45 AM. It was Nick's day off, and he'd really looked forward to sleeping late.

"We need to go," she told him as she stood at the foot of the bed.

He was half asleep and luxuriating under the warmth of the comforter.

"Go where?" he murmured.

"Nick. I broke my damned water!"

He snapped up into a seated position.

"I'm on it."

He jumped out of bed and went for his pants. Nora sat on the bed with a bath towel beneath her. It took him five minutes to dress, but Nora was going in in pajamas, slippers and a robe.

"I'll put the towel underneath me on the way in," she told him.

She was so completely calm and in control that it was Nick who had to restrain himself from becoming hysterical. He had to do the driving, after all.

He waited in the father's room for only forty-five minutes when the nurse came for him.

He tried to read her face, but it was blank.

"Oh, Jesus," he moaned.

"You have a healthy baby boy. Your wife is fine. Congratulations, Daddy."

She patted his right arm, and then she finally smiled.

"You ever play blackjack?" Nick asked her.

She furrowed her brows. Her surgical mask was tucked under her chin and she wore the pale blue cap, too.

"Huh?"

•　　　•　　　•　　　•　　　•

He had black hair, like his mother. There was no way to tell if he resembled either of them. His face was puckered up, as all newborn faces tended to be. They appeared like any mammal recently out of the womb. Their faces expressed astonishment.

"What the hell is this and where am I?"

Hard to blame them, Nick thought. They came from a nice, warm, wet place and they wound up here, instead. What a shock to the system!

They brought the boy into a room where they gave him his Vitamin K shot. He was very unhappy with the turn of events, but he quieted down after a brief squall. They had him cleaned up with a little knit cap on his head and he was wrapped in a blue blanket. They'd already printed his foot. Nick saw the print. It was hard to believe its tiny size.

He'd cleaned up nicely. He was beginning to take on a human form in a hurry.

They brought his son into Nora's room, and she was just waking up when the maternity nurse laid him in her arms.

"Let's call him Gus," she declared.

"I like it," Nick concurred.

"Good Greek name, huh, Gus?" Nora asked her son.

Gus blinked. Then he bawled a little, but after a while he seemed to recognize his mother, and then he went back to sleep while Nick held his diminutive hand.

Gus was seven pounds fourteen ounces.

CHAPTER TWENTY-THREE

Mara went down with the flu, and it was a hard fall. Nick called her at her apartment and asked what she needed.

"Stay the hell away from me. I've got the Black Plague."

"Let me bring you something."

"There's no medicine for this crap. Just flat-on-my-ass time. Already saw the doctor. I should be good in a week or ten days, and don't you dare come around. You have a baby to protect. I feel like I'm deserting you, Nick."

"Cut the self-pity. It doesn't help recovery. I ought to know."

"I'm really exhausted. Give me a couple days and you can stick pins in me again."

"Mara—"

"Your voice is fading, Detective Karras."

He gave it up and ended the call.

•　　•　　•　　•　　•

He went it alone. It had been a long time since he had no partner, and now it was Mara who went down. She sounded worse than she let on. But she was right. He couldn't take a chance on visiting her when it was Gus and Nora who might pay. All he could do was check up on her by phone.

He did the drive-by on the plastic surgeon during the afternoon, but Nick figured that the best-case scenario was that Dr. Kramer had already given Murphy a heads up. If he was lucky, Nick thought, Murphy hadn't undergone the knife yet.

They checked the calls that came into the surgeon's office, and only two offered possibilities. The two were made from a payphone near Wrigley Field on two separate days. He thought he'd give it a shot on surveilling the booth near the ballpark. It was his only lead from the calls into Kramer in the last three weeks, and the two in question were made before and after Mara and he had braced Kramer in his office.

The plastic surgeon was *wrong,* Karras decided. He was reconstructing dubious patients for yet more dubious reasons. It wasn't about nose jobs or cleft palates. This prick was creating new mugs for bad actors. It was likely why Kramer got the heave-ho from that group of doctors.

When Nick interviewed the other surgeons, they all became tight-assed and circled the wagons. It was typical of the profession to protect their own, even if Kramer were an outlaw swashbuckler.

Nick sat across from the booth on Sawyer for two hours. He was ready to give it up when a Chevy beater pulled to the curb near the payphone.

He was the right height and he was clean shaven, but it was too dark and the street light had been popped by some local punk, so Karras had to get out of the vehicle.

He walked across the street slowly with his weapon palmed in his right hand. He should have called for back-up, but he didn't want him loose in the neighborhood.

The man was engaged in a call, and the light was bright enough in the booth for Nick to make out the features. They matched Randall Murphy. Nick firmed his hold on the .38, but when he was ten feet from the booth, Murphy looked up, dropped the receiver and bolted out of the phone booth.

He sprinted a few yards and then stopped dead, turned toward the detective, and raised his right hand. Murphy pulled the trigger before Nick could unload his own piece at the Coast to Coast killer. Karras felt a lightning jolt in his right shoulder, and the round spun him around and then knocked him flat on the sidewalk. When he managed to get up, he saw that Murphy had a half-block lead on him.

The wound stung like a nest of African bees, but he was able to take off after him. He figured he'd only been grazed, but there was no way to tell. More importantly, this prick was not getting away this time. There was no time to call in the cavalry. Not yet.

Nick closed the gap to a quarter block or so, and then he stopped, raised the .38, and pulled off a round.

Murphy flopped on his face.

Karras sprinted ahead, but he was becoming a bit woozy. Still, he had him, this time.

But when he cut the distance to fifty feet or so, Murphy clambered to his feet somehow, and took off down Sawyer again. He took a hard left at the corner. When Nick made it there, he felt his legs giving out, and he sunk to his knees.

An old woman with a white poodle on a leash yelled out to Karras.

"Are you hurt, sir?"

Nick remained on his knees, but he couldn't hold onto the .38 any longer.

"*Top of the morning, Ma,*" escaped from his lips.

Then everything went black.

• • • • •

He woke up in St. Luke's near the Lake.

When his eyes focused, he made out Nora, holding the baby, standing over him.

"You lost some blood," she understated.

"I feel like a few quarts low," he tried to smile.

"You were able to mumble to a few detectives who came to see you when the nurses found your ID," Nora told him. "You said it was somebody named Murphy who shot you."

"Did they ask me where I was?"

"The nurse said they became very agitated, maybe excited, when you told them that name."

"I can imagine."

"It's him, isn't it," Nora said.

He looked at his wife. Gus seemed to be asleep and oblivious to his surroundings.

"The doctor said it could have been a lot worse if it had been a few inches to the right, near the middle of your chest."

"I've been hit worse, lady love. The Koreans were better shots."

"It isn't amusing, Nick."

"I know. I'm half out of it. They gave me some really fine shit. You could shoot me again and I wouldn't notice it."

"Do you see me laughing, Nick?"

"I'm going to be fine."

"The detectives told me you should have called for back-up."

"They're absolutely correct. My bad."

"What were you thinking, Nick? You're a father and you're forty."

"I just wanted to kill him."

Nora stared at her husband.

"You have to think of us. You're not alone, anymore."

She wasn't having any of his John Wayne bullshit.

"I'll call for back-up if I see that son of a bitch again. I promise, Nora...Why don't you go home and put Gus down and both of you get some sleep. I'll be all right, and you can come and burn me to the ground again tomorrow."

A smile flickered on her lips.

"It's just the job, lady love. Sometimes it happens. You knew the risks coming in, right?"

She didn't respond.

"I'll be back tomorrow. Prepare for the torch again."

She smiled and backed off and left his hospital room.

•   •   •   •   •

Magrette was there during what passed for breakfast at St. Luke's. The Captain came bearing jelly donuts and coffee.

"I'll save them for later," Nick apologized.

"Give them to your nurse and impress her. Maybe she'll up your dosage of sweet euphoria."

"She's fifty and road-tested. I don't think she likes me any more than my wife does, currently."

Magrette sat down next to him.

"It was laughing boy, for real?"

"Or his fucking identical twin. And my suspicion became fact when he turned the gun on me. It's personal, now, Captain."

"You know you'll be flying a desk when you're on your feet."

"You're going to have to cuff me to the table, then."

"No heroics, Detective. You ain't Wyatt fucking Earp."

"I feel like I've been sideswiped by a brick. She needs to stick me pretty soon."

"Push the button, Nick."

"Not until we're done, here. That crap waylays me pretty good...The phone booth says that he's been in contact with Kramer, the plastic surgeon. Have somebody check the payphone for last night. I'm betting he's trying to get the doc to meet him somewhere other than his office. Murphy's far from stupid. He knows Mara and I were likely keeping an eye on that cutter. If we watch Kramer, he might still lead us to our guy."

"Maybe he'll boogie out of town, Nick. If he's not stupid he's not stubborn, either. It's the logical move for him to run. He's used to being mobile."

"He's stuck around because he's telling us he's smarter than we are. We know where he is, but he's always a step beyond our reach. It's his game. If I know anything about him is that he likes the chase, and he figures this is his home court advantage."

"Fucker's nuts, Nick. It's one huge disadvantage."

Karras grimaced. Magrette stood, walked over to the head of the bed, and squeezed the button for the nurse.

"Too bad they don't use heroin," the Captain grinned. "I hear the pain eats it up and you don't get hooked."

"Morphine is only slightly less lethal," Nick answered.

"We'll check the payphone and watch Kramer. Relax and get better. We need you back. You've gotten closer to him than the whole fucking Federal Bureau of Investigation. Miss Abigail probably really hates you now. I'm sure her sources know about the Gunfight at the OK Corral last night on Sawyer Avenue. Nothing gets by that Amazon."

•   •   •   •   •

It was five days at St. Luke's before they sprung him. The doctors were concerned about infection, but by the fifth day Nick was given the all-clear to head home.

Nora was softer when she came to take him back to the apartment, but there was still a little tightness in her jaws. Gus was in the baby seat in the back of their Chevy.

It was late April and the bloom had burst forth all over the city. They drove Lakeshore to get to the expressway, and the Lake's water had turned stunningly blue. It wouldn't be long to Memorial Day, and then the sand would be clustered with swimmers and sunbathers.

Nick thought he'd start Gus early to learn how to swim. Lake Michigan was a frigid way to hit the water, but it was refreshing when the summer burned into July and August. Maybe in another year or two Gus could get used to the chill of the Great Lake.

He hated lying in bed. The pain in his right shoulder had turned into a dull numbness, but he was a fast healer. The few hits he'd taken in Korea twenty years ago had mended rapidly, too, and he was glad that the wound hadn't turned into other complications. Bullets fucked up human flesh much worse than the movies or TV led you to believe. He was fortunate, however, and his recovery went well.

Another doctor's visit and he'd be ready to ride the desk.

Mara was back. She'd visited him in the apartment after six days passed. His partner appeared a little more pale than usual—if a white girl could become alabaster, then she had arrived. But her eyes told a different story. They were alert and quick and blazing in intensity.

"I'm going to get him, Nick," she told Karras as Nick sat holding Gus on the couch.

He felt well enough to care for his son while Nora touched base back at the art studio. They'd given her six weeks' maternity leave at half pay, which was better than most mothers were receiving. At least she'd retain her job.

"Why don't you wait for me?" he asked her.

"Can't wait on this one," she warned.

"I know...Anything going with the plastic surgeon?"

"They've been on him. But he goes straight back to his apartment every night after he gets done slicing and dicing. The phone call was to Kramer's office on that night you got nicked. He likely won't be using that booth anymore, and I have the feeling his tuck job is on hold, maybe permanently. Maybe he'll resort to learning how to apply makeup, like actors do."

"You think he'll stay in town? Magrette thinks he won't."

"It'd be the logical move. But they're watching the highways and the bus stations and the railroad and O'Hare and Midway. I don't see how he'll slither out of Chicago, Nick."

"I hit him."

"They checked all the hospitals and clinics. Nothing. He has to be self-servicing and medicating."

"I think I clipped him up high. He went down hard. If I hurt him as bad as he hurt me, he won't be running anywhere for a while. If we're lucky, maybe he bled out and someone will nose the stink sooner or later."

"He seems to have the golden horseshoe up his backside."

"Everyone runs out of good fortune, inevitably, Red."

"You look tired...Gus is such a quiet baby. He's so good."

"Check him out at three AM. Showtime. His lungs are fine. Sounds like a tenor in the making."

She smiled and bent over and looked at Gus.

"I'll kiss you when that bug is absolutely out of my system. The doc says I'm okay for public consumption, but I want to wait a while. That crap laid me low, Nick."

"When I get back, I'll load you up with fat boy food."

"No, thanks. I got to get back. I don't like running solo. At least they're not talking about a new partner for me."

"Maybe you can get a guy with less mileage. And maybe you can get one who's a better shot."

"Maybe Murphy moved. Moving targets, right? I gotta go. I'll see you soon, I hope."

She waved to Gus, and then the child decided to break his silence. Mara hurried out of the apartment.

•　　　•　　　•　　　•　　　•

Two weeks later, in mid-May, Karras was back to his cubicle. He wasn't allowed to hit the streets. Paperwork was about as dangerous as it got.

He kept hoping they'd find a stiff with Murphy's fingerprints on it, but it didn't happen. Karras took only a little solace in the idea that he'd slowed the killer down a bit. He hoped Murphy didn't share his own powers of recuperation.

Nora's reaction to his wounding troubled him. As he told her, it was part of the job description. Sometimes the bad guys shot back. Hell, sometimes they initiated the gunplay. It didn't happen very often in Homicide because they usually weren't breathing when he encountered them. The Tacticals and the SWAT Team did more street combat than most detectives, but he'd been shot at three or four times in his tour of duty with the CPD.

If the bullet had only struck Murphy dead center then at least one very bad guy would be off his white board.

Bleed to death, you bastard, Nick thought to himself.

Bleed.

CHAPTER TWENTY-FOUR

And he bled.

Murphy managed to drag himself to a phone booth about a half mile from the site where he and the cop exchanged gunfire. Murphy had hoped he'd killed the copper, but the other man stood up as if he'd been resurrected in the spirit of the Easter season and had come loping after Murphy and then fired off a shot that clipped Randall in his right side.

The policeman seemed to fade. Murphy no longer heard his footsteps, and Randall made it to a phone booth before he leaked out.

"Now what?" the other voice asked.

"I need you to come pick me up. I got shot."

"The fuck."

Murphy was afraid he'd hang up.

"I got no one else. Come get me."

"This can't keep happening, Murph."

"I saved your ass. More than once."

There was silence on the line. Murphy peered out from the phone booth. He left the door open so the light wouldn't betray his presence.

"Where are you?" the other inquired.

Murphy gave the location of the pay phone.

"I'll be there in a few."

Randall held himself up by gripping the door to the booth. There wasn't much time before he'd lose consciousness. The minutes seemed to linger, and Murphy's knees started to buckle. He felt himself dripping down onto his shoes.

Finally, a car pulled up. Murphy weakly lifted his .38 toward the driver's side.

Gil Falcone appeared in front of him.

"Jesus Christ, Murph. You're running red down your fucking leg. You need to go to the hospital."

"You know I can't go there. You have to take me to one of your guys."

Falcone helped him to the car.

"Sit on my blanket."

Falcone went to the trunk of his Pontiac while Murphy tried to remain upright by the passenger's door. The shorter man threw a beach blanket over the seat and backrest.

"Try not to fuck up the interior. I just bought this fuckin' thing."

They pulled away from the curb. No one was outside to see their departure.

•　　　•　　　•　　　•　　　•

Dr. Pete Amalfi had lost his license six years ago when he was caught doing abortions for teenaged girls—underaged teenage girls. He spent six months in jail and he lost his livelihood. He did the only thing he knew. He set up an outlaw practice solely devoted to Outfit wiseguys who needed patchwork when they couldn't chance a visit to a legit medical facility. Business was better than it was when Amalfi was still legit, and abortions were a chancy way to make a living. Too many good Catholics and eyeball-rollers inhabited Chicago.

Gil Falcone had been in the shit with Murphy in 1968. The Irishman had saved Falcone's life in some villa when Falcone managed to get himself cut off from their platoon, and Gil wasn't the type to forget a debt. Even though Falcone went into the Outfit after he'd done his tour, he remembered how Murphy had extracted him from a very ugly situation.

The Mick had come charging into the villa with a Thompson chopper he'd appropriated through the black market in Saigon, and he'd dragged a wounded Gil Falcone out of harm's way. Gil had been popped with two rounds to his legs and would've bled out or been cut into chunks by some angry VC.

So, when he needed new ID, Gil came through. When he needed a new look, Falcone set him up with some shady surgeon on the southwest side.

But there were limits to his payback.

Amalfi sewed Murphy up and gave him a shot of antibiotics. He'd lost some blood, but Amalfi didn't have any to pump into him. He'd have to take his chances or give in and go to an ER.

Murphy took his chances.

"This is it, Murph. No more husses. We're even. Don't call me anymore. You get pinched, I go down with you."

He drove Murphy to his apartment and helped him up to his second-floor apartment on the northwest side. It was late, maybe past three, and no one saw them enter the building.

Falcone sat him down on the bed.

"Maybe you ought to give it up, Murph."

Randall flopped on his bedspread.

"There's no percentage. All those broads. The fuck do you get out of it? Then you killed Guido. Manfredi is very unhappy, but I talked him out of reciprocating. I told him our story, and he's soft about repaying debts. And you're lucky Guido was becoming a liability anyway.

"I'm done, Murph. You need to disappear. Get out of the city before the FBI or the cops catch you. I don't know why you stuck around here as long as you have. You got a fucking death wish? Our thing is about money, and killing only happens when it's necessary. Your luck has limits, Murph, and your run is done. You're lucky that cop didn't put one through your melon.

"I can still call for an ambulance. You need a few pints, pal."

Murphy shook his head slowly.

"I did what I could. We're quits."

Falcone turned and walked out.

Murphy was too weak to sit up, and he fell asleep a few minutes later.

• • • • •

There was a knock on the door and Randall tried to sit up. He looked at the clock next to the bed and noticed it was late afternoon. The April sun snuck a few rays past the borders of his blinds.

He labored and finally sat up and threw his legs over the edge of the bed. Falcone must have picked up his .38 at the booth and brought it back to the apartment because the piece lay on the nightstand. Murphy picked it up and staggered to his door.

"Who is it?" he demanded.

"Super. We need to put in a new shower head."

"Come back later. I'm sick."

Murphy began teetering in place.

"I can come back tomorrow, but we gotta get it done soon. Okay?"

"Yeah, okay."

He heard footsteps walking away from the door.

Jesus, he thought, I need a fucking transfusion.

He walked to his couch and nearly collapsed face first onto it.

The .38 hit the carpet, and he fell asleep again.

• • • • •

Murphy woke at 5:00 AM. It was still dark, and he was still flat on the living room couch. He was thirsty and hungry. He knew the dehydration and the blood loss were going to waste him. So, he forced himself into the kitchen and drank three glasses of water. He found a chunk of cheese and some leftover lunch meat, and he forced down as much of it as he could bear.

Then he wobbled back to the bedroom and lay down once more.

His bladder was about to burst. He got himself into the head and sat down on the toilet before he fell into it. He relieved himself with long, strong streams, and then he took a dump for the first time in two days. When he was empty, he felt a ravenous hunger, and he walked gingerly into the kitchen and began to stuff whatever he found into his mouth.

He tried sitting up on the couch and found that he felt slightly stronger.

He tilted over and fell asleep on his back again.

•   •   •   •   •

The pain reawakened him a few hours later. He wondered what happened to the super and his repairs on the showerhead, but he was relieved the guy didn't return as promised.

There were a few aspirins left in his medicine cabinet in the john, but he knew aspirin wouldn't relieve what ailed him. He'd need something far stronger.

•   •   •   •   •

He was able to get into his current ride, a road-worn Ford, and he knew where the action was. In the park, when the sun went down.

The Hispanic kid had a basic drug store in his car trunk.

"You don't look so good, hombre," the dealer told Murphy as he peered into Randall's driver's side window.

"I got some major league pain."

"You look whiter than white, amigo."

"Just find me something that'll make me sleep."

"You mean like morphine, bro?"

"Any time, bub."

"You hurtin' bad, huh?"

Murphy opened the car door and stepped out. He was parked at the curb just outside Ryan Park. The lights were on inside, but the street was badly illuminated where they stood.

Randall showed him the .38.

"Ah, man, you don't want to do that. Mi compadres would have to snuff you, man."

"Get me the fucking pills."

The drug dealer raised his hands and went to the trunk of his Mustang. He popped it open.

"Don't turn around with something besides the pills in your hands, asshole. I'll blow your ass into your trunk."

The other man raised his hands in surrender.

"Get me the pills."

He reached in and took out a bottle and handed it to Murphy. Murphy went into his back pocket and took out his wallet. He went inside and came out with a fifty- dollar bill.

The Hispanic began to carefully study Murphy's face.

"Ain't I seen you somewhere?" he grinned with large white teeth.

Murphy raised the .38 and pulled the trigger. The boom crashed the quiet spring night, and the dealer was blown back against his trunk. Murphy walked up and lifted him into the back end of the Mustang and then he shut the flap on him. He got back slowly into his own ride and headed back to the apartment.

•　　•　　•　　•　　•

Mara took the call. Someone on the street noticed the splash of gore on the rear end of the Mustang and when they approached the car, they smelled something "funny".

The techs popped the trunk and found the man stuffed inside.

He had a single wound in his forehead. The back of his head lay detached underneath him. The ME checked him out before he was removed, and he was the one who found what was left of the head.

• • • • •

"Where was this?" Nick asked as he sat back in his chair in his office.

She told him.

"Someone popped the pusher, right?"

"Looked like a freakin' Walgreens in that trunk. You name it, Nick, he was dealing it."

"I'm guessing it was stuff you can't get over the counter."

"Grass. Heroin. Morphine pain killers. All kinds of mother's little helpers."

"Why do you suppose he shot the poor goof?" Nick wondered aloud.

"Theft, probably. Straight up boost."

"Yeah, likely. But it's dangerous to go whacking street vendors. They tend to have armies behind them."

"We IDed him. Colombian. You're probably right. They'll come gunning for whoever it was. They don't take kindly to getting ripped off."

"But his stuff was still in the trunk when you found him, right?"

"Yeah. It doesn't fit with a rip-off, does it," Mara agreed.

"What would have caused him to shoot the fuck? It wasn't theft. Maybe it was personal."

"They never found any gunshot victims the night you got nicked," Mara said.

"No, they didn't."

"He'd be hurting pretty good, wouldn't he."

"You can't get happy at a drugstore with a gunshot wound, no."

"We could check the car for prints again, and this time look for a match with Murphy."

"Odds are pretty low. He got his painkillers...The dealer recognized him. So, he plugs him once in the face, takes his stash, and takes off for parts unknown."

"Murphy wouldn't be in any shape to wander the north side looking for medication," said Crosby.

"No, he'd look close to home. That park wouldn't be far away from where he's hiding. His apartment has to be close by. He can't be very mobile if he didn't check into an ER. He'd pick someone or some location he was familiar with. So, we canvas the immediate neighborhood where this went down."

"I'll send out the troops, Nick. You can't be among us. The Captain would hang us all if we took you along."

There was no argument from Karras. He knew his limitations.

But he really wanted to be there when they found the son of a bitch. It was the first time since the beginning of the case that he really felt hopeful that Randall Murphy was in their gunsights.

•   •   •   •   •

The Colombians were not happy. They were very upset that Enrique Chavez had been the recipient of a .38 caliber slug to the melon. There was some bigtime slicing and cutting to be done in response to losing one of their own. Killing an associate was not acceptable.

They sent a posse to scour the neighborhood, but they came up with no one who'd seen the assault and killing. But they were resolute in their cause, and they were confident they'd find the man who killed Enrique Chavez.

•   •   •   •   •

Mara and her colleagues went door-to-door in a square mile radius of the scene surrounding the park. No one saw anything, and no one recognized the likeness of Randall Murphy that they showed everyone they talked to.

Nick had one more week deskbound, and then he was joining the crew in search of the Coast to Coast killer.

Abigail Adams was not unaware of recent events. The story of the drug dealer's demise made the papers, and, somehow, she got wind that Randall

Murphy might be part of the scenario. There were loose lips in the CPD just like everywhere else.

Nick was cleared the next week and he was okayed for regular street duty.

The search went on in the area around the crime scene in the park.

The FBI was saturating the neighborhood with agents, as well. Abigail was becoming restless for results, and she didn't take disappointment well.

CHAPTER TWENTY-FIVE

Nora was more sensitive to Nick's job now that he'd been wounded. It was one thing to read about cops getting shot when that cop didn't belong to you, and now she'd seen his wound when he took off his shirt and came to bed.

There was Gus to think about, now. Nora couldn't picture the boy growing up without her husband. Nick doted on the child. It was his only son, and no matter what he said, a son was important in their heritage. Sure, it was the latter half of the 20th Century, and the old country was soil neither of them had placed a foot upon, but the genes were embedded in both of them, and although they considered themselves thoroughly modern and thoroughly American, a male child had some weight.

Especially since Penelope was all but lost, sitting in that mental facility just northwest of them. There was enough loss between the two of them, and Nick putting himself in harm's way every day was becoming increasingly harder to bear. Nora couldn't foretell the future like some charlatan with a crystal ball and tarot cards. There were things she sensed in advance, impressions she could visualize, but she didn't do parlor tricks for tragic old women who wanted to communicate with their dearly departed Harold or Freddy or Bob.

She was uneasy about Nick and his 'holy' quest for this horrible killer who occupied her husband's waking hours and inhabited his dreams, as well. Nick had several nights of writhing around in bed. It got to the point that she'd find him sitting in front of their bay window in the middle of the night looking out at the street as if he were waiting for this Randall Murphy to walk by so that he could run out into the darkness and pursue him in some nightmare landscape that had invaded Nick's consciousness.

Nora knew he was obsessed with Murphy without having to hear it from Nick. She could read him easily. It was why she was attracted to him in the first place. There was no duplicity in him, no façade. What she saw was what he was, and it pained her to see him with that bullet hole that might have torn him away from her and from Gus.

There was no point in talking about his retirement. He was a policeman and he knew nothing else, desired nothing else. It was who he was and what he did, and if she were successful in talking him into a new career, he'd be unhappy. Nora knew other women who had that kind of influence on their husbands. They'd talked them into early retirements or into career moves, and all it produced was misery for their spouses and for themselves.

He was too young to turn in his badge. He didn't have enough years behind him to take a full retirement. And Nora wondered what he'd be like when he put his thirty in. She'd read about men who quit their jobs and played golf and hung around the house watching TV. They didn't last long. Heart attacks, strokes, cancer.

Or just simply ennui—boredom. It sapped them, made them listless.

All this because they had no reason to get up in the morning.

She knew Nick loved her. Her gift allowed her more insight than most women had about what their partners really thought and felt. There was no indecision or doubt in him when it came to their relationship. But she didn't want to become the cliched policeman's wife. Divorce after a few years. Or living with him because it was easier than a breakup. Cops suffered from depression, anxiety, and their suicide rate was terrible.

Nora didn't see Nick swallowing his barrel. He was happy with her. She knew it completely and without reservation. Gus was another reason he was satisfied with things the way they were. He spent every moment off work being with his boy, and with his wife.

His first marriage was a disaster. He married young, just back from the war, and his first wife had issues, mostly mental. She took off on Nick, and her flight might have permanently scarred him, not to mention the tragedy with Penelope, their only child.

His daughter lay in a hospital bed, and even though she'd shown slight improvement, Penelope was still mute and almost motionless.

When Nora saw him on his own hospital bed, her first reaction was to cry out in fear. No, his wound was not life-threatening, but all it would have taken was a trajectory to the right, and she'd be a widow standing at an assembly of cops in their dress blues listening to the bagpipes and shuddering when the gunfire saluted the demise of one of their brothers in arms.

What was the solution?

Live with it.

So far, she'd had no premonitions about something worse happening to Nick. There were the anxiety and depression and frustration about this creature, this Randall Murphy, roaming freely in Nick's streets, in her streets, in everyone else's streets.

She wished she had the powers to visualize Murphy's whereabouts so her husband could find him and kill him or arrest him.

Nora knew Nick and Mara Crosby had a full white board of outstanding suspects to be found and dealt with. Murphy was just one on a long list of perpetrators to apprehend.

But Murphy was at the top of Nick's list. He didn't discuss the case very often with her, but she knew very well none of the other criminals he sought were making him sit in the living room well after midnight scouring the sidewalks for Randall Murphy, the Coast to Coast killer.

●　　　●　　　●　　　●　　　●

Nick still felt it, but it was nothing to keep him at that desk that he abhorred. He told himself to disregard the dregs of the discomfort, but the wound had healed properly, and the CPD doctor gave him the green light to return to the street.

Chicago wasn't like every other big city, Karras thought. He'd been to New York and LA and San Francisco and Philadelphia and Boston and

Atlanta and Dallas on police business, and his impression was that Chicago was unique. It was the ugliest and most beautiful city at the same time. There was the Loop, the Golden Mile, the Lake—and then there were the southside and the west side and the miles and miles of blacktop and concrete and stench from the nearby chemical factories. There was the fragrance of the Lake water in June and the rot from the barrios and 'hoods where the gangbangers ruled. There were museums like the Art Institute and the Natural History Museum and Navy Pier. And there were neighborhood parks where drug deals went south and required body bags to pick up the lifeless remains.

It was a contradictory kingdom, but Karras had no inclination or desire to leave it. It was his territory, his home, and his job was to pick up the human trash who defiled it.

•　　•　　•　　•　　•

Kramer went quiet. They tapped his home and office phones, and there was nothing to move on. Magrette said yes to everything Nick and Mara asked of him: warrants, phone taps, whatever they needed.

They kept watch on hospitals, looking for a gunshot victim that fit Murphy's description. Every ER in Cook and DuPage County was waiting for him to stumble in so they could make the call. It was the biggest manhunt since Richard Speck massacred all those nurses at Cook County Hospital.

Karen Manski and Ellen Prentice lurked in the city's conscience like Hamlet's ghost. They cried out for a special vengeance after all the elapsed time since they'd been brutalized and murdered.

The Mayor went silent because he knew that the CPD and the FBI were actively engaged in the manhunt, and there had already been enough bad publicity about Murphy running free in the city. No one was certain that Murphy was still in town, but Magrette and Karras and Crosby were playing it as if he were.

If he made it through the surveillance and the roadblocks, the killer had to be a phantom with a phantom's invisibility. His portrait was everywhere, in all its variations. Hair, no hair. Bald. Multiple hues of locks on his top knot. The posters were everywhere, in banks and supermarkets. The ticket reps at O'Hare and Midway had his likeness on their desks.

If he got through all that interference, he was truly a spook, a ghost, an apparition.

•   •   •   •   •

Gil Falcone's fatal flaw was his big mouth. He liked to brag about his exploits, real or fictional, and the word got back to Carl Manfredi that Gil had made bad choices with his friends. In other words, he had made an Army buddy out of a serial killer who was filling the media and air waves with interest. Carl was not a civic minded man. Unless the civic-mindedness led to profit, but when one of his soldiers told him that Falcone was hanging with a mass murderer, Manfredi thought all bets were off with this asshole Falcone. This kind of spotlight could be very bad for business if it ever got out that one of his guys was shielding a serial killer.

He brought Falcone in for a conversation.

Carl's office occupied the rear of the titty bar where he'd twice talked to Nick Karras, a cop he never wanted to have another little interview with.

Manfredi's office chair was expensive leather, and the folding chairs opposite him were uncomfortable and stiff by design.

Falcone sat in one of the metallic seaters, and Manfredi's personal storm goons stood by the door, looming in the darkness like two gargoyles ready to swoop down on the poor bastard Carl had summoned.

"You got a very special friend, I hear," Carl said.

Gil Falcone fidgeted.

"Save me some time and tell me the story."

Falcone slowly recounted how Murphy had saved him in the war.

"Why in the fuck did you let yourself get drafted?"

Falcone shrugged.

"You some kind of fucking goofy patriotic sap? Is that it?"

"I was just a kid. I thought I was doing the right thing, Carl."

Falcone was already sweating in spite of the chill of the office's air conditioning. Carl liked it clammy cold. It was a message to whomever sat before him on occasions like this.

"Every police agency in North America is looking for this cocksucker, and you go bailing him out with two of our contacts, the doctor and that faggot plastic surgeon."

"He saved my life, Mr. Manfredi."

The familiarity with 'Carl' disappeared.

"Yeah. You tried to repay this good deed by putting all of us in the shit. Are you getting the picture here, dumbass?"

Falcone shrugged again.

"What is this shrugging shit? You got a twitch in your fucking shoulders?"

"I'm sorry, Mr. Manfredi."

"The obvious move is for me to let those two have you so you can wind up in some watery place all over the county in little chunks."

Falcone sat up stiffly.

"But you got friends in your crew who might think it's a bit too harsh of me."

"I'm really sorry, Mr. Manfredi."

"Yeah, well. Stick the sorry up your ass. You're going to contact this little prick, tell him you got him a way out of the city. Bring him some place he'll feel safe."

"You're going to whack him?" Falcone protested.

"We could do you both. How's that sound, nickel-dick?"

Falcone slumped in his chair.

"No, we're not going to button him. We're going to give him up to the cops before the shitstorm rains all over us. You like the smell of shit, Falcone?"

He shook his head.

"Consider yourself lucky, then. This is your way out, and it ain't negotiable. Yes?"

"Yes."

"There cannot be an instant replay of this happy horseshit. I know he's your buddy, but you better know how to cut ties and deal with it. I want this done immediately. I want this serial killer cocksucker to become yesterday's bad news. Are we clear, shit-for-brains?"

One of the gargoyles opened the door for Gil Falcone, and the bodyguard smiled at him as he went out into the titty bar.

●　　　●　　　●　　　●　　　●

Falcone went over to the apartment at night. He didn't trust telephones, and he had a lot of company with that attitude in the Outfit. No one knew who was being tapped, lately. The FBI and the Sheriff and the US Marshals and the CPD—it was all like one big listening device. You had to do communication face-to-face, lately.

Even then they had audio gimmicks that could eavesdrop into an apartment or an office.

He knocked on the door since the entry lock to the three-flat was opened.

No one answered the door.

He turned the handle, and it too was open. Falcone took out his .45 and aimed it into the darkened flat.

"Randall?"

He proceeded inside.

"Randall, it's me, Gil."

He went into the bedroom first. The bed was disheveled. The sheets were tossed onto the floor and there was a distinct odor that suggested Murphy hadn't done a laundry in a long time.

Falcone walked out into the kitchenette and opened the refrigerator. There were hunks of molding cheese and lunch meat inside. The cheese was green and the bologna was black. Gil's gorge rose and he shut the fridge.

"Randall?"

There was silence.

"You motherfucker. You just signed my death warrant."

Then he left the apartment and walked down and out to the parking lot.

CHAPTER TWENTY-SIX

He who hesitates is fucked. Lost, too, Murphy understood.

The highways were sewn tight. There was no way out via either airport. The bus terminals were covered as well. And the only thing Randal had going for him was his newly-black hair and thick glasses with black horn rims and fake lenses. His eyesight was still 20-20.

His disguise would only work temporarily, and then either the FBI or Karras and his redheaded partner would move in. The die was cast and it wasn't a winning number. More like snake eyes.

There was no place to hide out. He couldn't tap Gil Falcone again. They'd be happy to see him go, too. Falcone had been taking a big risk by reaching out to him with the disgraced doctor and the plastic surgeon. There was no safe house to flee to. The apartment was not a safe haven, any longer. When he stayed in any one spot too long, he increased the odds that his run was over. Being on the road made it more difficult to trace him, but he'd made the mistake of sitting in his home town for far too long, and now there was no way out of here.

His only alternative was to make his own luck.

He drove the neighborhood looking for a straggler, perhaps a lone woman, but there were no available targets. Every female he saw as he cruised the blocks was accompanied, most of them by imposing looking males.

Next stop was the local supermarket. There were always lone females walking the aisles there.

He was drawn to one particular subject as he followed her up and down the aisles. He pushed an empty cart behind her. The thing that attracted him was that she was carrying cloth shopping bags. She wasn't pushing a cart of her own.

It took her twenty-five minutes to collect her goods. Randall picked up a six pack of beer and a bottle of white wine in his cart. He didn't have much cash left since he'd been out of work, and he couldn't very well go back to the job after being AWOL after Karras had clipped him.

She was a perfect selection. Not too old or young, maybe early or mid-thirties. No wedding band on her finger. If he was lucky, she'd be recently divorced or widowed, or maybe just what they used to call a spinster.

She had a bit of heft on her, but she wasn't in the ballpark of fat. Voluptuous, perhaps. Which made him wonder why she sported no wedding ring. It was possible she might be gay; you never knew. Randall didn't have a radar on their sexual proclivity.

Out into the parking lot she walked, and he was right behind her with his bag of beer and wine.

"Looks like a load," he said.

Her bags were overflowing.

She turned and looked at him, but there was no fatal flicker of recognition in her face. The black hair and the glasses were the best he could do, and it looked like it was working. Or perhaps she didn't read the papers or watch the news.

"Pardon me?" she smiled.

"I think I've seen you before in the neighborhood," he told her.

"You have? I don't think I've seen you," she grinned.

Easy pickings. She hadn't told him to buzz the fuck off, yet.

"I couldn't forget someone like you. Can I help you with your bags? I live close to here, and I could give you a lift."

"I don't know you."

Shoppers passed them on the way to the parking lot, but no one stopped and gave either of them a second look.

"I can change that. Come on, let me give you a lift. I only live a few blocks from here."

"Me, too. But I still don't know you."

"My name's Pat Stillman. You?"

"Theresa. I'll save the last name when I know you."

"I read like an open book. Come on, you look like you've had a long day."

"Where's your car?"

"I'll show you. If you're good, I've got some beer and wine with your name on it."

She laughed. But she followed him to his car.

He opened the trunk and put her groceries inside along with his two bags of booze.

He opened the door for her on the passenger's side.

"And a gentleman, too."

Randall finally had some luck. Lately, the noose had been tightening into a chokehold. But he'd found a woman with a hungry look. It hadn't taken much convincing. She was surprisingly attractive up close. It made him wonder what her story really was. Why was she alone? Her body appeared soft and pliable, comfortable. She didn't fit his usual type—lean and tall, a bit gangly. Theresa looked like the kind of woman you got to know a bit before you did the things you normally did when she became disposable.

She lived six blocks from the grocery story, maybe a mile from Murphy's last apartment. Randall had the feeling that Gil's Outfit buddies or the police had paid his old place a visit, by now.

"I don't want to seem pushy. If you're still a little leery, I can come back another time. It can be dangerous for a single, good-looking woman like you. I don't want to go too fast, but I'd like to get to know you, Theresa Whoever."

She laughed as they sat in Murphy's car.

"I don't usually accept rides from strange men," she smiled.

Her hair was blonde, likely bleached. It was almost platinum, with a few yellow streaks here and there.

"But since you've got all that alcohol in the trunk. I don't go to bars. Too many predators in taverns."

"I don't like bars, either."

"Why don't we go up to my place and see what you have in those paper bags? They'll get warm if we sit out here."

He got out and went to the trunk and retrieved her groceries and his two sacks. He followed her to the door of her three-flat and waited as she unlocked the door.

She was on the top floor, and she opened the entry and they walked in.

He followed her into the kitchen.

"Sit down, Pat Stillman."

He planted himself on one of her dinette chairs. The table was rectangular and seated four. There was no sign of a roommate or boyfriend or anyone other than her.

He watched while she put away the items she'd purchased. The kitchenette was clean and orderly, the way the living room appeared.

"You're thinking, what kind of girl lets herself get picked up at the supermarket? You must think I'm awfully easy, Pat."

"I think there's instant karma. That's what I think."

She sat down opposite him. He took out the six pack and yanked away two cans of Budweiser.

"Beer okay? I have wine in this sack. White wine."

"I like beer. Want a glass?"

He shook his head, but Theresa rose and went to a cabinet and pulled out a fancy glass beer mug with a handle. It had some label on it he couldn't make out.

Murphy saw the knives on the counter in a wooden holder. One of them appeared to be a large butcher blade, something you'd carve a roast beef or a turkey with.

She popped the can open and poured the beer into her mug.

"Can I have one of those glasses, too?"

She retrieved another mug.

He popped his open and watched as the blond liquid filled his glass.

They both drank in silence.

"What if I were the spider and *you* were the fly, Pat Stillman?"

She flashed him an evil grin.

"Maybe I enticed you, instead of the other way around."

"Are you armed, Theresa?"

"I have weapons of my own, yes. Right now, they're well-hidden."

"Should I be frightened?" he asked her with a smile.

"Terrified, that's what you should be."

"You have a gun? Or are you planning on using the cutlery on me?" he asked.

"Guns are too impersonal, don't you think? I like to get up close and personal."

"Me too," he smiled widely.

She took another drink.

"What's your story, Pat?"

"Story?"

"You pick up women from the market all the time?"

She took another hit from the mug. The glass was half-drained.

"I don't make a habit of it, no."

"Why me, then?"

"I like what I see. Why else?"

"Either one of us might have nefarious motives, right?"

Her blouse was unbuttoned at the top and her ample bosom was visible. She fingered the button below the opening.

"What is it that you really do?" she asked him.

"I used to drive trucks cross country, but then I lost my job. I'm getting kicked out of my apartment, as a matter of fact."

"When?"

"Next week. I'll have to find something I can afford, I guess. It's expensive, around here...How can you afford this place, if you don't mind my asking?"

She took another swallow, and her glass was almost empty. Murphy's mug was only half gone. He removed another can of brew and handed it to her. She popped it open and refilled her mug. He'd noticed a fifth of Jim Beam and a bottle of tequila on her counter by the knives. It was fine if she were a drunk. It would make things easier. And Theresa liked to play games. That was fine, also. She liked to tease him. Maybe she liked it dangerous. The bit about her weapons, hidden weapons. The spider and the fly, making her a black widow arachnid.

"I hope you find somewhere soon," she offered.

It would be his car if things didn't work out here.

The noose was pinching him, and he grimaced quickly.

"If I knew you better, I'd offer you the couch."

"I couldn't put you out like that."

She smiled.

"Like most things in this life, you have to play it by ear."

She took half of her refill down in one swallow.

"How about I make us something to eat? Beer makes my *hungry*."

"Hungry for what?"

"I have a voracious appetite. You do like red meat, don't you?"

"I live on it."

"I have a steak in the fridge. How do you like it?"

"Red. Rare. A little bloody."

"We already have something in common. Booze and steak. I wonder what else I'll find out about you tonight."

She went to the refrigerator and took out a package. She found a skillet in a cabinet and turned the gas on and the flame made a poof sound as it lit beneath the skillet.

"You need a vegetable?"

"Anything green'll do."

She found a can of green beans in her cabinet and she opened it with a can opener and poured them into a small pot and lit another burner and placed the green beans on the flame.

The steak was done in seven minutes. They ate at the table in silence, both of them wolfing down their meals.

"How about something with more of a kick?" she grinned.

"Sure."

She got the bottle of tequila and found two shot glasses in the cabinet that had housed the beer mugs.

She poured the clear liquid into the shot glasses.

"I don't have any lemon. Sorry."

She tossed down the tequila. Randall sipped at his. The booze was getting to his head slightly, but Theresa looked unfazed.

"I suppose I should go. You've been too good," he told her.

"You don't have to go if you don't want to."

"You can do better. I'm out of work and about to be homeless in a week, Theresa."

She was fingering the button beneath the cleavage, once again. She deftly undid the button, exposing her black brassiere.

She smiled.

"You don't have to leave. You can stay and crash on my couch. You're welcome here, Pat. It seems like good karma to me."

"I don't want to put you out, really."

"We're never going to get anywhere if you keep that up."

"Where are we going to get?"

She stood and opened her blouse all the way down the front.

He watched her as she unbuttoned. Murphy averted his eyes toward the cutlery on the counter.

Theresa walked around the dinette table and bent down and kissed him. He stood and embraced her, and then he unzipped her skirt in the back and pulled it down and let it fall around her ankles. She stepped out of the skirt and then hauled down her slip and panties and stepped out of them also.

She took Murphy by the hand and led him into the darkened bedroom. Theresa had a queen-sized bed with a comforter on top of the bedding and mattress. She turned on the bedside lamp and the dim glow illuminated the bedroom. He undid her bra and watched as the pendulous breasts descended slightly.

He forgot to grab the butcher knife from her countertop. It was too late to go back and retrieve it. She was too luscious to begin carving her up. He saw the erect nipples. They were pink with a small aureole circling each of them. He pressed her backward onto the bed. Then he undid his pants and let them fall to the carpet.

•   •   •   •   •

"I have to get up and go to work," she told him.

It was 6:00 AM.

"Where do you work?" he asked.

"I'm a paralegal downtown."

"Must be a good lawyer if you can afford to live here on your own."

They were lying on their backs, close to each other. The comforter had been thrown to the floor long ago.

"He pays well."

He turned to her and brushed her breasts with his palm. She groaned.

Murphy mounted her again, and it was over quickly and furiously.

"I like when it hurts a little. Is that too weird?"

"Why are you really alone?" he asked.

"You don't find out my secrets on the first date, Pat. You'd be bored with me if you did."

CHAPTER TWENTY-SEVEN

Carl Manfredi swore he was done talking to the police, but when Falcone came up empty on this serial killer who very much was bad for business as usual, he called Karras and let him know where Murphy last hung his hat.

The effect was the same as it had been for Gil Falcone, who now perched at the top of his boss' shit list. Falcone was fortunate that Carl was hesitant to whack one of his own crew, but Gil was relegated to bagman for the hookers on the north side, a pretty fair-sized demotion.

Nick and Mara hit the door courtesy of a uniform's swinging sledge, and all they found was the same decaying food that Gil Falcone had found in the refrigerator. Everything else had been removed from the apartment, and the building manager, of course, had no forwarding address for Randall Murphy since Murphy was not the name he knew his tenant by.

"He was a quiet guy. No problems. Kept to himself," Pete Johnson, the manager explained to Karras and Crosby.

"Where've we heard that story before?" Mara said to her partner on the ride back to Headquarters on the Lake.

The only information of value was that Johnson's recent renter had black hair and wore black horn-rimmed glasses. No facial hair, either, Pete informed them as they searched the previous digs of Randall Murphy, AKA the Coast to Coast killer.

"I don't see him making any long-distance trips. It's too dangerous," Nick said as they drove the Eisenhower east in dense afternoon traffic. "If he's consistent, he'll stay close to where he lived before. This is his comfort zone, now. His traveling days are over, I have a feeling. If we don't get him, the FBI will."

"But we have his new look and they don't, yet," she reminded her partner.

"True, but we cannot avoid sharing the wealth on him, either."

"I was never good at sharing. I liked being by myself, too. Didn't play well with others. My parents thought I was a problem child. They still do."

He looked over at the redhead and smiled.

"Maybe that explains your booked social life."

"Wow, that was below the belt."

"No harm intended. I'm just concerned you're not casting your bread on the waters is all I meant."

"Since when have you become my guardian angel, Nick?"

"I don't remember when it was."

They drove on in silence for a few minutes. Traffic was at a crawl, and June had opened the radiators for full blast heat. It was 97, the last time they passed a weather billboard on the expressway.

"You have any idea what we do next? It's like this prick is in our heads. He's always one jump ahead. It can't just be bad luck on our account. Maybe this guy has 'gifts' like your wife. Maybe he's fucking clairvoyant and sees us coming all the time."

"There's a difference between intelligent and sly and slimy. His instincts for survival are just sharper edged than most. Most of the perps we pursue are brain-deads. We catch them in a few days. Remember Quantico? Series killers get to be series killers because they're organized, they're planners, plotters."

"He can't go out in public. He's too much of a deviant rock star. He's a celebrity, for crissake. He goes out and all it takes is one eyeball to pop him. So, what does he do?"

"He finds a hole to hide in. Maybe someone to take him in. Murphy has nowhere to crash, so he finds a benefactor, likely a woman. The guy has charms. He's got looks that get him in the door. It's always been the way he operates. But if he does his thing, she's dead pretty quick, and then someone notices she's missing, and then he's got to move again. Every time he surfaces it's like another bullet in the gun for Russian roulette. So maybe he doesn't kill this one until he thinks it's safe to move on. Maybe he plays nice with this one until the urge won't let him, anymore."

"That's your theory?" Mara laughed.

"You got a better one? I'm all ears. You got to think the way your quarry thinks. Where would I go if I were Murphy?

"I think he hasn't rambled off too far, Mara. He'll keep ditching his rides, also. We should pay attention to the local stolen car reports. I'm guessing he'll do everything tight to the vest.

"What would you do if you were Murphy?" Nick asked her.

"I'm learning at the foot of the master," she grinned.

"You have any idea how many times I've been wrong?"

"How many?"

"My solved percentage has only approached fifty percent. Sixty percent on a very good month. These guys get away with it, sometimes."

"Not this time. Right?"

"No, not this time."

•   •   •   •   •

They went over the stolen car reports for the vicinity of Murphy's latest address. There were six cars reported missing in the last three weeks.

"Don't park your ride on the street," Mara mused.

"It's why you need insurance," Nick replied.

"He'll be switching plates constantly," she said.

"Without a doubt. But we'll have the guys in Auto Theft keep an eye out for these last six boosts. If they sight any of them, they'll stake out the car and watch to see who gets in and drives away.

"You and I, however, are back to expanding our search in a mile radius of his last address. Magrette said we could use some uniforms to hit the neighborhoods with us."

"If you're right about Murphy moving in with some woman, we better expedite. He doesn't seem like the type to get involved in a long-term commitment."

•　　•　　•　　•　　•

They scoured the nearby territory and flashed new pictures of Murphy in black locks and horn-rims. They came up empty for six days.

They took lunch at Pudgy's on Fullerton.

"He's submerged," Mara said as she tore into her corned beef sub. It was a footlong, but she told Karras it was going to be dinner tonight, also.

They were working four to midnight, and they had eight uniforms in four squads helping them search. They had heard nothing from any of the quartet of patrol cars, yet.

"He's trying to outlast us," she said with half a mouthful.

"He's doing a fine job, so far."

"We've got his new look out all over the city. How many dye jobs can he do?" Mara proposed.

"He's shut off from that Kramer guy. Last I heard, he picked up and moved to parts unknown, and I don't think he'll be getting any referrals from Gil Falcone, Manfredi's soldier."

"So, we're stuck with Murphy hiding out with a sweetie pie who hasn't seen his face on Channel 7 news."

"She'd better be a recluse. She gets drift of him, she's dead."

After their lunch break, they went back to the neighborhoods. Mara worked one side of the street, and Karras the other. Nick carried the hand-held in case there was word from the patrolmen working their detail. The hand-held never went off. Nick wondered if the batteries were any good.

Mara came up with a possible sighting.

The elderly woman said she'd seen someone who looked like the figure in the latest rendering. Her name was Julia Carpenter. She appeared to be approaching ninety, but she seemed sharp and lucid.

Julia invited Mara inside. Two cats rubbed against Crosby's ankles not long after she entered the old woman's apartment.

"Don't mind them," the old lady smiled. "They're harmless. The one with the spots is Fredo and the tabby is Sonny. I love gangster movies," Julia explained. "Would you like a cold drink? It's awfully hot out there."

"I'd take some ice water, if that's okay."

The elderly woman went into the kitchen.

She came back with a tumbler filled with ice and water.

"I've seen him down the block. He lives with some woman, but I didn't see a ring on her finger, if you know what I mean."

"Where exactly do they live? Do you know which building?"

"Oh, I think it's two down from here. A three-flat. Just north of us."

Mara took a gulp of the ice water and handed the old woman the tumbler.

"Thank you."

"It's awfully hot. Do you have to rush off?"

Mara thought the old girl was terribly lonely, cats or not. Sonny and Fredo rubbed up against Crosby's ankles again on her way out.

•　　•　　•　　•　　•

She hustled to Nick as he was coming out of another three-flat.

She repeated what Julia had told her and pointed out the building where the two people lived.

"Did she know which apartment?" he asked Mara.

Mara shook her head.

"We'll have to go inside and find out."

They crossed the street and walked toward the building. Nick used the hand-held and called for back-up. The batteries were charged, after all.

"Let's try the first floor first," Nick said.

They waited until two of the four patrol cars pulled up to the curb.

Then he punched the doorbell. He got a buzz from the intercom.

"Police," he explained.

When they got to the door, the entry was cracked open and Karras could see the chain. He flashed ID, and then the twenty-something woman undid the chain and widened the entry.

Nick showed her the latest version of Randall Murphy.

"Have you seen this man?" he asked.

She took the photo from him and stared at it for a few extended beats.

The woman's eyes were different colors—one blue and one brown. It took Karras aback, at first.

She popped a bubble from her chewing gum, and it startled both the detectives. The two uniforms were standing behind Mara Crosby.

"He lives upstairs. Third floor. Yeah. Guy's an asshole. Are we done?"

Nick backed out of the doorway, and the young woman shut the door in his face.

They trekked to the top floor. Nick palmed his .38 and Mara unholstered her own piece. The patrolmen did the same and followed them upstairs.

Karras knocked on the door. Not violently, but loud enough. They waited for a few seconds, and then the portal cracked open slowly.

"Police," Nick announced.

This female had a few decades on the girl on the first floor. She was around five feet eight and had long and curly blonde hair with a few highlights mixed in with the white, platinum hue.

She saw the gun in Nick's hand. He showed her the ID with his other hand.

Fear crossed her face.

"What's wrong?"

Nick walked at her and backed her into the apartment.

"Who else is in here?"

She looked at Mara and the uniforms.

"Jesus Christ! What the hell is going on?"

Nick showed her the rendition.

Then a man walked toward them from a rear bedroom. Nick raised the .38.

"Fuck!" the black-haired man in the tattered bathrobe bleated.

He was five or six inches too short. He was pudgy, with a beer gut, and he was going bald. But he did have the black locks on the fringes of a growing chrome-dome.

"Shit," Nick muttered.

"What are you doing in here?" the dark-haired man protested.

"Our mistake. My apologies," Karras offered as he put his piece back into his shoulder holster. "We were looking for this man."

He showed them the picture.

"How the hell did you get here, then?" the woman demanded.

"Someone said they saw him," Mara offered.

"They ought to have their fucking eyes examined. Please leave," the blonde told them.

•　　　•　　　•　　　•　　　•

The heat got to them, and Nick told the patrolmen to go coop where there was air conditioning. It was the end of their tour, anyway.

Karras drove to a nearby White Castle because it was open 24/7 and because it was air conditioned. Frigid, in fact, as they found out when the Arctic air met them coming in.

"There are only so many strikes in a game, and then it's over," he told her as they sat in the booth. "Do you believe in that karma crap?" he asked Crosby.

Her face was flushed, and perspiration made dark blotches in her navy-blue blouse. Nick was soaked to his waist, as well. The cold air sent a shock up his spine.

He ordered Cokes, but neither of them was hungry.

"The only thing I know, Nick, is that free will is vastly overrated. You ever read any Kurt Vonnegut, the sci-fi writer?"

"Not a fan of fantasy, no."

"He has these little guys he calls Tralfamadorans in his books. They look like plumber's helpers with their eyes on top of the handle, and they travel all over the universe."

"Cute," Nick smiled wearily.

"Thing is, they say that these creatures, these Earthlings, are the only crazy bastards in the entire universe who even talk about free will. The little guys insist that we're all bugs trapped in amber. Can you feature that? We're stuck with fate or determinism or whatever the hell, but we sure aren't free.

"Maybe our fate is to go after Murphy endlessly. Circling each other, like we're trapped in a loop."

"You really need to go out more," Karras told her.

"I'm serious. Maybe some stuff, maybe everything, is pre-planned."

"By whom?"

"God, the universe, the cosmos. Who knows?"

"You're a little too cosmic for me, and I'm too pooped to argue with you."

The waitress brought them their drinks as they sat in a booth near the door.

"Bugs in amber," Karras repeated. "Bugs. The hell is amber, anyway?"

"I'll lend you the book," she promised Karras.

"I can't hack fantasy, I told you."

"Science fiction. You have to expand your horizons, Nick."

CHAPTER TWENTY-EIGHT

Abigail was feeling the heat, and it had nothing to do with the July temperatures which had topped 100 three days in a row. The word 'sweltering' applied to the outdoors, but in her office on Michigan Avenue, the air conditioning did nothing to assuage her discomfort with the lack of results in nabbing Randall Murphy. There were no sightings on the highways or at the bus terminals or at the two airports. She was monitoring the CPD with moles the FBI planted at their Headquarters on Michigan Avenue near the Lake, and the closest thing to a nibble was when Karras and Crosby crashed an apartment and accosted a bald, fat guy living with his bleached blonde girlfriend.

It wasn't heartening, to understate the situation greatly. Abigail wasn't going to be reassigned to D.C. where the real action was—the growing business of anti-terrorism. Murphy was a lone wolf killer, but the Middle East was always rife with intrigue and conspiracy and threats to the United States. The Israelis were a continual hotbed of tension, and since America was a staunch ally, our nation was in the crosshairs of any crazy with a homemade bomb.

Murphy was small potatoes, and that was why Ms. Adams was upset with the lack of progress. Karras and Crosby were out stalking the north side, and her half-dozen agents assigned to locate the serial killer were coming up only with ineptitude. The thing to do, she decided is make heads roll before her own noggin was on the guillotine. Being black had helped her with the move toward diversity, but results were the only things that mattered to the old white men she served in the nation's capital.

She brought her people into her office for a very unpleasant (for them) interview, and she did a workman-like job of creating some sweat and squirming. Adams laid it on the line that they'd be headed for one-horse town positions if they didn't get a line on Murphy pronto—and she actually used the word 'pronto'.

No one found any humor in the word choice, and then she dismissed them in order to get their asses in gear. It was what a proper executive did, she figured.

The theory remained that Randall Murphy was still in the Cook County environs, that he hadn't resumed his MO of using the open road as kill scenes, the way he'd done with twenty outstanding homicide cases of young women. Karen Manski and Ellen Prentice were his latest victims, and his habit of strangling them and then cutting off their nipples hadn't re-emerged on the federal radar, to date. The details regarding the nipples were hidden from the public since publishing them might lead to copycats, who were tiresome and who complicated the search for Murphy.

This man kept moving, blending in, changing. He reminded Adams of Wells' *Invisible Man,* the phantom who became so dark that he disappeared. But Wells' character left footprints, at least. Murphy left nothing behind but corpses.

This was no way to move toward elected office, Abigail understood. There was no way to move into that Senator's or Representative's slot by failing at her current profession. You had to have scalps. You had to have statistics behind you. Bullshit only went so far at the FBI, and then it came down to your arrests. Big-time pinches. Headliners.

Was playing the blame game helping her cause? Did the buck stop with her? It was easier to lash out at her underlings, but it wouldn't put Murphy in a federal shithole. Abigail didn't want Murphy dead. She wanted a live specimen they could trot into a courtroom with all the attendant hoopla that major cases brought about. They didn't photograph FBI agents, usually, but the positive pub from a bust like Murphy could get her rockets off the launching pad.

Should she have another sitdown with Karras and Crosby? She already had a plant in Homicide. The guy was ex-vice and he was very pliable when it came to federal favors. The favors were information that was ostensibly privileged—the feds weren't to dabble in monetary payoffs. Not to other cops, anyway. They paid big money for information on the top ten list that was posted on most postal bulletin boards.

Abigail slunk down on her swivel chair and looked out the window at Lake Michigan. She could see dots that were in reality beach-goers, lying on the baked sand, roasting like barbequed meat.

She knew the sand was draining to the bottom of her professional hourglass. She needed the weight of the Coast to Coast killer removed from her shoulders.

•　　•　　•　　•　　•

Theresa Kelly hated television. She didn't subscribe to the newspapers. She had no female friends, and the last time she allowed a man near her was the recent encounters with Pat Stillman. She'd had an affair with a married guy three years ago, and it hadn't ended well. His wife hired a private detective who took unflattering photos of Theresa in various poses of coitus and fellatio. The wife confronted the hubby, and all bets were off. The adulterer had promised Theresa he was leaving his old lady, but of course it was all fiction. Theresa was a paralegal, and the wife came from old money in Highland Park. No contest. It was over, and Theresa had no recourse but to slink away with her perfect, round tail in disarray.

Humiliating, yes. She'd actually felt something for the bastard. He'd taken her to Vegas on her two-week vacation—his excuse with the wife was a business trip to San Diego. Apparently, his spouse didn't check on her husband's itinerary very carefully.

That wound had finally been cauterized, but Theresa developed a sincere lack of trust in the male members of the species. It was difficult because she also was passionate in nature. She enjoyed physical contact with men. She just didn't think it was worth being disappointed again.

All that distrust flew out the window when she found herself with her feet wrapped over Pat Stillman's shoulders and when he was slamming into her again and again and when she didn't think she could cum one more time after he thrust her into yet another explosive orgasm.

There was something odd about his eyes, however. Perhaps it was the dim lighting in the bedroom, but she could've sworn that there was a red tinge to his pupils as he bore into her own eyes with his. At other times the orbs seemed coal black and colorless. Perhaps it should have frightened her, but it only seemed to spur another eruption in her loins.

He seemed dangerous. There was something sinister in him, but it only made Pat more appealing. This was forbidden territory, but she was in her thirties now, and playing it safe didn't occur to her. Her best years were dwindling, and finding a man you were passionate about seemed less likely as the months melted into each other. She wasn't meant to live alone, sleep alone. There was so little pleasure in life. There was only her job. Movies and TV didn't interest her. Becoming close to the other women at the office never entered her thoughts. She wanted a man who moved her, made her feel alive.

It was idiotic to allow herself to be picked up at a goddamned grocery store by a complete stranger, but it seemed she was swept up into it as if all her reserve and good judgment had flown from her. He was charming and handsome, but that didn't do it. There was something magnetic about him that shot out at her at her first sight of him. She hadn't the will to rebuff him and walk away. Certainly, she understood that there might be payback in her hasty assessment of Pat Stillman. He might very well be as duplicitous as the lover who'd discarded her like some candy wrapper and left her fluttering in the wind on her way to the curb.

It was the chance you took when you decided to literally let someone in.

Did she think it was love? Theresa didn't buy into love at first sight. She hardly knew him. But he did things to her that no one had ever done. Not the wayward husband, not anyone else. There had never been a response like the one she had with this gorgeous man.

His only flaw was a scar near his abdomen. He told her it was an old, boring war story, and she let it go at that. He was between jobs and he was low on cash, and those two details should have been red flags. But none of it seemed to matter to her. She just needed to feel his heat, his lust. There was no transferring that want to anything remotely like love. Maybe it would blossom. She hoped so. She'd never been this reckless and wanton with anyone else, and the thrill, the juice, the buzz seemed enough for her.

It had been long, cold months since the two-faced amour had chucked her out. Maybe it wouldn't last. The second Pat asked her for money, she'd throw him out. She kept waiting over the past few days for him to reach out and try to tap her for cash, but he hadn't. He offered to find an apartment of his own, but Theresa figured he'd be sleeping in his car, instead. She wasn't ready to give him up, yet.

She asked him to move in with her until he got on his feet and found employment. Then he led her into the bedroom and he proceeded to mount her and make her beg him never to stop, never to stop, never to stop.

•　　•　　•　　•　　•

On the fifth day of cohabitation, Pat left the apartment and didn't return until 11:00 PM.

"I was afraid you weren't coming back," she told him.

"Don't you want me to come back?" he whispered.

He kissed her and thrust his tongue deeply into her mouth.

She felt him press against her below her waist.

"I thought you might have become tired of me."

"Does it feel like I'm tired of you?"

She shook her head, and Theresa was surprised to feel tears tracing themselves down her cheeks.

"I found a job."

"You did?" she smiled.

He licked her teardrops from her face.

Then he brushed his palms against her chest. She was wearing only a tee-shirt, and he could feel the tips of her breasts hardening.

"I'm working at a garage. A mechanic. Aren't you proud of me?"

He kissed her again, and this time their tongues met. Theresa found herself melting against him.

She told herself it was relief that she was feeling. When he hadn't come back to the apartment, she thought he'd just taken off, left her behind.

"I can find a place of my own, now," he said.

Her heart seemed to descend in her chest.

"Don't you like it here? I mean if you want to live on your own, I get it, but I thought you liked being here, with me."

"I don't want to take advantage of you. That's all."

"I'll let you know when I feel that way," she answered.

"You really looking for a roomie?" he smiled.

He clamped his hands on her buttocks and pulled her tighter to him. She could feel his arousal against her shorts. She never wore underwear in the apartment.

"No, I'm not looking for a roommate. No."

She lowered herself to her knees and unbuckled his jeans.

●　　　●　　　●　　　●　　　●

She wanted to tell him she loved him, but she wanted it to be reciprocal. There were times she wanted to tell the cheating husband the same thing, but fortunately she held out against voicing her affections for that miserable son of a bitch. Theresa had learned the hard way about letting yourself get close to another, and she wanted to see where Pat was really leading her.

It wasn't likely this would add up to anything long-term, she knew. Incredible flames were likely to burn themselves out, if the sex was all they had. But the sex was extraordinary. It didn't seem to diminish, even after a few weeks together. It always seemed new. There was no repetition to it. Even though the coupling was similar, the passion he brought to her seemed original on every encounter. It never became stale, and she knew that the physical act of coitus was limited. There were only so many ways you could conjoin two bodies.

But every time he took her, it seemed unique, different from the last time.

Theresa was religious about using birth control. She wasn't a foolish novice at this kind of thing. She used the pill because of its reliability. There were times she wondered if Pat would mind if she skipped them and let nature take its course, but she also understood they still hardly knew each other.

The blackness in his eyes titillated her. He could be some madman who was stalking the neighborhood looking for his newest victim. A predator who hadn't yet toyed enough with her before he got around to his real business.

Pat was physical with her, but he was never abusive. The only pain he inflicted was the pain that she begged for. There were times he put his hands on her throat and began to squeeze the air out of her, but it only served to make her orgasms even more intense. But he let go of her just as it seemed she was going to lose consciousness, and she'd suck in the oxygen and she'd throb for a long time after he'd finished inside her.

He paid a lot of attention to her breasts, but it wasn't uncommon for her partners to be impressed by them. They were large, but they didn't sag much yet. All of which would likely change around middle age. For now, they were perfect, and she knew men were well aware of their attractions.

He liked to nip at her and suckle her, and it made her respond deliriously.

It's only sex, she tried to remind herself. You can get weary of anything with repetition.

The wolf had not arrived at her door, just yet. The pleasure seemed to expand and expand every time they lay on the bed or the floor or the kitchenette table or in the shower. The *ennui* hadn't arrived to ruin their version of Eden, just yet.

•   •   •   •   •

They lived like husband and wife. He went off to his small garage on Western Avenue, not far from the apartment, and she rode the El to her job at the attorney's. But the mundane disappeared when dinner was over and when he touched her electrically and when their work clothes were scattered all over the living room floor. It wouldn't dissipate. The energy grew and grew.

She was deliriously happy and hoped it would never end.

Only when she peered up at him and saw the absence of color in his eyes did she have the slightest pause about where they were headed.

•   •   •   •   •

It was fine with her that they never went out. To movies or to eat or to the beach. He was enough. They needed no one else to feel complete. Others were a distraction from their time together, and Theresa was jealous of the hours after they finished work, and he seemed to be in concert with her desire to cut themselves off from the outsiders that threatened to encroach upon them. There was no need for anything outside the apartment they shared. They only went out to work and to buy groceries.

"How come you don't watch TV?" he asked.

The 26- inch set sat silent in the corner by the living room window. It hadn't been turned on since he'd moved in.

"Nothing on it to interest me."

"I heard the war might be ending soon."

"That's in their world, Pat, not ours."

"I fought in that war, you know."

"I saw the scar," she said.

She traced her fingertips against the spot underneath his tee-shirt.

"No more scars for us," she told him.

He smiled, but his eyes lost color as his lips parted.

CHAPTER TWENTY-NINE

The grind was getting to Mara, and she couldn't understand why it hadn't burned out Nick, as well. But he was like concrete; nothing seemed to move him. He was like that cliched bulldog in copper-dom. He just kept coming relentlessly after Randall Murphy. They'd had leads that evaporated, roads that became dead ends, and still he pursued this multiple murderer. She knew better than to ask him why he was so adamant about catching a man that the FBI, the State Police, the US Marshals and no one else had been able to capture.

It was in his nature never to let go. That was what they meant by a 'bulldog'. The mutt grabs hold of your trouser cuff and he just won't let go. No matter that a big chunk of the names went unsolved on their white board at HQ. He just kept coming, so who was she to tell him to back off, cease and desist? They had other cases on their plate, but this was the case.

On her few off hours, Mara liked to go to a book shop on Clark Street and drink espresso and read science fiction. She loved Arthur C. Clarke and Philip K. Dick. She admired imagination, and sci-fi let her escape from the gravity of the real and mostly ugly planet Earth. Off she went to alien worlds and dimensions, and the escape was refreshing and invigorating. It was nothing like the mundane, grim environment that she lived and worked in, picking up the remains of killers and sadists.

She also had to admit to herself that she found one of the baristas to her liking. He was about her own age, and he seemed to sport a special smile for Mara as he asked for her order. She went for the espresso every time, but he let her tell him her order anyway.

"Too much caffeine," he grinned.

He was tall and thin and had a bedraggled mustache and goatee. His eyes were gray, though, and the unique color caught her attention the first time she saw him in Del's Books. Mara had no idea who Del was or if there were an actual Del.

The name on his ID read Sam.

The book store was virtually deserted. It was one of the reasons she enjoyed going there when she was off shift.

Mara waited as he filled her order. There was but one lonesome-looking senior male sitting at a table by the window that looked out onto Clark Street.

"Are you guys going to be able to stay open much longer?" she asked him as he placed her drink on the counter.

"Why do you ask?" he smiled.

"You're not exactly overrun, are you."

He snorted.

"That's because you only come in at night. We're jammed at breakfast and lunch. It's always slow at night. Too many barflies in this neighborhood, and we don't supply their alcohol fix. But caffeine seems necessary in the morning after they've wasted themselves on debauchery the night before."

She laughed in reply.

"Debauchery?"

"You're young. You must understand the need for buzz time. Caffeine in the morning to spark you up, and booze in the PM to put you to sleep."

"Excuse me for asking, but is the bookstore full-time for you?" she queried.

"I'm finishing my master's in psychology at Northwestern, as a matter of fact. Hope to do my PhD there starting next fall, and I've got a teaching assistant's position in place starting next autumn. Hope to be a full-time psychologist whenever I finish up my dissertation. So, no, this is not my life's work."

She smiled.

"I hope you don't feel like I'm interrogating you."

"And what are you doing to save the planet?" he retorted.

"I'm a detective."

His eyebrows shot up.

"No you're not."

Mara dug in her purse and pulled out the badge.

"Homicide, actually."

"You're too young, aren't you?"

"I'm older than you think, then."

"Wow."

"Wow?"

"Yes, wow."

"I'm a quick study. Went from patrol to Burglary to Homicide in eight years."

"You're a prodigy."

"My name's Mara, by the way."

"Sam," he replied and pointed to his ID.

"Who the hell is Del?" she grinned.

"The owner. He's in and out. That's him by the window."

She looked over at the old man reading *The New Yorker* magazine.

"Isn't he ready for retirement, yet?" she asked.

"His son wants to sell the store. Maybe he'll find someone who'll keep the ambiance alive, here...I don't suppose you have time for the mating ritual."

She laughed, and Del looked over at them from the window with a scowl.

"You mean dating?" she asked him.

"I suppose that's what I mean."

"Are you proposing we begin the mating dance here and now?"

"You like movies?"

"Sure."

"Want to take one in when you're free?"

"I have a strange schedule, but I suppose I could slip one in on my next day off, which just happens to be Sunday."

It was Friday night in late August, and there was no hint that the tropical weather was going to give in to the cool of fall and September.

"I just happen to be off Sunday night. Who'd a thunk it?"

"Call me and let me know what time. Sam."

She borrowed a ballpoint from the barista and wrote her phone number on a napkin with Del's monogram on it.

Sam smiled, and Mara thought she noticed the slightest blush in his pale cheeks. Then he flashed her his gray eyes again.

"Only wolves have gray eyes," she told him.

"I get that a lot. But the full moon does absolutely nothing for me, and it took me two years to grow this failure of a mustache and goatee. I'm thinking of shaving, and to hell with it."

"Let it stay. It goes with your face."

Mara perceived another slight coloration on his cheeks.

"Are you able to tell me what you're investigating at work?"

"I guess I can trust you. We're looking for a man they call the Coast to Coast killer."

His eyebrows shot up again.

"I read about him in the *Sun Times*. How many women?"

"Twenty, that we know about."

"And I read that the FBI is after him, too."

"You're the wanna-be shrink. Who do you think he is?"

"He sounds like he fits the sociopath characterization. No feelings, no emotions. Maybe a dose of narcissism, as well. Hard to tell without actually talking to him. They do studies at Quantico, I've read."

"Been there."

"Wow, again."

"It's standard, pretty much for Homicide detectives. We run into the breed, now and then."

"I've read they get away with it more often than other murderers. Right?"

"The only people I ever seem to talk shop with are other cops."

"I'm sorry. You must be tired of going over what you do every day."

Del looked over at Mara and Sam and seemed to be snarling.

"I'm sorry," she laughed. "I seem to be loitering."

Her espresso had gone cold by now.

"Let me get you another, on the house," he apologized.

"That's okay. I've got to be going. I'll warm it up at home."

"I'll call you about that movie. Sunday night, right?"

She stared at him.

"I can't believe I just got picked up at a bookstore. How often do you think that happens?"

She picked up her drink. It had a sipping lid on it.

"Still pretty hot...Call me."

Then she walked to the door, stopped, and peered down at Del.

"Don't lose that young man. He's very personable."

Del looked up at her and huffed, and then Mara went out the door.

●　　　●　　　●　　　●　　　●

"You look happy. What's up?" Nick asked as they headed back to the neighborhood they were scouring for Murphy.

"Didn't I look happy before?"

"Cut the crap, Red. You look pronouncedly jubilant. So tell me."

"I had a date, last night."

"You're not joining the nunnery after all."

"No one likes a wiseguy, Nick."

"You lost your pale. Is it love?"

"We went to the movies."

"Did he become amorous?"

"None of your damn business!"

"You're lovely when you're aroused."

"I'm easy, aren't I."

"Mara, I'm happy for you. It's about time. How many kids are the two of you planning on?"

"Jesus. Let's get to work."

They got out of the Crown Vic. Mara took the west side of the street and Nick took the east. This was the ninth consecutive tour that they spent the first half of their watch going from building to building in search of a killer with hair as black as his soul. It didn't help that the heat was beyond oppressive.

They retreated to the ride after each block and sat in front of the air conditioning until they were somewhat revived. Nick brought along a cooler packed with ice and Cokes. They greedily sucked the bottles dry after every finished block.

They were on days, so Nick figured they'd devote the mornings to searching for Randall. They worked their other cases in the PM until their tours were over.

Another day passed without a sighting. Nick began to think that his resolve might be decaying. There were some cases that simply got away from you. No one got them all done with a happy ending. No one. Maybe he was a perfectionist, but he couldn't imagine going at his job any other way.

He'd come on strong in front of Mara so she wouldn't lose heart this early in her career, but the redhead was no dummy. She knew that the deck wasn't always going to play out in your favor. Some things were simply not meant to be. Like those goofy characters in that sci-fi book she described. The little plumber's helpers' guys who sailed the universe and could not believe that Earthlings were dumb enough to believe in anything other than fate. Bugs in amber, she'd told Nick. It might be nuts enough to be true.

•   •   •   •   •

After they'd finished the afternoon half of their tour, and after making one satisfying bust of a drive-by shooter who'd killed a six-year-old boy on the west side, they took dinner break to finish off their last hour of the days' shift. To make Mara happy, he drove them to Standby's Grill near the Lake. It was moderately priced for something as close to the water as it was, and she could order healthy food there. Meaning stuff colored green that didn't have parents.

So, naturally, she ordered a medium rare sirloin steak and an order of onion rings. It sounded right to Nick, so he chose the same thing.

The place wasn't swank, but it was clean. There were no empty booths or tables, so Karras figured Standby's was doing something right.

"We're running out of city blocks," she told him as she sipped her Coke.

Nick had hooked her on the caramel-colored dose of sugar and caffeine. It was too hot to think about coffee.

"Indeed," Nick concurred. "But something will pop. Trust me."

He sat across from his partner in a booth with a table covered in white cloth.

The glasses were sweating, even inside in the air conditioning. The cubes seemed to dissipate a little too quickly.

"Do you really think it will, Nick?" she smiled somberly.

"Would I lie to you?"

She laughed.

"It's the job, Red. You have to learn to get back up when you get kicked on your ass. You have to get back up when the bell rings between rounds. You get hit pretty often, and you live with your bruises. You have to harden yourself to the dead, especially when they're kids, like today. Six fucking years old, and this brain-dead sprays the corner, misses his real target, but the boy is still dead anyway.

"When I was in Korea, I tried to learn to live with the shit we all saw. Don't worry. No old war stories. I won't waste your time, kid. You see shit no one should see, but it's there even when you turn away from it. Part of the job. It's like building callouses when you swing a sledge or a baseball bat. And then there are people who can't seem to harden their hearts. Totally understandable. And they come home and cut their wife's throat because it's just way too much to absorb and then endure.

"Am I lightening up your day, Red?"

She looked down at her empty plate. She picked up her drink and finished it.

"There really can't be a God," she whispered. "Who'd make this kind of fucking mess?"

"Maybe there really are those plumber's helpers' guys. I can picture them now, the way you described them to me. Maybe I should read the books."

"The guy who wrote them survived the Dresden firebomb raids in World War II. He was stuck in a meat locker."

"Yeah?"

"He was an atheist. Guess he preferred plumbers' helpers."

"I baptized Gus. Isn't that a hoot?"

"You baptized your own kid?"

"The Catholics say any Christian can baptize another Christian."

"So, you're hedging your bets," Mara smiled.

"Something like that. What the hell can it harm?"

She looked at her partner sadly.

"Yeah, what can it harm?"

CHAPTER THIRTY

Gus had a cough and Nora took the day off from the art studio to watch him. They wanted to bring him to Elgin for the visit, but they were worried about bringing the virus or the bacteria into the hospital with them. Nick went alone and walked into Penelope's room. There was no sense in bringing flowers because she wouldn't notice them, of course.

"Any news?" he asked the blonde nurse.

She looked fifty and had some mileage on her face from working in a mental institution.

The nurse shook her head with a sad smile, and she left Karras alone with his daughter.

He sat next to her bed. She was lying, as always, on her side, facing him.

"We were going to bring your little brother to see you, but he's got a cold or something. We'll bring him next time, when he's better."

Her eyes were closed. Her breathing was regular. It was the only sound emanating from Penelope.

The anxiety that came from the visits was beginning to ratchet up. The way it always did.

"We're looking for the man who did this to you. We think he's still in the city, and I'm going to find him, honey, so he can't hurt anybody again. We've had some leads and we're going to get him. I feel sure of it."

If she couldn't hear him anyway, what was the harm of lying to his daughter? He felt no confidence at all that they were going to arrest Randall Murphy in the near future or any time after that.

"Nora sends her love. The baby's getting huge. He'll be a big boy. Must come from Nora's side of the family. We're all short, on our side. You're more like your mother, tall and slender. You're still beautiful, Penelope.

"Nora said you were in there trying to come out. I want to be here the moment you do. Don't give up on it. We're waiting to get you back. Don't let this bastard steal your life, honey. Please don't. He will never hurt you again, I swear to Christ. Just don't give up. I pray for you all the time.

"Isn't that a laugh? Me praying? When did I ever walk into a church? Hell, I'd burst into flames. Your old man in a church. If I thought it'd do any good, I would have gone every week since...

"I'd do anything to see your eyes again. I swear it. Light candles, anything. Just don't stay in there forever, Penelope. Don't."

His eyes began to sting.

Then her fingers seemed to move just slightly, and he thought he saw her eyelids quiver electrically.

"Honey?"

This time the flutter of her lids was definite. He wanted to call for the nurse, but he couldn't move.

Penelope opened her eyes and moaned.

He reached for her hand and gripped it tightly. He could feel pressure being returned. Her eyes seemed out of focus, glazed, but she was blinking and he could see them scanning his face tentatively.

She moaned once more.

"Are you thirsty? Do you want something? Want me to call the nurse?"

The stinging in his eyes evolved to free flow. He didn't want to weep and sob and scare the hell out of her.

"You see me, Penelope? Do you know me?"

She squeezed his hand more firmly and tried to say something to him.

"Let me get the nurse, honey."

"No."

The answer made him tremble.

"No," she said again.

"All right. Okay. I'm not going anywhere."

"Where?" she asked.

"You're here. In the hospital."

Her eyes were fully focused on him now.

"Where?"

"The hospital. Elgin. You've been here a long time. I thought we'd never..."

She squeezed his hand harder.

"Thirsty. I'm thirsty."

There was a pitcher of water and a plastic cup by the window.

He poured a half-glass and put the lid on so he could insert a straw.

Nick brought the cup near to her lips and guided the straw into her mouth. Penelope took a tug at the water.

Then she looked at him intently. Focused on him squarely.

"Daddy?"

"Jesus Christ," he whispered.

"Jesus?"

He bent over and kissed her on the forehead.

"How long?" she asked again.

"Doesn't matter, Penelope. It doesn't matter."

He kissed her on the forehead again.

"What...What day is it?"

"Saturday. It's Saturday. It's September. It's very hot outside."

"September? Hot?"

The blonde nurse entered the room.

"Who?" Penelope asked her father.

"Her name is Myra. She's your nurse."

"Oh my good God!" Myra blurted.

Karras looked at Myra.

"This is my daughter, Penelope, Myra."

Myra looked a bit unsteady, but her professional demeanor took over and she straightened up.

"Penelope," Myra uttered.

"I'm hungry. Thirsty, too."

Karras gave her some more water out of the cup with the red straw.

"I'll go get the doctor right away. He won't believe it. He just won't."

Myra looked a bit misty in the eyes.

"He will not believe it."

The nurse bolted out of the room.

"Think you can sit up?" he asked Penelope.

She nodded faintly.

He helped her up and arranged the pillows to support her head and back.

"I'm hungry. Starved."

They'd been feeding her using intravenous tubes, of course. But she'd been breathing on her own, at least.

He hadn't released her hand until he helped her sit up.

"Need to go."

"You want me to help you?"

"You better," she told him.

He pulled back her covers and lifted her off the bed. She was light, a featherweight. She'd never been heavy a day in her life.

He took her into the bathroom and got her onto the toilet. There were bars on either side that she could grip to steady herself. When she was in position and after he'd helped her raise her gown, Penelope took hold of the bars and steadied herself.

"You good to go on your own?"

"Don't leave. Maybe. Turn around…I'm okay, but stay in here with me."

He heard the flow, and then it stopped.

"Okay. You better help," she said.

He lifted her off the commode and carried her back to bed just as the doctor and the nurse, Myra, entered the room.

The doctor's nametag read 'McGann'. He looked as Irish as his redheaded partner, Mara. But he had sandy-brown hair. He was young, couldn't have been far past thirty-five, Karras decided.

"Penelope?" McGann asked.

She looked to Nick, again.

"I'm Dr. McGann. I'm your doctor—one of them."

"Daddy?" she asked Nick.

"It's okay. He's your doctor. It's okay."

Penelope snuck a look at McGann, and then at Myra.

"I'm hungry," she told them both.

"I can imagine," McGann smiled. "We're not going to be able to start you off on steak and potatoes, I'm afraid, but you'll get there."

"I like tacos."

"You're going to have to build up to that stuff, Penelope. But Myra can get you something you can handle and we'll go from there."

McGann looked at Nick, studying him.

"Maybe we could talk while she's eating, Mr. Karras."

Nick didn't correct him about the 'mister'.

They waited until Myra came back in with a bowl of light brown broth and some orange juice in a plastic cup with a straw.

Then Karras went out with the psychiatrist and walked into his office in the adjoining wing.

He motioned for Nick to sit opposite him.

"I cannot imagine what you're feeling, about now."

"*I* can't imagine what I'm thinking right now."

McGann smiled in response.

"Things like this just don't happen. Rarely or never, as a matter of fact. Your daughter was catatonic, as you know. I'm as amazed as you are. But I'm sure happy that she fooled us all.

"But this is just a first step. A huge first step, but she'll have a lot of therapy to endure before you can bring her home."

"Bring her home?" Nick asked.

"I don't see why not, some day. But there's a lot of work to be done before that happens."

Now Nick let it happen, and the waterworks flooded his face and he couldn't hold back the sobs that he'd held back in Penelope's room. McGann handed him a box of tissues.

"Let 'er rip," the doctor comforted him.

After the squall subsided, Nick was back.

"She was raped and mutilated," McGann said. "I know you're well aware of the details. You're a policeman, right?"

"Homicide detective, yes."

"I've been told the man who did this might be that killer everyone's looking for. What do they call him? The Coast to Coast killer?"

"Yes."

"So, it's very personal with you."

"Yes, it is."

McGann hesitated. Nick was waiting for him to whip out the professorial pipe, but it didn't happen.

"Have you ever considered therapy for yourself, Detective?"

"I've had therapy after two shootings I was involved in. They cleared me to go back to work."

"I mean therapy for what happened with your daughter."

"I've been too busy looking for the motherfucker who did this to my kid."

Nick's swarthy face turned a shade darker.

"I understand."

"No, you don't," Nick shot back.

"I'm sorry. You're right. I really don't."

"I apologize, Doctor. You didn't deserve that."

McGann raised his hands to waive it off.

"Would you consider getting a little help? Because when she does get out of here, if she does, you're going to need some help in dealing with her recovery. She'll never wipe out what this man did. She'll have to learn to live with it and learn not to let it take control of her life from now on. You'll need some tools of your own to help her.

"I wish I could tell you she'll be recovered in a short time, but her trauma was massive, as you already understand. She might not have to stay here, but she'll need in- patient help for a substantial period.

"I know you want to take her with you when you leave, but I'm sure you understand this is something like her rebirth. She's going to have to re-learn a lot of things before she's ready to be on her own.

"That being said, don't let me dampen this moment. Are you religious, Detective?"

"Not guilty."

McGann smiled.

"Then you don't buy into miracles."

"Not until recently."

"I don't know if 'miracle' is the right word because I'm a scientist, but I hope I'm not dumb enough to think I have an answer for everything because I know my limitations. Certainly, there are surprises, now and then. People fool you. They teach you to avoid assumptions.

"Anyway. Go back to your daughter's room and spend some time. She'll be here for a while, yet, and I know you'll want to visit her more frequently. It must have been heart-breaking, until today."

Nick rose and shook hands with the psychiatrist.

"What?" Nora asked.

She was holding Gus and feeding him a bottle.

When he clamped onto the two of them, his wife cried out.

He let them go and stepped back, here in their kitchenette.

"It's Penelope," Nora said.

Nick nodded but started to cry again.

"She's back again," Nora said.

Karras couldn't talk.

"Can I tell you 'I told you so' now?" his wife beamed.

He grabbed hold of two-thirds of his family.

"Will she be coming home soon?" Nora asked.

"The doctor said it'll be a while before they can release her."

Tears began to meander down his wife's cheeks.

"We'll need a bigger place to live, Nick. We better start looking."

CHAPTER THIRTY-ONE

She'd felt Penelope struggling to rise. Nora hadn't told Nick the extent of her 'gift', however. Everyone had secrets. She supposed her husband hadn't told her everything about his past, especially about the years with his first wife. Some things are kept dark and hidden. Some things you don't tell a priest or an analyst or your best friend or your spouse. Families do indeed have skeletons clanking in closets, and sometimes they're best left undisturbed.

Nora felt it was purely genetic, this thing she had that most others did not. Second sight, insight, whatever it really was. It was passed down into the generations that followed. And occasionally generations were skipped over. So it was, with Nora's mother. It was her grandmother, Yianna, who lived near Athens in a town called Plaka. Yianna died in the United States, and Nora's father and mother had been immigrants to America back in the Great Depression. Yianna lived long enough to be a permanent memory for Nora. She'd survived until a few weeks after Nora's twelfth birthday.

They were close. Yianna's husband, Peter, died in the granddaughter's infancy, so Nora never knew him. Yianna spent considerable time with the young girl, and it was from her grandmother that she learned about this legacy that Nora had inherited from her. It was a way of seeing things that were not visible to the eye.

But there was more than just this exceptional sight, more than these mystical-like visions that occurred to both of them from time to time. And the events were never summoned consciously by either of them. They arrived unannounced. And when they were emotionally aroused or disturbed by something, there was something else.

They both could make someone who caused them emotional distress feel pain or discomfort. Occasionally they could cause the source of their arousal to suffer injury. Yianna and Nora had never had occasion to cause permanent damage or death to anyone. But they were able to vanquish anyone who seemed to want to harm them seriously, emotionally or physically.

Fortunately, they hadn't had a reason to unleash what they might have been able to if circumstances warranted retaliation. Yianna taught Nora that she must control that darker 'gift' she was given. Her grandmother had struggled all her life to keep it leashed, and she had been mostly successful. It was the granddaughter's obligation to keep what she might be able to do in check. There had been times, especially in high school, when she felt it necessary to let it come forth, but Yianna's warning had prevented her, each time. Teenaged girls were very capable of bringing out violence from their classmates, but mostly it was all talk. Nora learned to let it go and to make strategic retreats when anyone aimed their bile at her.

There was also the constant fear that she might let her abilities overcome her reason, and then there'd be punishment to endure. Nora always wondered how far it might go if she were properly provoked.

Nick had certainly given her no reason to let the Gorgon loose. He was loving and gentle in spite of his profession. She could understand why cops took to booze and drugs and why they had such a high rate of divorce and suicide. Homicide was a brutal job to endure. They dealt with the worst crime of all, taking a life. But he never took home his work. He rarely even discussed it. But she knew he was hung up on this latest case with Randall Murphy. She wondered if Mara Crosby shared his obsession. She knew that Homicide detectives lived with their work twenty-four-seven. It wasn't like chasing after car thieves or busting prostitutes. It was a different species altogether.

Yet he never aimed his frustration or anger at her, nor did he take it out on Gus when he woke up yelling with an upset tummy at 3:00 AM when Nick was on days.

Nora knew you were supposed to be forthright with your husband. But there were limits to complete disclosure. He kept the sordid details to himself about the man who maimed his daughter Penelope. Penelope who'd been trapped in her own dark labyrinth for years because of the horror she'd gone through. His daughter was facing years, perhaps, of further therapy.

She wondered how she would have reacted if Murphy had found her on some dark avenue. Might she have summoned it up and hurled it at this Coast to Coast killer? Wasn't he worthy of any wrath she could unleash at him?

Yianna made it through her life by rarely summoning up hell against anyone. Her grandmother warned her that a red rage could be destructive not only to another but also to herself.

"You are not a monster," her grandmother told her when she was ten. "You cannot allow yourself to become such a beast. It would make you like the evil one, and you cannot have him inside you."

Then why did it dwell inside them both? Nora wondered. If it was not meant to be used, then why were they both equipped with this dark gift?

It wasn't a parlor game. It wasn't like bending spoons with your concentration, without touching the spoon. It wasn't telekinesis, hurling objects into the ceiling. It was worse than those magic tricks that you might see on TV late at night on a talk show when the hosts ran out of Hollywood celebrities.

It wasn't magic and it wasn't a game. She couldn't bend inanimate objects or lift dishes and silverware off the table. It was not entertainment.

Nora and Yianni could somehow slip inside someone who was threatening them or enraging them and assault their nervous systems with great pain, crippling pain. It's what Yianna warned the little girl she *could* do but should never allow herself to do.

How would Nora explain all that to her husband? Nick was barely able to accept that she had impressions about other people that went beyond logic and science. What Yianna had told her was something she could not share with anyone. If she told Nick about it, how could he sleep in the same bed with her at night wondering if his wife was about to let it out of its cage?

Some are born with perfect pitch, an uncanny ability to detect a sour note in music. Some can play musical instruments by ear, not being able to read a note on the score sheet. Others are gifted by 'seeing' mathematics in their heads. No one sees anything paranormal in those exceptional instincts. Drifting into another's soul is something altogether different.

She'd felt the absolute loneliness of Karen Manski in the dead girl's apartment. Nick never brought her to a crime scene again. Perhaps he understood the chill it sent throughout Nora when she walked into that killing room. She would leave it there and not mention it to him again. She hadn't been able to sense anything about Randall Murphy. He was nothing, non-existent. He was empty, a vacuum. No human being was inside that flesh, as far as Nora could sense.

Everyone has secrets, things they bury inside themselves where no one can find them. Everyone has sins that are so completely black that they cannot summon them to the surface, into the light.

So far, Nora had done what her grandmother had commanded her to do for her own well-being and safety. She'd kept her silent monster at bay. She wasn't a killer like Randall Murphy. She could not harm another unless it was absolutely self-defense. Nora didn't believe in God, not the God that Yianna believed in in the Orthodox faith. But there were right and wrong—that much was immutable.

Nora picked Gus up just after he awoke in his crib in their bedroom. If they bought a house, Gus could have his own room, and now that Penelope returned, Nick's daughter would need a place to stay once her therapy concluded. Nora made it clear that Penelope was welcome to live with them until she could live independently.

"Gus, you got something special about you? You carrying a secret inside you, too?"

The toddler burped and then smiled as she held him in her arms.

"You got some Grandma Yianna in you? I hope it passed you over. It's no bargain."

Gus burped and frowned.

"It's overrated, being special. Believe me. Happy is far better."

She placed the bottle to his lips and he took the nipple greedily.

"Maybe you'll be a policeman, like your dad. He gets the bad guys. Some of the time."

She stopped and burped him before he chugged the entire thing down.

"Maybe you'll be a college professor. Live with ideas instead of chasing bad guys...Maybe we can take you to Grandma Yianna's village. Plaka, right next to Athens. She used to tell me about the blue doors on the white houses and about the narrow brick streets and about the marketplace where they sold everything. Like feta, the goat's cheese. Everyone greeted you with a *ti kaneis*—It means 'how are you?' There were fishermen in the marketplace displaying their catch.

"I've never been there, never been to Greece, and neither has daddy.

"No, I hope it's passed you by, what Grandma Yianna and I have. I hope you're the most average, normal, happy little boy ever. That's what your mama hopes."

•   •   •   •   •

Nick came home a few hours later after his days shift.

He found Gus crawling on the floor as Nora watched him with a smile. Gus made his way over to the couch as his father watched, and then the boy hoisted himself up, turned around in a 180, and took three tentative steps toward his father before he flopped to the plush carpet.

They found a possible dwelling on the northwest side. Nick had to live in the city or forfeit his job. It was the way it worked with the police. You had to reside locally. Some guys lived in the 'burbs and gave the department one of their relative's city addresses, but Karras preferred to be honest about his location. And he had a pension to think about, as well.

It was a ranch with three bedrooms. There was a finished basement without tell-tale signs of water damage, and that was a plus to them both. The present owners were 'motivated', the real estate agent told them.

That meant they'd consider a lower price.

Gus was on his best behavior, and the boy brightened considerably when they walked out into a spacious backyard with a six-foot chain link fence enclosing it.

The real estate agent was a middle-aged woman with short strawberry blonde hair. She appeared to be a bit weary because it was late afternoon, about 4:30. She told them she had three more showings that evening. Her name was Angela.

"I think we can get them down to your price range," Angela said, out in the clean-cut lawn of the yard. "They're moving to Tampa/St. Pete as soon as they can unload this place. He and she are both retired. They both worked at GE for thirty years. They're looking to buy a condo and they both play golf."

Gus smiled.

"Gas," she told Nick.

Angela giggled. It sounded a bit forced. She was wearing heels and her dogs were probably barking.

"You're a policeman?" she asked Nick.

He nodded.

"They'll be happy to have a cop in the neighborhood."

"If they don't kill each other."

Angela looked at Karras strangely. He didn't explain his specific role in the CPD.

"He works in Homicide," Nora finally informed the agent.

"Oh...Oh! Are you involved in that serial killer case?"

"You say they're motivated?" Nick asked Angela.

"Oh, yes. Very. They want to go south before winter arrives. You know. Hit the beaches and the links. They'll be living their dream."

"How old is the roof?" Karras asked.

"They replaced it just five years ago."

"How about the furnace?" he queried.

"New, four years ago. Central air—I think I already told you that."

"You did, right," Nora added. "How much does the electric bill go? You said there was natural gas for the heat, right?"

Angela was staring at Nick.

"I thought I saw your picture in the *Tribune*," Angela went on. "It said you were the detective on that serial killer thing. Now I remember your name, Karras."

Angela's white face began to color.

"I'm sorry. You don't like to talk shop."

"Everybody's got their own stuff they don't like to talk about," Nora grinned.

•   •   •   •   •

They made an offer, and the GE couple accepted on the first try. They signed the papers a week later after Nick secured the loan from the bank. They got a break because they were first-time buyers. The monthly payments were steep, but do-able.

"The overtime on Murphy finally paid off," Nick told his wife as they moved in in October.

Gus was at the daycare center at the Methodist church where they'd enrolled him once Nora went back to work at the art studio. Gus loved the other kids, and Nick and Nora especially liked the variety of races of the children who went there. They took in everyone, regardless of skin tone.

Nick and Nora thought it would be good for Gus to avoid a monochrome environment.

They liked the hardwood floors, and the house had already been treated for termites. Nothing demanded immediate repairs, and the apartment had been too cramped after Gus arrived.

• • • • •

"So how do you like your new casa?" Nick asked her as they lay in bed.

"Love it...Nick?"

"Yeah?"

"You think people should keep secrets between them?"

"Are you having an affair at work?" he laughed.

She slapped his bare chest.

"I'm not having an affair with Mara. She looks at me and thinks 'grandpa'."

"I'm not kidding around. You think people should keep secrets?"

"What kind of secrets?"

"You know. Stuff you wouldn't tell a shrink."

He peered over at her.

"You're a Soviet spy, right?"

She slapped his chest again.

"Christ, you made a red mark."

"Do you tell me everything, Nick?"

"I already told you nothing's happening with Mara, and she's been going out with some guy from a bookstore—"

"Be serious for one minute. Okay?"

"Ask me anything."

She studied his eyes.

"I just don't want you to think I'm holding out on you."

"What would you be holding out about?" he grinned.

"You already know about my weird thing."

"The second sight."

"Yeah. I know you think it's a little nuts."

"You're the sanest woman I ever knew."

"I'm not a Soviet spy. It's nothing like that."

"Too bad. The idea was kind of a turn-on, Comrade."

"You can ask me anything, too, you know."

"I know everything about you, my love, and it's all good."

He kissed her and drew her to him.

"I know all there is to know about you, Nora, my love."

CHAPTER THIRTY-TWO

When a few of his fellow mechanics started to eye him cautiously, Murphy knew it was time to move on. He quit on a Friday in September, took his check and cashed it at a check-cashing service a half-block from the auto shop. His boss watched him closely as he picked up his last paycheck, and he hurried out the door to get his money. He couldn't very well use a standard bank because they all had his poster glued to their walls.

He got back to the apartment, but he didn't tell Theresa he was unemployed again. It was hardly a good idea to tell her why, so he kept it to himself. The problem with Theresa was that he was tiring of her talking about commitment and about deepening their relationship. Murphy enjoyed fucking her, but listening to her was becoming boring. The reason he was bored was because he had to refrain from choking the bitch and slicing off her ample nipples. The whole idea of living with her was to hide in place without drawing attention to himself, so if he killed her, he'd have to get rid of the body, and the neighbors were used to seeing her come and go.

Murphy figured that those neighbors thought that the two of them were a couple, by now. If he took her out, his refuge was gone. So, he allowed them to think they were both a tranquil domestic pair living in what passed for bliss.

"You're home early, aren't you?" Theresa smiled at him.

"It's six. Why's that early?" he snapped.

"Had a bad day?"

They sat at the kitchenette table while she began preparing a meal.

"What are you making?" he asked.

"Meatloaf."

"I hate that crap."

She dropped a spoon on top of the stove with a clang.

"What is wrong with you, Pat?"

"There's nothing fucking wrong with me."

"You want to go out to eat?"

"No, I don't want to go out!"

"You never want to go out anywhere with me. Are you ashamed to be seen with me?"

He laughed.

She turned off the burner on the stove and dumped the sauce pan into the sink.

"Did something happen at work?" she demanded.

"I got fired. That's what happened."

"I'm sorry, Pat. I—"

"I'm not sorry, and will you just lay the fuck off me?"

Murphy got up from his chair and slammed it into the table.

He wanted to leave her and the apartment, but he had no idea where to go and little cash to go anywhere. He felt confined, trapped.

"You don't need to talk to me like that," she spat at him.

"Talking's not your strong suit. You only have the one talent."

He looked toward the bedroom.

"Get out! Get your shit and get out!"

He stepped toward her aggressively, and fear took over her face.

"You don't tell me to do anything. You know that, don't you, Theresa? I leave when I want to. You hear me?"

His hands were clenched at his sides.

"I've never seen you like this," she whispered.

"Here I am."

"I want you to leave. I'll call the police."

He unclenched his hands.

"I'm sorry...I don't know why I was saying all that to you. You know I don't mean any of it, baby. Don't you?"

She watched him carefully.

"You had no call to talk to me like that."

"No, you're right. I'm sorry, baby."

"I've been good to you."

"I know. I said I'm sorry."

"Don't take your shit out on me again, okay?"

"I won't. I promise."

"You can look for a new job, a better one."

"You're right. I will."

He moved toward her, and Theresa flinched slightly.

"C'mon. Let me make it up to you. Please."

"Then take me out somewhere. To a movie. To eat. I don't care, but we've been cooped up in here for weeks."

Murphy didn't see any options remaining for him.

•   •   •   •   •

He wore a Cubs baseball cap and dark sunglasses. When they got to Luigi's Italian Restaurant two blocks from the apartment, he took off the cap and left the shades on. He tried to will himself into invisibility. No one seemed to notice either of them when they walked in. The restaurant was half-occupied, but it was quiet, and everyone else seemed oblivious to the two of them.

A waitress seated them in a booth in the back. There were no other customers near them.

Luigi's was comfortable and laid back. The music from overhead was muted and sounded like an elevator's greatest hits. Mostly it was Dean Martin and Frank Sinatra accompanied by sentimental-sounding strings.

"See? Is this so awful?" she smiled.

"You're right, and I'm still sorry for yelling at you, Theresa."

He wouldn't have found an apartment with the scrawny final check he cashed from the auto shop. She was paying for the rent and the utilities and the food. What the fuck was he thinking when he exploded at her? If he could just outwait the CPD and the feds when they tired of looking for him, he'd make a move.

Maybe he could talk her into putting his name on her checks and bank account. He could propose to her, marry her in Vegas, say, where he could play fast and loose with the paperwork. A civil ceremony would convince her to share the wealth. Then he'd take care of her when they flew back to Chicago. Find some slough to dump her in, maybe Lake Michigan off one of the piers in the middle of the night.

Then he'd be free. He could buy another rig. He'd seen her bank statement after she'd left it opened on the kitchen table. Theresa had about fifty grand socked in a savings account, and another thirty K in certificates of deposit. She apparently saved every nickel she ever made. And here he was, a few hours ago, ready to kill the golden goose. What was he thinking?

He ordered some red wine and he refilled her glass three times before their meal was consumed.

"What would you think about marrying me?"

She almost choked on her wine.

"What?"

"I'm serious. You know I love you. I was just all pent up from getting canned. You know that, right? Haven't we got along good, up until that? I know what a good thing I've got in you, Theresa, and I'll make it up to you. I swear I will. You know what a good thing *we've* got. Don't let that one thing tear us down, because I love you.

"Where did you think we were headed, baby? I can't see living without you. You understand that? Let's get married. Take a flight out of O'Hare tonight and go to Vegas and make it legal. This'll be my chance to make it up to you, so you can forgive me for being an asshole."

Her eyes seemed a little hazy, and then a few droplets came loose and dribbled onto her cheeks.

"You can't ever talk to me like that again."

"I won't. I swear it, Theresa. Let's leave tonight."

He poured her another glass of the red.

• • • • •

They took a late flight out of O'Hare for Sin City, and an hour after they arrived at the Hotel Vegas, they found a JP and they were married. The JP never asked for his ID or for hers. He looked pretty ripped, and Murphy gave him a twenty for a tip.

They stayed overnight and then took an afternoon flight back to Chicago. It was Saturday, but Theresa had to be back to work on Monday.

When they got back to the apartment, he began to undress her immediately. Anything that might have lingered with his eruption at her had disappeared by now and they were back to the way they'd been up until Murphy had lost his job.

He undid her bra and her great breasts seemed to jump out at him. He got on his knees and pulled down her skirt after he'd unzipped it in the back. Theresa moaned, and then he pulled down her panties and buried his face in her nest. She moaned again.

Murphy stood, and she knelt down and undid his belt and pants and pulled down his shorts and took him in her mouth.

• • • • •

He waited two weeks. It was mid-October.

"Why don't we sign up for a joint account? You could put my name on everything, and that would make it easier to take care of the money."

He found a job as a night watchman on a used car lot. It wasn't much money, but it made her feel like he was trying to carry his own weight.

Their sex had been even more volcanic than it was before, even in the beginning when he'd picked her up at the supermarket. He was doting, sweet. The complete reversal of the savage he'd become when he jumped all over her, just before his reversal and Vegas.

He made her cry out when she went into her throes. Murphy was concerned the neighbors might complain, but by now everyone in the building knew they were man and wife. Theresa made it her business to tell all the neighbors.

"Sure. It would make it more convenient, Pat."

"I'll start depositing my checks in our account. Maybe I can throw a few bucks into savings and we can buy a few more CDs, huh?"

"For our retirement...You like Florida?"

"Only been there twice."

One Hispanic bitch, and one white cunt, he remembered. Six months apart. They were two of his highlights.

The memory aroused him. They were in bed, late at night on a Thursday.

"Oh, what have we here?"

She went down, and Murphy was caught by surprise with her enthusiasm.

Then he mounted her and slammed into her as if he were trying to skewer her into the mattress. She cried out even more loudly than she usually did. He figured they were providing some late-night entertainment for the next- door neighbors. No one had complained about her vocalization, yet.

"We both have to get up early," she murmured.

She was still quivering.

Not for much longer, Murphy said to himself.

•   •   •   •   •

He had to make arrangements to drain her accounts when she wasn't around to suspect him. She'd have to be removed before he emptied her funds—they were legally his, now, since his moniker had been added to her checking and savings and CDs.

The trouble was he'd become addicted to the couplings. In spite of his better judgment, he liked making her yelp and beg and throb and explode against him. When he killed all of the others, the happy ending wasn't nearly as intense as it was now with Theresa who he allowed to survive after each encounter.

What was his hurry? He couldn't come up with a reason to end it just yet. They weren't going out in public, and his job at night kept him from the interested stares that he'd come up against at the auto shop before he walked off the job. The money was accumulating, and Theresa's CDs were pulling in 10%, so what the fuck was he in a hurry about? He was still going to sink her into some water somewhere when he tired of her, finally, so there was no reason to get out when the money was accumulating and while he was getting off watching her writhe beneath him once or twice every night.

No one from the autobody joint had come forth to identify him, it didn't look like. He was in the clear. He could live with Theresa for a little while longer. All good things came to a conclusion. Sooner or later he'd become careless and take her out into public and some pain in the ass bystander would recognize him and then he'd never live to spend Theresa's life savings on the road or wherever he took off for.

Maybe he'd hit Florida again. Or California or Texas or the Pacific Northwest or New England. They'd never be expecting a return tour for the Coast to Coast killer. They probably thought he went underground or that he was dead. Karras was one of those cops who couldn't give it up, but anyone was capable of hitting a dead-end street. He'd become a cold case sooner or later. He'd outlast the Greek cop and that skinny bitch Mick partner of his, Crosby.

He was too slick to get caught, he smiled while Theresa fellated him below the covers.

Then she mounted him and took him astride and she lifted her head back and literally howled like a she-wolf at the rising of the moon.

•   •   •   •   •

He plotted Theresa's demise at the lot where he worked from 10:00 PM to 6:00 AM. They had to schedule their coitus for the evenings before he went to work and for the mornings after he got home and before she left to catch the El for the law office in the Loop.

•   •   •   •   •

Karras was stubborn. Murphy still could feel him coming after all this time. The accepted wisdom was that you didn't go after policemen. It would enrage the rest of the brothers in blue and they would turn the city upside down to find you.

That's if you weren't sly, Murphy figured. They weren't nearly as slick as he was. Look how long he'd roamed free after all those twenty bitches had succumbed to his hands and his steel. How many months had he remained on the loose in spite of pursuit from every police agency in the country?

Was he uncatchable? Was that his so-called narcissism talking or was he as good as he thought he was? The reality was that he was fucking Theresa and had managed his way into her life's savings and was on the verge of sending her wherever all those previous kills were. It was laid out in front of him like a road map. No one could catch him. If they were able, it would have happened by now.

Was he as good as he thought he was, or was it just ill-fated arrogance?

It was money for nothing at the lot where he worked. The nights passed without incident, and he picked up his meagre check on Fridays and deposited them at Theresa's bank.

Where would he really go when he disposed of his new bride? Would he really buy a rig and start it all up again? Perhaps he'd head for new, virgin territory in Canada. Perhaps he might choose the more temperate clime of Mexico. He could learn Spanish, blend in with the natives, the mestizos.

It was all sprawled out before him, like some personal mural on a whitewashed wall.

CHAPTER THIRTY-THREE

Mrs. Harrison lived on the first floor of the apartment building where Theresa Kelly lived. She was happy that Theresa had finally found a boyfriend because the young woman had lived alone for too many years. Mrs. Harrison was spry for an eighty-year-old, but she'd had problems with cataracts, until recently. She had the surgery, and now her vision was better than it had been for twenty-five years. It was amazing what those eye surgeons could do, these days. She still had to wear glasses, but now her vision was clear and sharp. Everything had been a blur before, but now she was able to see the way she had before the doctor miraculously restored her sight.

She'd never been able to see this boyfriend Pat before now. He was a cloud-like mass. Now she could make out his features perfectly. There was something familiar about him. It seemed to Mrs. Harrison that he used to have dark hair, but now she saw that his hair was mousey brown. Maybe he was coloring his locks, but most men didn't go in for that sort of thing, she figured, unless he was a little light in the loafers, but it was pretty obvious he and Theresa were living together, and she doubted Theresa would be harboring a gay roommate.

Television was no comfort to Mrs. Harrison because the picture was all foggy before she'd had her eyes done, and reading the newspapers or magazines was a trial as well, but now she could enjoy TV and she decided to subscribe to the *Tribune.* It was a conservative, Republican paper, and

Mrs. Harrison really liked Ike, although she didn't much care for Nixon. The man's upper lip was always beading with perspiration. There was something shady about him, but she had never voted for a Democrat in her life, even though Chicago was a Democratic city, what with that tub of lard Daley and his terrible henchmen.

The paper had begun to arrive at her building only a day ago, and she felt empowered by her new ability to make out the newsprint clearly. She could listen to television, but it bored her, mostly. Reading was something she always enjoyed before her eyes went bad. Now she read voraciously. She hoped her eyes wouldn't go bad again because of her age, but so far so good. She read everything, from the front page to sports to the comic section.

Today, on the front page, was a story that was meant to revive interest in the murder of a young woman named Karen Manski. There was also mention of a second murder of a young girl named Ellen Prentice. Both were victims of some maniac called the Coast to Coast killer, Randall Murphy. He had seemed to disappear, the article read. It continued on page 17, where there were pictures of the two victims, and below was a rendering of Randall Murphy.

It was a black and white picture, but when Mrs. Harrison looked at the photo of Murphy closely, her jaw literally dropped.

·   ·   ·   ·   ·

Nick received the call around 3:50 PM on a Wednesday in mid-October. It had finally begun to cool down, and the breeze emanated out of the northwest. The sky turned a different color of blue, minus the haze of July and August and early September. It felt like fall, outside, and the cooler temperatures seemed to invigorate everyone in the city.

"This is Detective Karras."

"I've seen him."

The voice on the other end sounded fragile with age.

"Who is this?"

"Mrs. Agnes Harrison."

She gave her address without being asked. Then she recited her telephone number, as well.

"Who've you seen, Agnes?"

"Him."

She sounded a little frightened. There was a tremor in her voice.

"Who, Agnes?"

"That man you've been looking for."

Nick sat up straight. Mara was downstairs in the cafeteria getting them a couple of Cokes.

"And who am I looking for?"

There was silence on the line.

"I'm afraid to tell you. He lives right upstairs with Theresa."

"Theresa who, ma'am?"

"Theresa Kelly."

"Tell me his name, Agnes."

"I think it's that murderer, Randall Murphy."

"Are you sure, Agnes?"

She explained how she'd had cataract surgery, how her eyesight had been poor but how it was clear and how she was able to read the story in the *Tribune* and how she was able to see his face clearly in the picture.

Agnes was almost out of breath.

"Slow down, Agnes. Are you very certain that it's who you say it is?"

"He lives with Theresa Kelly. He's been with her for weeks. I'm frightened for her, and they just got married. She told me all about it when I saw her at the mailboxes a few days ago. She's living with that…thing."

"You just stay inside. Lock your door, and we'll come see you as soon as we can. Can you do that for me, Agnes?"

Agnes Harrison began to whimper.

•   •   •   •   •

Nick caught Mara in the cafeteria as she was paying for the two soft drinks. He didn't need to tell her anything. She read it in his eyes. She dropped the cans of Coke on the counter.

"Hey, you paid for these," the elderly female cashier complained.

"They're on me," Mara shot back.

•   •   •   •   •

Nick called for backup on the way to Mrs. Harrison's building. Two cruisers were going to meet them there.

Karras recounted the phone call for her.

"Woman has cataract surgery and she suddenly recognizes Murphy as her upstairs neighbor?"

"She says the surgery was miraculous," Nick smiled at her.

"How many times have we gone through this prick tease before?" she wondered aloud.

"What if Agnes isn't a dementia patient? What've we got to lose except our late afternoon break?"

"I'm a bit tired of all the foreplay with this bastard. Aren't you?"

"It's nice out. We'll get a little fresh air, now that the oven's been turned off."

They pulled to the curb in front of the address that Agnes gave Karras.

The two cruisers arrived with a pair of uniforms inside each.

All six of them got out of their rides.

"You two go around the back and watch the rear," Nick told one pair of patrolmen. "You two follow us upstairs."

They entered the building. Nick buzzed Agnes Harrison, and she buzzed them in.

They climbed the half-dozen steps to her apartment.

Nick tapped on her door softly. The old lady opened it, but it was still fastened with a chain. Karras showed her ID, and the woman let Mara and Nick inside. The unis waited out in the hallway.

"I'm Detective Karras. We talked on the phone."

The old girl was quivering.

Mara approached her and put an arm around her shoulders.

"You're safe, Agnes," Crosby told her.

Mara showed her their photo of Randall Murphy.

"Is this the man upstairs?" she asked the old woman.

Agnes shot a tiny fist to her mouth.

"Are you sure, Agnes?" Nick asked again.

Agnes nodded.

"It's him. He's been here for weeks, but I never *saw* him before..."

"This patrolman will stay here with you while we go upstairs, Agnes," Mara reassured her.

The uniform came inside. Nick used the handheld to call in for more backup.

"They'll be here in a few minutes," he explained to Mrs. Harrison. "You'll be fine. Is anyone up there?" he asked.

"She doesn't come home until six."

It was 5:30 PM.

"What about him?" Mara asked Agnes.

"He comes and goes at odd hours. I think he works late at night, but I'm not sure. I go to bed around ten."

They waited until the other squads arrived. Mara saw them pull up outside.

"Do you mind if we wait until Theresa Kelly gets home?" Nick asked.

"No, it's all right with me," Agnes replied.

"If he's in there, we'll wait until she arrives. Then we'll let her unlock the door."

Agnes looked at him with a question on her face.

"Maybe no one gets hurt if he thinks it's just Theresa at the door."

Nick went outside and told the other uniforms to park further down the street so that they wouldn't spook Theresa Kelly. Hopefully, Murphy was either asleep or he hadn't taken a peek out the front window. Agnes said he worked nights, so Murphy might not yet be awake.

Nick and Mara and the patrolman waited in the old woman's apartment. It was just past six when they heard someone out in the hall. Nick went to the door and Mara and the uniform followed him.

Theresa Kelly was ascending the stairs when Nick stopped her.

"Ms. Kelly?"

Theresa turned around and saw the three of them below her on the staircase.

Karras showed her his shield.

Her eyebrows elevated.

"What is this?"

"Please step down here, ma'am," Mara said gently.

Kelly descended the several steps.

"What is this? What do you want?"

Nick showed her the by-now famous portrait.

"You know this man?"

Her shock was obvious.

"Is this man your husband?" Nick asked.

"No, that's not Pat. Can't be."

"His name is Randall Murphy. Is this the man you're married to?" Karras asked.

"It can't be him. It cannot be him. No."

Mara stepped toward her and took her arm.

"We want you to unlock the door and let us in. Then you need to go back outside and wait for us."

"Oh my God. It's not Pat. It can't be him. You've made a mistake."

Mara guided her upstairs to her door.

"Please," Crosby whispered. "Unlock it."

Theresa unlocked the entry. Then Mara walked her outside.

Karras turned the door handle and opened it slowly, his service weapon in his right hand. He and the uniform entered, their guns aimed in front of them.

There was no one in the living room. There was no one in the small dining area. They headed for the bedroom, and they found the bed unmade and the sheets disheveled.

No one home.

Nick went out and brought Theresa Kelly back inside. He told the patrolmen to stick around in case Murphy showed up.

Mara and Karras and Theresa Kelly reentered the apartment on the second floor.

Theresa had gone pale and was shaking. Mara sat her down on the couch and then sat next to her. Nick sat in a chair opposite them.

"You know who he is?" Nick asked.

"He's not the man in that picture. I know he's not."

"You've never seen that photo before?" Mara asked.

"I don't read the papers."

"Never seen it on TV?" Crosby queried.

"I don't watch that thing. Maybe an old movie, now and then. I like to read. I like to listen to music."

She pointed to the stereo in the corner with a rack of vinyl albums below the turntable.

"Your neighbor seems to think this is a picture of Randall Murphy. You haven't heard of him before?" Nick asked softly.

"I told you. Pat and I stay in, mostly. We just got married."

"Where'd you meet Pat?" Mara asked.

Theresa had calmed slightly.

"I met him in the neighborhood. At the supermarket. He used to live not far from here. We hit it off right away, you know? We were...what do you call it—smitten. He moved in, we were together for a few weeks, and then we went to Las Vegas and we were married.

"He is not the man in that photograph!"

"Do you know where he is now?" Mara asked her. "We'd like to ask him a few questions, and then we'll straighten everything out. I'm sure you're right. It's probably all a big misunderstanding. Your neighbor was probably mistaken. So, we'll clear everything up. But we need to talk to Pat so that we can eliminate him from our list of suspects. I'm sure you understand how it works."

"I'm a paralegal, and we don't deal with criminal law. Just business concerns."

"Where does Pat work?" Nick asked.

"He's got a temporary job as a night watchman. He works ten to six in the morning. I don't know where he could be. Maybe he went out to buy some beer. I don't know."

They sat with her for an hour. Then Karras told her to call him as soon as 'Pat' came home. He handed her his card.

Agnes had told them that she'd lived alone for a very long time. Theresa was lonely, a familiar complaint for a lot of people, Nick thought. He remembered his first wife taking off, and then Penelope was attacked and Karras was left alone. It had been a long while until Nora entered his scene.

Theresa Kelly lived sheltered in this small apartment. The TV sat in the corner of the living room like a piece of un-used furniture. She didn't read the newspapers. She lived in her own cocoon, untouched by everything that happened around her.

But she recognized the photograph of Randall Murphy. It registered in her eyes as soon as she saw it. Who wouldn't deny they were living with a serial rapist-murderer? Someone had entered Theresa Kelly's life after all these years, and it had to be Randall Murphy.

He'd let her live so he could hide out with her here in that tiny, safe shelter. Nick wondered how long he intended to let her survive before he took off again.

At least she was still alive. At least they'd arrived before he got the itch for blood again. There was that, even if they'd come up empty on him once more.

Nick and Mara left Theresa Kelly with a reminder to call them if he showed up.

They walked outside and got back in the Crown Vic. They'd be sitting at the curb working overtime tonight, and so would the patrolmen who were parked down the block.

There was no place for Randall to run to, was there?

CHAPTER THIRTY-FOUR

He walked to the grocery store where he'd picked up Theresa all those weeks before. Murphy was beginning to wonder if he was ever going to get around to getting rid of her and move on. His excuse had been that there was too much heat on him to try and make a run, but now he was thinking he was pressing his luck even more by sticking around.

The sex was distracting him. Before, he got off killing them and raping them, but he told himself if he strangled Theresa and then cut her, he wouldn't be able to fuck her again. Necro-sex was not his thing. His victims had to be breathing.

And Theresa did have that luscious body, those full breasts with prominent pink nipples. Her waistline was still in good shape, and her ass was only a little bit too ample. It was a comfortable fit, and he knew he shouldn't get used to her.

He walked back the few blocks to their apartment carrying a six pack of beer and a bottle of mescale. Maybe they'd get drunk tonight and he could try a few new tricks with her.

When he got a half-block away from their building, he spotted the Ford with a man and a woman sitting in the front seat. They weren't sitting close, and he thought he recognized the male. They were close enough to the street light that he could barely make out the swarthy complexion. Karras came to mind, and Murphy did a hasty 180. He was hoping that the detective, if that's who it really was, hadn't seen him. His heart began to thump and his pulse quickened as he walked back toward the supermarket.

Reality didn't take long to sink in. They were onto him. Someone had recognized him in the building or nearby. It could have been anyone who came into contact with him on the way to work or during the few forays he'd gone on with Theresa.

It figured that a living woman had done him in.

He scanned the next block for a likely ride that he might boost. He knew how to hotwire most cars, and he picked a non-descript blue Chevy. He'd have to steal some plates when he could get hold of a screwdriver, and then he'd lose the existing plates on the Chevy.

Murphy got under the dashboard of the unlocked car and had it hotwired in less than ten minutes. He figured the owner would report it, so he headed to a twenty-four-hour hardware store on Fullerton Avenue. His cash was dwindling. He'd put a chunk in their account and kept a few bucks for spending money. If he could get to the bank in the morning, he might be able to unload their checking and savings accounts.

That was if the cop hadn't talked to Theresa and shown her the police photograph. She didn't read papers or watch much TV, and he'd had that going for him until now.

Would she believe Karras and that female Homicide if they told her she was living with Randall Murphy, AKA the Coast to Coast killer? The odds were pretty fair that she'd dump her initial denial and take a good look at that flyer with his face all over it.

If he could empty the accounts when the bank opened at nine, he might have a chance to buy a car off a lot, legit, and then try to avoid main highways and head south. Mexico sounded good. You could buy anything with cash, and the farther south he drifted, the less likely it was that he'd get pinched. Mexican cops, the rurales and federales, were notoriously corrupt and were known to be bribable.

This guy Karras was that classic thorn in Murphy's side. Randall wanted to reach out to him personally before he took off for parts unknown in the wilds of rural Mexico. Killing a cop was supposed to be taboo. It just wasn't done. The Outfit avoided it like syphilis, and the other gangs in the city and across the country felt it was very bad business to off one of the boys or girls in blue. Then they'd really come for you, balls out.

How many times could he wait his turn on death row? They could only fry you once. Then why not go out in a blaze of glory? Maybe this cop had a wife, perhaps a kid. What a headline that would make. If he did have an old lady, Randall could have a little fun with her while this Greek prick watched, bleeding out on his own floor.

It wasn't likely he'd make it across the border, but Karras wouldn't be expecting Murphy to come after him personally. Again, it just wasn't done. Surprise was always a primo element.

So, he decided to take a ride by the CPD on Michigan Avenue where the Homicide Bureau was housed. If he could follow Karras from work to his home, he might have a shot at making one last, very bad day for the Homicide detective.

•　　•　　•　　•　　•

Randall boosted a pair of plates a few blocks from where he picked up his new ride, and he left the actual plates from the Chevy in its trunk. Then he drove downtown and parked opposite the coppers' lot on Michigan Avenue. He didn't put any change in the meter. Why bother? He was here watching for a policeman he was going to kill.

•　　•　　•　　•　　•

Karras must have been working a lot of overtime watching Theresa's apartment building because he didn't show up with Crosby until 4:45 AM. Murphy figured he'd follow him home, and then leave and go wait by the bank for it to open. Once he had the cash, he could return anytime to take care of the policeman and his better half, if he had one. If there were children, it'd make it even sweeter. He'd never murdered an entire family before.

He gave the cop a good interval as Karras drove his old heap of a Chevy in the direction of the northwest side. It took twenty-five minutes in pre-dawn traffic for the Greek to arrive at a ranch dwelling. Murphy thought it was a plus that the detective owned his own place. It made it more likely that he didn't live there alone.

He let Karras get inside. The light came on in the front room, but he didn't see anyone but the detective in the front window of the house. His wife and whoever else would be asleep at this hour.

Ten minutes later, the lamp was extinguished, and Murphy pulled away from the curb.

•   •   •   •   •

Randall stopped in an all-night diner on Cermak and had a big breakfast. He was famished because he hadn't eaten since lunch the day before. He couldn't linger too long because the word might be out that Randall was spotted and on the loose on the north side of town. These patrons were sitting in booths and at the counter reading newspapers. The place was maybe half-full. They were the early workers, the factory, blue-collar drones who occupied these kinds of twenty-four- hour dives.

It was 7:30 when he left the restaurant. The sun had risen about 6:15. Now he had to blow an hour and a half before the bank opened. He took a ride out to the lake figuring the stolen plates would keep Burglary/Auto Theft off his ass.

He parked at a beach lot on the near north. The beach itself was closed since Labor Day, but the lot wasn't blocked off since joggers and runners used the paths to exercise early in the morning before they traipsed off to push their pencils in the Loop. He hated those yuppie bastards living their predictable lives that led to predictable retirements in Florida and California and any place with year-long greenery. How could they stand it? Marking off days on a calendar until July or August and then taking two weeks at some half-assed resort and sitting by a pool or atop sand and watching the lake or a rectangle of chlorinated water.

It was 8:30 when he left the lot and headed for the bank. He was counting on the fact that Theresa hadn't told Karras about the joint checking and banking accounts.

He was parked at the curb in front of the bank on Western and Kedzie. This time he put change in the meter. No use drawing attention from some meter maid.

He was at the door at nine, first in line. He went to a female teller whom he found appealing in a familiar way. She was tall and thin with a pale complexion—just his type. But he wasted no time getting down to business. He asked for a withdrawal slip for checking and savings after he found out the two balances from the teller. Murphy figured he'd play it safe and leave some cash in both accounts.

The tall girl never blinked an eye after he showed her his fake ID with his new married name on it. It was the last false identification that little prick wop created for Murphy.

She came back with the cash. It was stacked high on the counter. Murphy looked around to see if anyone was watching him.

"Have you got some kind of bag I could put it in? I wouldn't want to walk outside with all that uncovered. It's dangerous out there, you know."

"We can spare some cash bags, sure," she smiled.

She retrieved a few cloth sacks from under the counter. There was sixty thousand in hundreds lying there before she stuffed the bills into two bags.

"You should've hired a Brinks truck," she smiled again.

He'd left Theresa with about ten grand, total, in both accounts. This skinny bitch looked lame enough to have allowed him to remove it all. She never even called for the manager to okay the transaction.

Murphy turned from her and walked out the door. There were only a few customers inside that morning. Randall thought he might have knocked over the whole bank, but he hadn't taken up the heist business so far in his career.

•　　•　　•　　•　　•

The money was in the trunk. He needed to get this thing with Karras over with in a hurry and try to head south. He figured if illegal immigrants could get into the States, he ought to be able to get out of the country and into Mexico. The place to cross, he figured, would be Tijuana. He'd have to buy some new clothes before he departed anyway, so he headed for a discount clothing store nearby. They sold cheap shit, but Randall figured he could improve his wardrobe in Mexico. Things were even cheaper down there.

He bought shirts, pants, underwear and socks. He bought a jacket because he had no idea what the weather was like that far south in October.

Murphy headed back toward Karras' house. It took longer, this time, because it was mid-morning, but he thought the cop had to be in bed after his long night parked by Theresa's building.

Had she gone crazy when Karras informed her who he really was? Maybe he hadn't even talked to her. The cop might have been waiting for him to come home instead of bracing Theresa. He couldn't be sure. It was all guesswork, but he wasn't imagining seeing Karras parked out by the building. He'd seen his face in the papers in those articles about Manski and Prentice. It was the Greek cop, all right.

When he pulled in front of the detective's house, the beater Chevy was gone. How could this bastard have slept a couple of hours and have taken off again? They had to have someone else sitting outside Theresa's apartment. Did this guy have that big a hardon that he was going sleepless to arrest him? What kind of crazy was he?

Was he that hung up on snapping the bracelets on Murphy?

A tremor traveled up Randall's back. This guy was someone to avoid. He was someone to fear. He just kept coming. The son of a bitch probably came home to change clothes and eat, and then he'd head back to Theresa's so he could personally cuff Murphy. This cop had made Randall his life's fucking work.

Murphy could sit here at the curb and wait, or he could go inside and make himself comfortable. If Karras had a wife, she'd likely be at work, and if they had a young kid or kids, they'd be in school by now, so the place was probably vacated. Either way, he couldn't keep driving around aimlessly. His trip to Mexico could wait until he took care of the Greek and whomever else was temporarily alive in that house.

•　　•　　•　　•　　•

Nora had a bad feeling. It wasn't about Gus. He was with the daycare people at the Methodist church and the sitters there were first rate. They were competent and caring and they called her if her son sniffled or coughed. They let her know what was going on with Gus as if they were the boy's own parents.

The bad feeling wasn't about him. She'd only seen Nick for a few minutes this morning. He was in and out, and he wouldn't share any information about why he'd been out nearly all night and then was headed back only after breakfast and a shave.

She could sense it in his tightness, facially. Something was up. He kept mute about whatever it was and he hadn't enough time to get into it, he told her.

The first thing that came to mind was Randall Murphy, of course. It was his main course of business all these months, and they'd talked about it a few times. It wasn't difficult to figure out that Murphy had been consuming Nick night and day. Nora didn't need a second sight to figure it out. There had been several near misses with Murphy, and it had to be eating at her husband that this killer remained elusive.

Nora wondered if these murderers ever attempted to stop their pursuers from catching them. She asked Nick about it, and he said it was rarely and never that perps tried kill cops. It was bad business and these criminals knew they'd have the entire blue horde coming down on them if they ever harmed a police officer or their families. It was simply unthinkable, Karras told her. They'd have to be insane.

She knew Murphy qualified under that category—lunatic. Nuts. Batshit.

Twenty women that the police knew about. That kind of animal had no boundaries. But he couldn't know about her or about Gus or about their new location at the house.

Nick took her to the firing range three or four times. She hated guns, but she was married to a policeman and Chicago was a hard, unforgiving city, sometimes, and you had to be ready to defend yourself, Nick had told her. So, he bought her a snub-nosed .38. He told her it had great stopping power, and he bought some ammo that most cops didn't use on the street. There was something about the heads of the bullets that flattened on contact with human flesh, and on the way out of the body it made huge holes about the size of a softball. All his graphic detail made her shudder.

"If you ever have to use this piece, you won't have to worry about knocking down what you're aiming at. If you hit him, they'll be generous chunks of him on whatever's behind him."

"That's horrible," she protested.

"Better him than you, and self-defense is a moral obligation, even though you're about as devout as I am."

The .38 had a kick, all right. It numbed her right hand and wrist until she became used to it. He taught her to use two hands, the way the coppers did, and she was surprised to find out that she could hit the bullseyes from time to time.

"You don't have to be William Tell, and it ain't no apple you're aiming for. Just know, Nora, that shooting at paper is nothing like shooting at a live body."

"Are you used to shooting at people?"

"Anyone who is needs Dr. Freud. I never got used to it in Korea or on the streets, I'm happy to report. But I sure as hell know I'd rather be the shooter than the shootee."

The pistol was locked in a drawer in the bedroom. Nick and Nora kept the keys on their rings with the house key and the car keys. The rings were never left lying around in Gus's sight, even though he was still too little to work a lock.

She hated the sight of the ugly revolver. Nora never pictured herself having anything to do with firearms, and the fact she was pretty handy with the thing gave her no cause for celebration. She prayed to Christ she'd never have the occasion to aim it or shoot it at anything with two legs.

The bad feeling would not leave her alone. She couldn't concentrate on the portrait she'd been commissioned to do, and she walked around her corner of the studio as if something or someone were stalking her.

She had to pick up Gus at 5:30. God only knew when Nick was coming home.

CHAPTER THIRTY-FIVE

Gus was teething and let Nora know about it all the way home in her ageing VW Bug. She had him in the child's seat, but he was whimpering enroute.

When she had him in her arms, she felt what a load he was becoming. He wasn't fat, but he was heavily muscled for a little guy. Dense muscles or whatever, but no baby flab. It was unusual in a boy so young. He had green eyes, unlike his parents' Aegean brown. He looked more Anglo than Greek, but he was far from full-grown.

She stopped abruptly at the front door. Something made her hesitate to unlock the door.

Then she decided her arms were getting weary from Gus's bulk, and she stuck the key in the deadbolt lock. When she walked inside with the boy, she halted again.

It was silent inside. The furnace wasn't running, and there was nothing to disturb the still air inside the ranch. She couldn't put Gus down, so she headed for the bedroom.

Nora felt the presence of another in the house. It was a distinct feeling that she and the boy were not alone. She also felt the urge to unlock the drawer where the .38 was, but she was interrupted halfway across the bedroom floor.

"What a good-looking boy."

She spun around and saw him in the doorway. No one had to identify him for her.

"Get out of this house!"

"I just got here," he smiled.

The beard was gone and his hair was brown, unlike the black she'd seen on the poster on TV.

"*Get out of this house.*"

She laid Gus on their bed, and then she tried to back up to the cabinet where the gun was.

"I'll be here a while. I'm waiting until your husband comes home."

He showed her the gun in his right hand. He had a length of rope in the other.

"Where's the kid's room?"

She nodded out into the hallway.

"Put him there."

He followed her to Gus's room, and Nora laid her boy in his crib. He'd be needing a bigger bed soon.

"Back into the bedroom."

Gus had stopped his whimpering the moment Murphy appeared.

Murphy pointed the gun to her back as he led her back into the master bedroom.

"I never had a cop's wife before. You think he'd mind?"

She stopped in the middle of the room and eyed the cabinet, but it was hopeless. He wasn't about to let her unlock it and then find out what was inside. She turned and faced him again.

"You'll have to kill me."

"I intend to, but not until your hubby arrives. First, we're going to have some fun...Take off your clothes."

"You wouldn't hurt my baby."

"I can't leave him without parents, now can I?"

Nora sent her hand to her mouth.

"I've never done a whole family before. It's on my to-do list before I disappear into the wilds of Mexico *lindo*."

Nora dropped her fists to her sides. A sudden calm took her over. She bored her eyes into Murphy's and it caused him to smile.

"You going to stare me down, sweet lady?"

Nora stopped blinking.

The smile evaporated from Randall's face. His face displayed something like concern.

"Cut that shit out, you crazy bitch. First I'm going to tie you up on that bed and then I'm going to..."

His words drifted off, and a look of discomfort crossed his visage.

"Cut out that goddamned staring."

A droplet of blood meandered out of his right nostril.

"The fuck is that?" he said as he dabbed at the droplet.

She remained locked in on him.

He dropped the weapon and the rope to the carpet, and then he palmed both sides of his head.

"What the fuck is going on here?"

He closed his eyes, but Nora didn't move. She kept aiming her gaze at Murphy as he went down to his knees.

Then he seemed to regain control of himself, and he struggled to his feet with an enormous effort.

The pistol was back in his hand. Slowly, steadily, he raised the piece toward Nora's face, and then the silence was shattered by an explosion.

Murphy was flung forward, and at the same time a chunk of his forehead flew toward the wall behind Nora. Randall flopped down face first next to her, and it was then that she saw Nick standing in the doorway with the smoking handgun's barrel pointed at the prone body on the floor.

Blood was pooling on the carpet beneath Murphy's head, or what was left of it.

"*Oh oh oh oh,*" Nora whispered.

Nick bent down and felt for a pulse. Then he picked up Murphy's weapon and dropped it on the bed. He saw the rope lying on the bed behind his wife.

He holstered his piece and put his arms around his wife and led her into Gus's room. Gus was playing with a toy attached to the crib and was standing up. Then he looked at his parents.

"Mama?" he asked.

She reached in and pulled him out of the bed and hugged him tightly.

"Mama?" he asked again.

Nick went out to the kitchen phone and made the call.

Forensics arrived, and the ME came into their newly-bought ranch shortly after. Nick sat with his wife and his child in the living room. They had no other place to go. All three sat on the sectional couch.

Mara Crosby came a short while after the techs showed up. She walked over to them on the couch.

"I'd ask you all if you're okay, but I figure it's the stupidest question I could ask."

Nora looked up at the redheaded detective, and then Nora began to weep.

She was still holding Gus.

"Mama?" the boy repeated a third time.

"How about Daddy?" Nick asked the child.

Gus smiled a mostly toothless smile at his father.

"Gas," Nick told his partner.

"The hell you say," Mara laughed.

Nora slowly turned off the waterworks.

"He was going to kill all three of us, he told me."

Nick grabbed hold of both of them and pulled them toward him.

"He told me that, Nick. He said he'd never done a whole family before."

Mara reached down and touched Nora's shoulder.

"I better go do my job," she told the three of them.

"How did he get in here? The front door was locked," Nora asked her husband.

"One of the techs found a broken window in the kitchen door. He must have gotten in in the back," Nick told her.

He kissed her and the boy.

"The ME said there was some blood in his nose that wasn't likely the result of the bullet. What? Did you hit that prick or something?"

"I never touched him."

She looked into Karras' eyes.

"Then what happened?"

"I didn't have time to get the gun out of the cabinet. He was behind me before I knew it."

"So?"

"Like I said, I never touched him."

"You mean he just miraculously had a nosebleed."

"Maybe the ME is wrong. Maybe it was a result of the gunshot."

"You're not telling me something," Nick said.

He was still holding them tightly.

Then he released Nora and Gus and prodded her with a stare of his own.

"It's the detective in you. You can't stand a mystery, can you."

Her face relaxed, finally, and she smiled and hugged Gus and bent to Nick and kissed him.

"You're in shock, you know... If I hadn't left my wallet at home...Christ, it was just dumb luck I came home when I did," he told her.

"I'm fine."

"You're going to the hospital anyway," Nick told her.

"What about Gus?" she asked.

"He's making a return engagement. We're all going together."

"Don't they have to interview us?" Nora asked.

"That can wait...Nora, did you do something to that bastard before I got here?"

"What could I have possibly done? He had the gun; I didn't."

"Yeah, he had the gun."

"If we have to go to the ER, let's go. I'd like to get us out of here while all these people are in the house, Nick."

She clasped her son and stood up.

"Incredible," he murmured.

"What?"

"You."

She gave him a Mona Lisa smile.

Mysterious.

• • • • •

The ER doctor checked her out and said she was all right, but that she needed to take off work for a week or so. He made an appointment for her with the hospital trauma shrink. She didn't fight the issue.

She had no physical injuries. She changed her blouse before they'd left the house because there were blood gouts on the front from Murphy's wound. Other than the stains, she was unscathed.

Nick wasn't sure she was solid mentally, however. He was fairly certain that his wife had never witnessed anyone's brains being blown out right in front of her. It wasn't the usual kind of thing for most civilians.

While they waited at the ER to be seen by the doc, he couldn't get anything else out of her.

She had her secrets, like everyone else, he supposed, and it seemed pointless to keep after her about it. He had just returned home as a result of exhaustion after surveilling Theresa Kelly's building for something like thirty-six hours. He and Mara had had enough, and someone else took over for them. He'd needed sleep and food and the forgotten wallet, and when he heard a male voice coming out of the bedroom, the gun was unholstered, and he found Randall Murphy pointing a piece at his wife. Pulling the trigger came automatically, and Randall Murphy met the floor less several ounces of blood and brain matter.

He'd shot men before, but this wasn't like Korea or the few other times he'd been compelled to use deadly force on the streets during a tour.

No one had ever threatened his wife and child before—except for the horror of what had happened to Penelope. Murphy aimed a gun at Nora with Gus lying a few feet away in his bedroom. Murphy had raped and mutilated his elder child and left her in a vegetative state at Elgin. She'd only recently come back to Nick and the world. He had plenty of motivation to kill the son of a bitch. It was absolutely and obviously personal.

He'd still be behind a desk for a week or two while they investigated the shoot. It wasn't likely there'd be an issue. He'd be back with Mara fairly soon.

But there would be the compulsory visit to the department psychiatrist. He'd been there a few times before.

•　　•　　•　　•　　•

Nora wanted new carpet in the bedroom. It was understandable. Nick brought in a professional cleaning outfit to get the other stains taken care of.

"We could sell the house," he offered to Nora.

"Are you nuts? We just moved in here."

"Yeah, but the house has some history, now."

"He's not here anymore," she told Nick. "Not a trace. I think I'd know."

"I suppose you would...I'd still like to know what happened in the bedroom before I got there."

She smiled slyly and ignored him.

•　　•　　•　　•　　•

Nick visited the graves of Karen Manski and Ellen Prentice. He placed a white rose by each marker. He planned on doing it for them both annually.

Magrette was happy. He brought Nick in for a personal audience.

"One less piece of poop walking among us."

"You have a way with words, Captain."

"One of the reasons I hauled you in here. I'm getting a promotion. Assistant Chief of Police. You gave me that last little shove, Karras."

"I'm sure you deserved it anyway, Sir."

"Is your wife all right?"

"So far," Nick smiled.

"Shit like that has to be a shock to the system."

Karras looked out Magrette's spacious window that faced Lake Michigan. The water was already turning gray. Fall would chill into winter soon enough and The Hawk would be blowing inland off the water, sending the first Arctic blast of the oncoming end of seasons.

"My wife is unique."

"How so?" Magrette asked.

"Do you believe in paranormal stuff, Sir?"

"You mean Halloween shit?"

"I mean like extra sensory perception."

"Fucking tarot cards? Eenie beanie chilly beanie the spirits are moving?" Magrette grinned.

"I mean for real stuff. No bullshit."

"You think your wife put the evil eye on this guy before you blew his shit up?"

"I don't know. She won't tell me. She did tell me before that she can sense things before they happen."

"Take her to Vegas."

"I'd like to, but she says she doesn't do that kind of thing."

"Too bad. You could take an early retirement...Does your wife scare you a little, Detective Karras?"

Nick pondered the question.

Then he smiled and turned and walked out the Captain's door.

EPILOGUE

Nick couldn't remember the last time he saw his daughter Penelope smile. It must have been when she was a pre-teen. After her teenaged years began, he couldn't recall a single glimmer on her countenance.

Here she was now, sitting in the shrink's office at the hospital, and Penelope flashed him some bright white that damn near blinded him.

Nick was here to participate in a family session. Nora would be asked to join in a little later, perhaps in a few months.

But seeing her smiling made him lift his lips into a facial expression that almost made his jaws ache. Penelope rose from her chair and embraced her father. Nick gripped her as tightly as he could without squeezing her airless.

"Daddy," she grinned.

He was still waiting to hear that term from Gus, but he figured the boy was just being stubborn.

"Here," he told her.

Karras handed her an envelope.

"It's your baby brother. Half-brother, technically, but screw the technically. He's your brother, Penelope."

She opened the envelope and looked over the snapshots.

"He's handsome, like his dad," she said.

"You're almost twins. Look at his face."

The psychiatrist's name was Wilson Jordan, a black man who looked a little like Sidney Poitier. Very handsome guy, and he could see why his daughter might have a crush on her therapist.

"Please sit down. Let's begin," he told Nick and Penelope.

· · · · ·

Nick and Penelope walked the grounds outside the building. They were spacious and pocked with beds of colorful flowers and thriving shrubbery. The landscape was well-tended, and it smelled like the season, early spring.

She wore a light jacket, and Nick wore a sport coat to conceal his holster and weapon. He had to go to work in a half hour.

They walked the path that circled the multiple acres of grounds. The sun was sinking in the west, but the days were progressively getting warmer and longer. It was April, but Easter came late, this year.

"I saw them talking about a peace treaty in the war," Penelope said. "They were interviewing Kissinger, that guy who sounds like he should be a Nazi in a World War II movie."

He laughed and so did his daughter.

The doctor said a sense of humor was a very encouraging sign.

"They said I might be able to come home in a few months. The doc also suggested I look into plastic surgery."

"What do you think?" Nick asked.

"Can you afford it? I'm broke."

She smiled widely.

"I've got some money put aside for you. I've been putting some in a savings account ever since you were born and there's a decent pile in there...I saved some money in case you ever wanted to go to school."

She halted and looked at Karras. Her eyes were watering up.

"Don't do that," he grinned. "I like the other look better."

She grabbed hold of him.

"I was going to tell you I want to go get my GED and then go to some junior college."

"We can afford a little better than a juco, honey."

"I want to get the required general stuff out of the way, and a two-year school is lots cheaper. I've been reading up on the ones around the city. Then, when I get that out of the way, we can look at a four-year deal to finish my degree. I think I want to major in psychology, maybe help abused kids."

Not too many months ago, there'd been no talk of a future for his girl, let alone for a plan for a professional life.

"I'm glad you killed that man. I shouldn't feel happy that you had to end a life, but if anyone had it coming, it was Murphy. I had trouble even saying his name until a few weeks ago. Dr. Jordan said it was a big step, just to say it."

"I didn't have a choice."

"I know. You told me."

"It doesn't really matter how much they've got it coming."

She began to walk again, and he stayed with her.

"I know guys who fought in a war don't like to talk about it...Did you kill anybody in Korea?"

"Yes."

"Was it hard?"

"It was very hard, especially at first. And it was just as hard when I had to do it on the street, on the job. There's a reason they make you sit down with a therapist when it happens. Some guys never have to even draw their pieces during a tour. I wasn't as lucky as they are."

"Do you like what you do, Dad?"

"When I catch people who need to be caught, yes. Like I said, I'd prefer not to shoot them, however."

She smiled, and they continued to walk the path that was surrounded on either side by color and fragrance. There were roses and lilac bushes and zinnias and a host of other flowers and shrubbery.

"I've got to go to work soon," he told her.

"Dr. Jordan says I might be able to come home by the fall."

Nick stopped.

"We can't wait. Nora and Gus and I. We've got your room ready. You can live with us as long as you want. I assume you'll want to live on campus when you reach that point, though."

"I don't think I want to become one of those middle-aged basement dwellers, Dad. No."

"We better head back."

Then he stopped and faced her.

"I thought I lost you forever," he told Penelope.

"No chance, Dad. It was just a long climb back, that's all."

"Are you going to try and contact your mother?" Karras asked.

"I don't think so. If she gives a damn about me, she'll reach out to me. Otherwise, you're all the family I need."

She hugged Karras again.

"You're gonna be late for work," she told him, and they walked back to the main building.

·　　·　　·　　·　　·

Mara's relationship was progressing nicely, she informed her partner. The young man from the bookstore had graduated from Northwestern with his master's and was now a teaching assistant full-time as he progressed to his dissertation and PhD in psychology.

They were currently living together at Mara's apartment, but they were looking for something bigger. He hadn't broached the marriage subject yet, but Mara was in no hurry.

"We're getting used to each other. He's easy. Me, not so much. But he's very tolerant, and I love him for it. These hours are ridiculous."

Nick had looked into taking the sergeant's test. It meant more money, and then he figured on trying to do lieutenant, which was more money yet.

The lieutenant's rank would basically get him off the streets and maybe into nine to five hours, mostly.

Karras didn't want to be robbed of watching Gus grow and of missing time with Nora. And now there was Penelope added to his cast of characters. A chunk of her life had been stolen by Randall Murphy.

But if he rose two steps in the ranks, it was time to make up for all those lost years. He could be a better husband to Nora, be there more of the time. He could come home like everyone else in the evening and read to his son and take his family out to dinner. Do the things that normal people do and spend less time pursuing monsters like Murphy.

He could get used to sitting in a bigger office and sending other detectives out into the field to catch the bad guys.

A new office might even have a view of the Lake.

ABOUT THE AUTHOR

Thomas Laird was born in Kansas City, Missouri, in 1947. He grew up in Chicago, Illinois, and was educated in the public schools. He graduated from Northern Illinois University with a BA in English in 1971.

He moved to Peoria, Illinois in 1973 and has taught English and Creative Writing at Spalding High School and Notre Dame High School for 43 years. Laird finished his Master's in English at Bradley University (December, 2010), and taught composition at Bradley University for four years.

His first story was published in the *Pacific Sun Literary Quarterly* in 1976, and he subsequently published several other stories in literary journals around the country. *Blue Color & Other Stories*, a collection of short fiction, was published by the *Dan River Press* in Maine in 1994. The two printings sold out. *Cutter* (2001), his first novel, was published by Constable & Robinson in London, England, and by Carroll & Graf in New York. *Season of the Assassin* (2003) and *Black Dog* (2004) were published by the same houses, and all three were translated into Czech by Domino Publishers in the Czech Republic. *Season of the Assassin* was also published in Dutch in the Netherlands. Domino published *Voices of the Dead* in 2006. *The Underground Detective*, Laird's fifth novel, was published by Parkgate/Dionysus on April 14, 2012. *Desert Storm Heart* was published by Parkgate in 2013, and the ebooks of *Underground* and *Desert* came out in 2013-2014. Recent publications are: *The Ruin of Souls* (Ecanus, April 2015), and from Endeavour Press in London, England, in 2015-2016: *The Long Midnight, My Brother's Keeper, Healer, Boats Against the Current* (recently a Number 1 Bestseller on Amazon Kindle), *In the Forests of the Night, The Last Sleep*, and *Black Widower. Cutter, Season of the Assasin*, and *Black Dog* were all reprinted in ebook and in paperback. All the Endeavour Press books are available in paperback and ebook.

Laird lives with his wife, Marsha, and Mick the Australian shepherd, Tar the Amazon yellow nape parrot, and Jimmy the cat near Germantown Hills, Illinois.

NOTE FROM THE AUTHOR

Word-of-mouth is crucial for any author to succeed. If you enjoyed *Ferocious*, please leave a review online—anywhere you are able. Even if it's just a sentence or two. It would make all the difference and would be very much appreciated.

Thanks!
Thomas Laird

We hope you enjoyed reading this title from:

BLACK ROSE
writing™

www.blackrosewriting.com

Subscribe to our mailing list – *The Rosevine* – and receive **FREE** books, daily
deals, and stay current with news about upcoming
releases and our hottest authors.
Scan the QR code below to sign up.

Already a subscriber? Please accept a sincere thank you for being a fan of
Black Rose Writing authors.

View other Black Rose Writing titles at
www.blackrosewriting.com/books and use promo code
PRINT to receive a **20% discount** when purchasing.